RUTH AND ANN'S GUIDE TO TIME TRAVEL

VOLUME I

RUTH AND ANN'S GUIDE TO TIME TRAVEL

VOLUME I

Edited by
Ann Stolinsky, Ruth Littner, and Cindy Snyder

CELESTIAL ECHO PRESS
ROSLYN, PA, USA
2024

Celestial Echo Press
An imprint of Gemini Wordsmiths, LLC
P.O. Box 1191
Roslyn, PA 19001
celestialechopress.com

Copyright © 2024 Celestial Echo Press
ISBN: 978-1-951967-03-1

The authors of the stories featured in this anthology retain the copyright of their individual stories. Jonathan Maberry's Joe Ledger Adventure © 2024 Jonathan Maberry Productions

All persons, places, and events in this book are fictitious and any resemblance to actual persons, places, or events is purely coincidental.

All rights reserved. No part of the contents of this book may be reproduced or stored in a retrieval system or transmitted in any form or by any means, electronic, mechanical, photocopy, recording, or otherwise, without express written permission of the authors.

Cover art and design: Don Dyen

Acquisitions and editing: Gemini Wordsmiths, LLC

Image by Iconic Panda 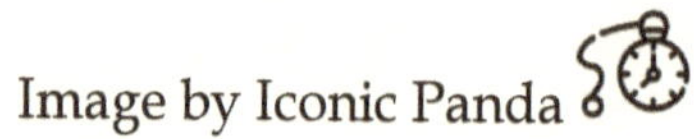

Dedication

This book is dedicated to the pioneers in the science fiction genre, especially to those whose minds traveled through time and brought readers their incredible and creative stories.

We also dedicate this to our friends and families.

Contents

Jonathan Maberry
Against That Time, if Ever That Time Come 1

James Ryan
The Rooftop Session...................................…..........25

Teel James Glenn
The Legend of Wyatt Ape!.......…....…....................29

David C. Strickler
Buried Beneath the Gallows.....................…...............49

Phil Giunta
A Thorne in Time....................................…..........61

Joanne McLaughlin
Way, Way Out of the Building.............................…....75

Gordon Linzner
Privileged Inca Nations.....................................…....89

Judith Field
Somewhere, Somewhen....................................….....103

Carol Gyzander
Time for Adventure......................................…........113

Ken Altabef
Schrödinger's Razor.......................................129

Charles Barouch
It Started at the Never Mind 135

Grigory Lukin
How to Prepare for Time Travelers in the Workplace 159

Gary Every
Tadpole's Time Travel........... 163

Ef Deal
Uchronia 181

Neal Wiser
Have We Met?..191

Brenda W. Clough
The Red-headed League...................................209

Daniel Lumpkin
The Biography..225

John Bukowski
Literary Time Machine....................................247

Stephen W. Chappell
Zach and Deke's Stumbling, Bumbling Adventure in
Time 253

Karen Eisenbrey
Sarah's Assistant 269

Jon McGoran
Time Changes Everything................................283

Praise for
Ruth and Ann's Guide to Time Travel, Volume I

"These stories take one of the most venerable tropes of science fiction and spin some brilliant, thoughtful, clever, mind-twisting yarns. Bravo to all and sundry!"

--- **Keith R.A. DeCandido**, award-winning author of *Star Trek: The Klingon Art of War*, DeCandido.net

~~~~~~

"A great collection of time travel stories with some of my favorite authors! You'll want to go back in time to read each one again to enjoy them anew!"

-- **Michael A. Ventrella**, editor of *Three Time Travelers Walk Into...* and author of *Big Stick*, www.MichaelAVentrella.com

~~~~~~

"From time traveling detectives trying to prevent murders to Cold War time machines, this collection has everything to keep your imagination in overdrive and swimming through the timestream with delight."

-- **Jacob Jones-Goldstein**, Author and Editor for Oddity Prodigy Productions, oddityprodigy.com

Foreword

It's All About the Butterflies

By way of introduction, I am the publisher of *Amazing Stories*, the world's first magazine devoted entirely to the publication of science fiction stories, a magazine first established in 1926 that will soon be approaching its 100th anniversary.

I mention this because, while the idea of manipulating time as a story element has been with us almost from the beginnings of literature, it wasn't until the pulp magazines arrived on the scene in the first decades of the twentieth century that a ready and eager market became available to authors who wished to explore this theme.

Wells, of course, was among the first, if not the first author to mediate time travel through technology, where previously it had been the stuff of dreams or magic. Wells' treatment made the subject more accessible to the science fiction genre, by introducing the need for some scientific plausibility and rigor. And it wasn't until this kind of story made its way into the SF genre that some of its strongest elements – time paradoxes, alternate timelines, questions of causality, to name a few that we are very familiar with today, found their first expressions.

I won't delve into the literary history of this trope – *The Encyclopedia of Science Fiction* does more than an adequate job. Instead, I wish to address its allure.

Science Fiction, as a genre, often presents itself as one in which problem solving plays a major role. The problem may be inherent in the story – a spaceship lacks enough fuel to make its return trip from an unliveable environment, the story then centering on the crew's scientific solution to the problem (strip it of everything they don't need) (a trope that should be recognizable from both *Destination Moon* and *The Martian*) – or it may be a societal issue that the story addresses by offering alternatives found or used elsewhere in the cosmos, such as that offered in Star Trek's *A Taste of Armageddon*, and presented as either advocacy or warning.

Fictionally solving humankind's problems has long been the playground of Science Fiction, but it is only through Time Travel that our problems can be actually undone, to be made to never have happened in the first place.

Who among us has no regrets regarding the decisions we've made in our own lives, let alone those made collectively by our societies?

I find it terribly interesting and instructive that as our literary field has continued to explore this theme, the primary lesson it seems to be relating is this: It's less dangerous to deal with the consequences than it is to try and undo the past.

Although as any fan of these kinds of stories can tell you, learning that lesson is not only instructive, but the journey can be a heck of a lot of fun.

Which is the experience we know you'll have while reading this volume.

Steve Davidson is the Owner and Publisher of *Amazing Stories* and a Co-Chair of SF100, the 100th anniversary celebration of Science Fiction and *Amazing Stories*, scheduled for April 2026.

Against That Time, if Ever That Time Come
A Joe Ledger Adventure
Jonathan Maberry

-1-

This started tomorrow and ended yesterday.

I know how that sounds. I wish it was a joke.

-2-

It started with a video message someone left on my cell phone. Sometimes it's as simple as that.

The video-mail was from a semi-friend of mine named Richard Spadaro. He looked like a fifth-grade math teacher—nondescript and mousy—but he was an investigative journalist. Has a shelf full of Pulitzers, and a whole bunch of interesting scars. He has been shot, stabbed, beaten nearly to death, tortured, and poisoned. Tough S.O.B. Relentless.

First time I met him was during a rescue op back when I was running Echo Team for the Department of Military Sciences. Spadaro had been gathering intel on troop buildup as part of what became the invasion of Ukraine. He got photos and other intel, made some calls, and then had to go dark because someone tipped off both the FSB (Federal Security Service of the Russian Federation) and the SVR (Foreign Intelligence Service). They tried real damn hard to capture Spadaro and left some bodies behind them in the process. A couple of Spadaro's most reliable contacts were butchered along with their families. He managed to get a message to someone who knows my boss, Mr. Church, and my team was sent in.

We found him hiding in a false room in a farmhouse. His hidey-hole was no bigger than a gas station men's room, and by the time we got there, he was scared out of his mind and half-starved. Finding him was tough; getting him out of there was messy. We had to spank some of the Russians pretty hard, but that's the cost of doing business.

The suckiest part was that the information Spadaro managed to send took too long to be vetted by political gatekeepers, and longer to reach the right desks in Washington, and by that time the Russians had rolled over the border into Luhansk Oblast. You know the rest.

I spoke with Spadaro on that trip home, and he had some tales to tell. Like all investigative journalists he was a pragmatic conspiracy theorist. He believed a lot of the chatter on the least well-monitored corners of the Net, but instead of making a tinfoil hat, he tended to go into the field to see for himself.

"Eight, nine times out of ten," he told me when we were halfway across the Atlantic, "it's a nothingburger. Some villager talking trash and then it's whisper down the lane until people either start freaking or it all fades to dust."

"And the other time?"

"The Russians are definitely going to invade Ukraine," he said. "My guess is that by spring 2021 they'll be at the gates of Kyiv."

He was close enough.

But he also said that once things cooled down and he could build a new background and get new false documents, he was going back into Russia because there was something weird he wanted to check out.

"Weird how?" I asked.

"Not sure yet, Joe, but weird enough to make me want to go back and see for myself," he said. "Been hearing rumors about it for years … and I mean since I was in journalism school. Something about a new kind of power plant they're working on that, if it works, could do two separate things. One good and one very bad."

I said, "Tell me."

"The good is that they're working on a new kind of induced-weather system. Something that will use artificially generated lightning and manipulate weather patterns. I don't yet understand how and will have to read up on it before I go back. The goal—at least officially—is to control and increase rainfall in those parts of Russia that have poor soil. They plan to use this tech to restore soil so that desert areas can be made farmable. The more Russia can feed its own people, the less grabby they'll get about Ukraine and elsewhere."

"Sounds like a good plan."

"If it's true, it's a great plan," said Spadaro. "The intel I got was that they are going to field test it in the Astrakhan Nature Reserve. That's Russia's largest desert and it has a pretty low annual precipitation."

"So, what's the bad?"

Spadaro laughed. "Oh, it's probably nothing."

"Tell me anyway."

The plane flew a lot of miles before he said, "Look, back in the seventies, the Soviets built what they called a High Voltage Research Center. HVRC. Also known as the Tesla Generators Research Facility. It's just outside of Istra, about twenty-five miles west of Moscow. It's officially run by the Moscow Power Engineering Institute."

"Wow," I said, "that's not even a little exciting. Can you dull it up even more?"

"It gets better."

"It would have to."

He grinned. "They built a Marx generator—"

"Marx as in Karl?" I asked.

"Marx as in Erwin Otto Marx, a German electrical engineer. His machine looks like a standard Tesla coil but isn't. Look, Joe, these Marx generators are used in a bunch of high-energy physics experiments, some of which are very much off the record. The U.S. has a whole bank of them—thirty-six—at the

Sandia facility, which is part of the United States Department of Energy's National Nuclear Security Administration. I've filed a ton of Freedom of Information requests, but they hit the National Security wall and that's that. My focus has been on the ones in Russia because that government claims they are relics of past power projects that were canned after the Wall fell."

I smiled. "Which you don't believe?"

"Of course not. I don't trust what anyone has to say about anything developed during the Cold War. Secrecy was raised to the status of a cult. Still is, really."

"That's fair enough."

"One of the Russian officials I asked said that their Marx generator was being used to test the effects of lightning on airplane landing gear. I mean, sure, I was born at night, but it wasn't *last* night. Besides, a contact of mine who's usefully placed inside the Kremlin told me on the downlow that when the generator is running at full tilt it could generate power equal to— or maybe surpassing—every single operating generator and nuclear power plant in the country combined."

"Uh huh," I said, and grabbed some Cheetos from a bag. I offered one to Spadaro. He took two, but since they're cheddar jalapeno Cheetos, he gets a pass.

"Thing is, they didn't actually use the power," he said. "None of what was generated was distributed across their power grid, and we're talking the Soviet Union in the '70s. Providing cheap power to their people would have been a massive political win. It would have gone a long way to whitewashing their global image, too. Their economy would have boomed with all of the new plant-based commodities they could sell. And yet the whole thing was covered up. Every now and then they run the test again; the most recent I know of was back in August of 2014. They run it, it works, it generates tons of power, and then they switch it off and don't do anything with that power."

"What *do* they do with it?" I asked.

"That's just it, no one seems to know," he said, emphasizing his point by jabbing the Cheeto in my direction. "That power has to be used for something. I mean, they built these giant storage batteries. Whole farms of them, actually. They get charged, and after X-number of years they get charged again. There's enough juice in those batteries to light all of Russia and still have enough left to sell to other countries. They could be making hundreds of billions off of it, but they don't even try. Why?"

We ate a few Cheetos and thought about it.

"Russia's supposed to have a bunch of off-book places," I said. "Black prisons, secret labs, all of that. Maybe they're keeping lights on there."

"They already do that by lying about mass production from the nuclear power plants."

"Hmmm."

He peered into the bag. "There's one Cheeto left. If I tell you something really cool, can I have that last one?"

I shook the bag. "Better be good."

He said, "I uncovered a source that said they built a second Marx generator. Work was begun on August 15, 1972, and it was commissioned for use on September 26, 1977. This was a much bigger one. And that they hid it inside a nuclear power station to erase all traces. Except on April 26, 1986, something went wrong."

"Chernobyl?" I asked.

"Yup."

"And now the Russians want Ukraine back."

"Yup. And isn't that a big ol' coincidence?"

I considered that, then plucked the Cheeto from the bag and offered it to him.

He chomped, and then grinned, showing me cheese gunk on his teeth.

-3-

That was 2020.

Since then, the old DMS was closed down and my boss, Mr. Church, opened a new agency, Rogue Team International, based in Greece. Church got tired of the political games and red tape that had slowed the DMS to a crawl. We're now freelance troubleshooters, doing odd jobs for the U.N, NATO, the World Health Organization, and sometimes picking our own fights when we trip over some nutcase wanting to deploy a bioweapon in Tokyo or truck a bunch of man-portable nukes into downtown London, or weaponize Ebola so that it's airborne. The world is mad and that keeps us busy.

Last time I heard from Spadaro—about eight months ago—he was planning on heading back into Russia to try and get to the bottom of the Marx generator mystery. Truth to tell, I've been so busy with other cases that he spilled completely out of my mind.

Until I got the e-video message.

It was waiting on my personal cell phone when I was on a plane after closing a case in Eastern Pennsylvania. It wasn't the kind of gig where one takes any kind of device that has a link to one's own identity into the field. The co-pilot handed me my stuff, and when we were airborne I opened my cell and there was the message. I played it.

"Joe, listen, I don't have much time," Spadaro said, then gave an odd little laugh. "Funny. Not much '*time*.' Jesus. Anyway, I found out what they've been doing with the Marx generator. It's bad, man. It's really bad. And it's weird, which I know is your sort of thing." He was perspiring badly and mopped his face with a wadded-up tissue. "Holy shit, Joe, you have to do something. I'm going back there now. If you don't hear from me, just do whatever you can to shut this down. I mean it. You *have* to stop this, or it'll all go to shit. Not just Russia, but everything. Look at me. That

6

should be enough. Okay, wish me luck. Maybe I'll see you in there."

The video ended. I played it again.

And then like six more times.

Then I sent it to my boss, Mr. Church, and Bug, the tech wizard at our HQ on Omfori Island. Seven minutes later I was on a video conference call with them.

"Help me understand this, Colonel," said Church. "Who is the person in the video?"

"That's the problem. He sounds like Rich Spadaro. He *looks* like Spadaro. Has the same moles on his cheek. Same eyes. Everything's the same."

"Except ...."

"Except the guy in the video is too old. Like forty years too old. Spadaro's thirty and the guy in the video is seventy if he's a day. And a seventy-year-old who's been through some shit."

Bug said, "Joe, I ran voice analysis and facial recognition and as of right now I am one hundred percent freaked out."

"Hit me," I said.

He did. "Everything matches Richard Anthony Spadaro, thirty-one, of Claymont, Delaware. The video was clear enough that I could zoom in for a retina scan. It's a clean match. And we did measurements on the face—ear shape and size, distance of nose to lips, width of the philtrum, lip thickness, orientation and slant of each eye."

"So what are we talking here, Bug? A double? Some AI deepfake aging software? Spadaro's grandfather?"

"Joe," said Bug, "that *is* Richard Spadaro. There's no doubt."

"Has to be AI."

He gave a terse little laugh. "We have MindReader Q1, Joe. It analyzed this down to micropixels. It's not a fake."

"Then explain to me how a thirty-one-year-old guy suddenly ages forty years in eight months."

Neither of them had an answer.

I felt the jet tilting, accelerating, changing direction. I looked at Church.

"Wait, where am I going?"

Church asked, "How's your Russian?"

-4-

Bug had everything set up before I even landed. He's like that. A guy accosted me in the men's room of the Pushkin International Airport. He had been taking a long time washing his hands and when we were the only two left there, he walked past me and deftly handed off a thick envelope. I took it into a stall with me and opened it to find all new papers—licenses, IDs, travel documents, the works. I was now Vladimir Zhirov, a location scout for Walt Disney Company CIS—aka Disney Russia, a movie production company.

Everything was good and would stand up to even the closest scrutiny. I became Zhirov and then I went to work.

-5-

Eleven hours later I was hanging by a thin cable down the inside of an air duct.

Long story short, I got in. No need for details. I have all kinds of cool toys—gadgets that would make the prop guys for the *Mission: Impossible* flicks cry in their beers. Mind you, for most places I'd have been inside and back out in under three hours. The Istra High Voltage Research Center had so many levels of safeguards, biometric scanners, active and passive listening devices, drone surveillances, guard patrols with dogs, and alarms that I'd have stolen the British Crown Jewels in half the time.

Which says everything. Spadaro was right. Something was super hinky here, and that began to scare me a little. For a couple of reasons—the first of which is that they don't even have this kind of sophisticated security at nuclear power plants. This is the level of protection they use for bioweapons labs or some kind of sneaky new missile system. The second reason is that getting caught there wasn't going to be an arrest and some awkward political bullshit. In situations like this they would put a bag over my head and ship me off to a black site that would make Gitmo look like the Sandals Royal Caribbean resort. And then after they carved everything I know out of me they'd put two in the back of my head and bury me somewhere in Siberia.

So, yeah. I was scared.

And mighty damn curious, too.

Why all this security? And what in the wide blue fuck goes on here that it made Richard Spadaro look like his own grandfather?

I hung from my cable and very carefully removed the cover to an electrical access panel. I had a camera on the front of my equipment harness and a comms unit in my ear. Bug was watching and I let him take a good look at the panel.

"Jeez Louise," he said. "They're really not messing around. Some of that stuff is so new it isn't even in this year's catalog. Some really sexy tech there."

"When you're done having quality time with it, Bug," I said, "remember that I'm hanging upside down in a vent. Tell me if this is something you can bypass."

He laughed. "Silly mortal."

Then he told me what to plug where, what to clip and splice, and what to absolutely not touch. I was a dutiful padawan and followed his instructions to the letter.

"Okay, here's the sitch, Joe," he said. "As soon as I send this software patch, that system is going to be under my control. I'm already recording loops to play back on their security office monitors. But they have a self-correcting self-learning AI backup to their whole system. It cycles at random intervals, so you'll have—tops—thirty minutes. Safe zone is twenty-two."

"That's not much time."

"It's what we have."

We meaning *me*.

"Send the patch," I said and pressed the timer on my watch.

He did. Nothing visibly happened, which is exactly the kind of thing you *want*.

"Go," he said. I went.

Four minutes later I was spooking my way through a series of hallways. I wore Scout Glasses, which are a proprietary tech Church obtained for us. Goggles that can go from deep zoom to microscopic; variable light settings ranging from UV to infrared; and a data scroll down one lens. Schematics popped onto the left lens, and I followed those. The place was enormous but also pretty damned empty. There were huge rooms filled with machinery of a kind I'd never seen before. I had a whole bagful of No-see-um bugs—tiny surveillance devices that I placed on walls at levels where the eye would not typically fall. The bugs had a chemical coating that read the background color and then took on the same color, allowing them to blend in. Once I was gone and my mission clock ran out, tiny acid pouches would open and melt everything in each bug.

I placed several in each room, and hoped the bunch of mad scientists back in HQ were paying attention. My job was to gather intel, theirs was to make sense of it.

Then I ran down several flights of stairs to what felt like the center of the Earth. The clock was ticking and in my nervous head I swore I could hear it chopping off each second. There was a door guarded by two sentries. They stood in front of what looked like an airlock. The soldiers were heavily armed and looked tough as nails. They were not the kind of bored third-string apes in uniforms you'd expect at a facility that's been around this long. These guys were sharp and alert.

"Call it," I said very quietly.

Church said, "We need to know what's behind that door, Outlaw," he said, using my combat call sign. "That is a three-million-dollar security portal. Whatever they're hiding in there, it's not a power station or a lightning generator."

"What about the clock? It's going to take time to get in there and I can't do that covertly with those guards."

"As of right now the clock doesn't matter. We need to know what's behind that door."

"Sandman?" I asked.

"Sandman," he agreed.

So, I pulled my Snellig 22A-Max gas dart pistol, took very steady aim, and shot them both. The pistol shoots high-velocity collagen-shell darts filled with a cocktail of chemicals designed around the veterinary drug ketamine, but with BZ — 3-Quinuclidinyl benzilate — to cause intense and immediate confusion and DMHP — Dimethylheptylpyran, a derivative of THC — for muscle failure. We call it Sandman because when you get hit, you go down and you go to sleep. Not a nice sleep, mind you, but into a version of the *Twilight Zone* that Rod Serling would have done if he was both high and mad at you.

They puddled down and I ran forward.

I used several of Bug's gadgets to access the computer controlling the airlock. It took him almost three minutes to bypass the system, and that's disturbing because it usually takes him thirty seconds. The airlock went clickety-click and swung open. Gun in hand, I crept inside. There were two more guards walking patrol around a catwalk forty feet off the ground. I waited until they were close and then darted them, too.

It was the middle of the night, so I expected to find no active technicians, and that was the case. For the moment I was the only person awake in that room.

Then I stood and looked at the thing that all of this security was built to protect. Church was right, this wasn't a generator. Not of any kind. There were power cables coming *into* the chamber. Big ones, and they were plugged into a machine that stood about eighty feet high and fifty wide. It was bizarre looking, with several large screens on which images and data flowed. There was a cold-room at the bottom in which I saw a whole line of big-ass computers. I recognized them because we had a bunch at our HQ in Greece. OLCF-5 exascale supercomputers. The fastest of their kind anywhere in the world, and they had fifty of them.

In my ear, Bug said, "Holy fucking shitballs. What the hell do they need that kind of processing power for? NASA doesn't use a fifth as many boxes as that."

"I guess it's for whatever *that* thing is," I said, facing a gigantic machine that filled most of the big room. It was not a design configuration I'd ever seen before. It was all curves and planes and odd shapes that didn't begin to hint at purpose. It looked like the inside of one of those spaceships from the old *Alien* movies. There was a cruel sensuality to the flowing lines, and some of the thick cables twitched and pulsed in an unnerving imitation of life.

"Anybody want to tell me what I'm looking at?"

Doc Holliday was on the command channel. She is a certified multidisciplinary super genius and runs our Integrated Sciences Division. She knows everything about everything.

"I have no idea," she said.

"Not what I want to hear, Doc. Can you at least make a guess?"

"No. I cannot. Take a lot of pictures and then get the hell out of there," she cautioned. "I don't like the look of that one little bit."

"Copy that."

I went down zigzagging metal stairs to the bottom and saw that there were worktables covered with tools, several panels standing open on the main housing near one of the screens, and complex schematics smoothed out on a bench. I bent over the papers, letting my bodycam record everything. On the screen there was what looked like newsreel footage of the Russian invasion of Berlin at the end of World War II. Seemed like an odd entertainment choice, unless that thing was the world's biggest flatscreen TV and this was Russia's version of *The History Channel.*

But my attention was drawn by something on the top of one of the schematics. The diagram coincided with the exposed guts of the open panel. I frowned at the heading.

"*Vremennoy Regulyator Potoka,*" I read. "Umm … guys?"

There was a beat.

Then Doc said, "No."

"No … what?"

"They can't really be building that."

"Stop being shocked and cryptic," I snapped. "I speak Russian. That says *Temporal Flow Regulator.* Please tell me this is just a really big clock."

"Turn the page," ordered Doc.

I did. The heading on the next sheet was, *Instrument Vremennoy Fokusirovki Volnovogo Sostoyaniya.*

Doc translated it in a hollow, devastated voice. "*Temporal wave-state focusing tool.* God almighty. Outlaw, check the rest of the pages; see if there's one that says, *Prognoziruyushchiy simulyator.*" From her tone, it was clear she was hoping I wouldn't find it.

But I did. It was on the sixteenth page.

"What is a *predictive simulator?*" I asked. When there was no immediate answer, I barked at her. "I'm standing here with my dick in my hands, Doc. How about you focus and give me some useful intel."

"Let me see the screen again," she said, and there was a definite nervous tremolo in her voice. I showed her, then I heard her talking to Church. "It's the Fyodor Rokotov project. Christ, I thought all of that was destroyed back in '86 while it was still a theoretical model."

"It was," said Church. He never lets emotion show in his voice. Until now. "And Grace Courtland took out the last of the science team working on it. It was her first mission with the DMS."

Grace.

That name was a knife to the heart.

When I joined the DMS, Grace was their senior field agent. We worked some absolutely crazy cases, and in doing so saved the world. Not an exaggeration—the actual world. Like three separate times. And we fell in love while all that was happening. Then on the third case, an assassin shot her, and she died in my arms. It was years ago, but I could still feel the heat of her last breath. I was holding her so closely, trying to keep her with me. Failing so very badly.

"Grace never told me," I said.

"There were likely many things she did not have time to share, Outlaw," said Church with surprising gentleness. "In fact, we nearly lost her on that operation and her memories of what happened were spotty at best. We pieced together most of what happened. There was a power surge at the station she had infiltrated. She lost a lot of her equipment including an entire bag of modified C4. It was never found. She said that it was taken from her by someone during that power surge, but she never discovered who. Once the surge abated, she had to find another way to destroy the facility. Luckily she was an exceptional operative, as you know. She managed to remove the surge protectors on the generator and then run a feedback loop so that it fed the power it generated into itself. The blast was significant. A local asset found her dazed and wounded and got her to a safe house. Her memories end shortly before the explosion, so Grace had no idea of how she even escaped."

"Jesus. And she blew the whole place up?"

"She did."

"Was that machine the same as this one here?"

"Same design," said Doc. "But the one she destroyed was about one tenth the size of that one there."

"Swell. And I don't have anywhere near enough explosives to do much damage. I can cripple it, but that's about it. Don't suppose we can risk a drone strike?"

"And start World War III?" asked Doc with a cold laugh. "Sure. It was bad enough back in the '80s. We destroyed Chernobyl to stop this madness, and *that* wasn't as big as the one Grace found."

"What makes this so scary?" I demanded. "The temporal stuff … that's time, right? Don't even begin to tell me the Russians are building a fucking time machine."

"It's a bit worse than that," said Church grimly. "Fyodor Rokotov was a genius who was obsessed with not just moving through time, but manipulating the *flow* of time. He was a dedicated Soviet whose father had been in Stalin's inner circle. People think that the Soviet Union bankrupted itself trying to outgun us in the nuclear arms race, but that was not the whole truth. They sank billions they could not afford into Rokotov's machine. Not to go back in time but to alter the flow of time, Outlaw, to change events that happened in order to steer history in a direction more in line with the Soviet goals."

I turned and looked up at the screen.

"Russians in Berlin," I said. "And the Cold War started right after Hitler fell. So what was their Plan B? Immediately declaring war on us?"

"That wouldn't be winnable," said Church. "We were too strong by that point, and they knew about the Manhattan Project. No, they wanted to use temporal focusing—a kind of lens that allowed them to look into any part of the past—and steal our nuclear secrets in 1945 or earlier, rather than August of 1949. That way they could drop atomic bombs on Berlin and Washington at the same time. London and Paris as well. Four bombs, even low-yield ones—would have changed the course of history."

"And allow the Soviet Union to become the dominant superpower," I said.

"In a nutshell, yes."

"But what they've built goes a step farther," said Doc. "If they've really cracked the science on this—and I'm terrified to say that it looks like they have—they can open limited windows to make direct actions in the past in order to change the future. Or, I suppose, the present."

"What about all that shit about time paradoxes? That you can't change the past because that will mean our future is not the future of that past, which means we could not have gone back and ... okay, this is messing with my head. Every sci-fi movie I ever watched said that what you're talking about won't work. It's self-defeating."

"Yes," said Church, "that is true. However, the same science suggests that if the past is changed, then that timeline splits off, creating a new reality."

"Meaning what? They find a way to defeat us after World War II and they go all Marvel Comics multiverse? Doesn't make sense, though, because whoever built this won't be *in* any resulting future."

"No," said Church and Doc at the same time.

I said, "What?"

"This is radical science, Outlaw," said Doc. "The energy field it generates will create a state—a kind of plasma bubble—of a certain size. When the machine is fully activated, anyone inside that bubble will be buffered from the effects. So, if Vladimir Putin and few hundred of his most trusted people are in the building in which you're standing, they would be protected, along with their memories, and would emerge unscathed."

"And," said Church, "before you ask, yes, it will require some management on their part to explain what happened to the people who are running this extended Soviet Union. No doubt they will bring documentation—history books, video archives, and the plans of the machine itself—to explain what they've done. It's a gamble, and given the paranoia the Soviets demonstrated with outside-the-box thinkers, they might be stood against a wall and shot. On the other hand, they could become the truest and most enduring heroes of this Soviet Empire they are trying to create."

I wanted to say something. Make some kind of snarky joke. But the words turned to dust on my tongue.

I stared in horror at the gigantic machine.

"Listen," I said hoarsely, "if I plug MindReader into their computers here can Bug run a tapeworm that will destroy all of their research?"

"All computer records, sure," said Bug. "But they will have copies of the schematics you're holding, Outlaw."

"We have to try, though, don't we?"

"We absolutely need to try," said Church. "Bug will send a tapeworm. He'll use a Trojan horse to plant spyware in their mainframes. If nothing else, it will help us identify key players in this project."

"And do what?" I asked. "Hunt them down and pop caps?"

Without pausing or flinching, Church said, "Yes. Exactly that."

I began to say something about that when there was a heavy *thrummmmm* sound, followed by a pulse of energy from the machine. It made the screen seem to bulge and then flash. The image changed from World War II to what looked like the same room I was in.

"Wait, something's happening here," I said.

"Your telemetry just went wonky," said Bug.

"Define 'wonky'."

"You were there, then you weren't. And … and this is weird … your mission clock just went out of alignment with ours."

"Trying unplugging and plugging back in," I suggested.

"Ha ha," he said. Pronouncing the words. "Must be some kind of interference from the machine and—"

His voice cut off abruptly.

"Outlaw to Bug, please say again."

Nothing.

"Outlaw to Merlin."

Nothing.

No Doc Holliday, either. There was no signal of any kind.

"Well ... shit—"

And a voice said, "Freeze."

-6-

A woman's voice, speaking Russian with a British accent.

I froze. Not because she told me to, but because I knew that voice. My heart turned to ice in my chest.

"Hands on your head," she ordered. "Turn slowly."

I did exactly that.

And there she was. Tall, pale, with long brown hair tied in a tight ponytail. High cheekbones and luminous eyes. Fit and strong. Wearing all black. Just like me. Wearing comms and a weapons harness and gunbelts. Just like me.

"You're no Russian," she said, pointing a Sig Sauer P226 at my chest. At my heart.

"No," I told her. "I'm not."

She frowned. "American?"

"Born and bred."

"Who sent you? The Agency? Delta?"

I looked her in the eyes and said, "Mr. Church sent me."

She stiffened. "What?"

"My callsign is Outlaw," I said. "I work for Church."

She tapped her comms. "Amazing to TOC. Do you copy."

The TOC was the tactical operations center. We had one at the old DMS and have one now with RTI. But I didn't think she was going to reach either. She tried again. And again.

"It won't work," I said. "My comms are out, too."

"I don't know of any operative in our group with the callsign of Outlaw."

"But I know you, Amazing," I said. It hurt to say it. It hurt to speak at all, and I could feel the Earth tilting under my feet. "Gus Dietrich gave you that callsign. Amazing Grace."

She eyed me with doubt and surprise. "You know my name?"

"Yes," I said. I could feel tears gathering in the corners of my eyes. "You are Major Grace Courtland, formerly of the SAS. Seconded to Church to help with the formation of the Department of Military Sciences."

"Who *are* you?"

"My name is Joe Ledger. I'm a colonel with Rogue Team International."

"I thought you said you worked for Church."

"I do." I took a risk and lowered my hands. "Listen to me. I don't know what's happening here, but I think I understand *why*. You're on a mission to destroy a Marx generator, but not really. The true mission is to stop the Russians from building an *Instrument Vremennoy Fokusirovki Volnovogo Sostoyaniya*. A temporal wave-state focusing tool."

Her gun wavered ever so slightly.

"I'm here to do the same thing, Grace."

"Bullshit." Her eyes flicked past me to the gigantic machine.

"This isn't the one you're looking for," I said. "It's a hell of a lot bigger."

"Yes," she said faintly.

"For what it's worth, you succeeded in your mission. That smaller one blew up." I nodded to the heavy bag slung across her back. "And, no, you didn't use the C4. You created a terminal feedback loop."

She patted her bag. "Why would I do that? There are—"

"—easier ways," I said. "Yes, I know. But … I think I understand what happened and why you had to change that plan."

"What are you talking about?"

I nodded to the schematics. "Take a look. Those are the plans for this machine. Check, you'll see."

She edged closer to the table, still holding me at gunpoint. Her eyes darted to the papers and then back up. "So?"

"You looked too fast, Grace. Look at the dates. They're stamped in the upper right of every page."

"That's a lame distraction."

"Just take a look."

She chewed her lower lip for a moment, then glanced down again. I saw the exact moment when she saw the date. Deep vertical lines appeared between her brows.

"That's … no. No way."

"It's a fucking time machine, Grace. The date is right. That's *my* date. My time, or close enough. Those schematics were printed out at least a year ago. It's a year later right now."

"No," she said. But she meant *yes*.

When she looked at me again there was fear in her eyes. There was wonder and awe and naked terror.

I took a very small step toward her, watching her eyes but aware of the gun.

"You just experienced a pulse when you were about to begin setting charges, right?"

"Y-yes."

"I felt a pulse, too. Just now. Right when you showed up here." I took another step. "You have to know that this isn't the same building you entered. I can show you my tech. You won't recognize much because it was made later. After your mission. After your time."

One of my tears fell down my cheek.

She looked at it, her frown deepening, then back up at me. "I don't …"

"I know. How do we even talk about this without sound-ing insane."

"No, I mean, why did they send you?"

"I'm one of Church's top field agents."

"That's not what I mean. Why you and not me? I have been following this case for two years. That's why I'm in … *was* in … Christ, how do I even talk about this? If you're here and I'm not, then where am I?"

Another tear fell.

I saw her understanding. "Did I … fail?"

"Grace, you never failed at anything. You completed every mission, every time. You will destroy that other machine. This--whatever we call this--is a blip or a glitch. But you did the job Church sent you to do. And you made it back home."

She did not ask the next obvious questions. She was too smart. Maybe if time machines were not part of the goddamn conversation she might have been confused. But not now. She understood.

That understanding hurt her. Hurt us both.

She lowered her gun. "Ledger … Joe … is it weird that there's something familiar about you?"

"No. We knew each other."

"'*Knew.*'" She echoed the word. It was immensely clumsy of me to have said it.

The machine *thrummmmmmed* again. We both looked at it.

"What do we do?" I asked, and a sob nearly cracked my question in half.

Grace stood there, her face white as snow, eyes big and filled with the most heartbreaking complexity of emotions.

Thrummmmm.

"Feedback loop?" she murmured.

"Yeah."

"And it worked?"

"Yeah."

Grace nodded and shrugged one shoulder, letting the strap of the equipment bag slide down. She caught it in the crook of her arm and lowered it carefully to the floor. I looked at it.

Understood.

Nodded.

I said, "When you get back … after you destroy that other machine … you won't remember."

"How do you know?"

"Because you would have told me."

She closed her eyes for a moment. Then I saw her reassemble her control and her strength back into place, one steel plate at a time.

Thrummmmm.

There was a faint shimmer in the air around her. She looked down at her hands. I looked, too. They were translucent. It was like looking through smoky crystal.

"I guess we both have missions to complete," she said.

"Yes."

She began to take a step toward me. I don't know why. Handshake, hug. Whatever. But she stopped herself, shook her head. Stepped back.

"Good luck, Colonel Joe Ledger."

"Good luck, Major Grace Courtland."

She snapped off a salute. There were tears in her eyes and a crooked smile on her lips.

I began to raise my hand to return the salute, but she was gone.

Just like that

Gone.

-7-

I was four klicks away when the place blew.

My comms had come back on, and I asked Doc where to place the charges for best effect.

"Outlaw, say again. Charges? Were you able to locate some explosives?"

"Copy that," I said, but offered no explanation. Then, or ever.

She had walked me through it. Placing the C4 around the batteries, the power generator, and a few other key spots. I set a timer and fled.

The explosion was enormous. First news reports mistakenly called it a nuclear accident. Russia spun the story five ways from Sunday. Obfuscation and a lack of oversight allows Putin to say what he wants.

I don't give much of a damn.

It took a few days to get out of the country. With all the world scrutiny I needed to rely on back routes. But I got out. It wasn't until I was crossing into Belarus that I noticed something weird on my passport. The visa stamped had the wrong date on it. It was yesterday's date. I was about to mention this to the customs officer when I spotted a TV monitor showing local news. The day, date, and time were clearly displayed.

Yesterday.

I was in … yesterday.

It stalled me. Hit me like a truck. I had no idea what kind of expression was on my face because three different people asked me if I was unwell. I said I had a cold.

Time.

Goddamn.

I got home. The conversation I had with Mr. Church was had over a bottle of very old brandy. He almost never drinks, but he had three glasses. We told Doc Holliday. She went over to the wet bar in Church's office, took down a bottle of George Dickle sour mash, gave us a maniacal smile that looked frozen onto her face, and walked out. She was drunk for three days.

We tried to find Richard Spadaro, but he was gone, and I suspected he was well beyond our reach. Was he somehow responsible for the pulse that allowed Grace to help me? I don't know. I like to think so, and that's how it'll be in my head until the world proves otherwise.

A few weeks after it was all over, I went to a cemetery and found a headstone and sat cross-legged on the grass, and cried.

I didn't leave a pebble on the headstone.

No.

I left a small clock. An ornate thing of brass and crystal. I stood touching the marker for a long time, listening to the clock ticking quietly.

"You saved the world," I said. "Again."

That's when I returned her salute, holding it for a long time.

Then I turned and left.

Jonathan Maberry is a NYTimes bestselling author, #1 Audible bestseller, 5-time Bram Stoker Award-winner, 4-time Scribe Award winner, Inkpot Award winner, comic book writer, and producer. He is the president of the International Association of Media Tie-in Writers, and editor of *Weird Tales Magazine*. Find him at www.jonathanmaberry.com.

The Rooftop Session
James Ryan

She was thankful she'd remembered to wear an extra layer as she walked over the rooftops. She had heard that London was really chilly in January but didn't think it'd be like this.

As far as she was concerned, London had never been this cold, in her experience.

As she swung around a chimney pipe she kept her focus on the roofs of Savile Row. She felt a certain anticipation tingle through her long legs and fingers; she thought she could see goosebumps peeking through her green stockings as she edged her way over the dividing walls between the buildings, trying not to trip on skirting masonry.

She also thought that if she'd taken an extra second, she would have dressed with the weather in mind, not the scene.

At last, she thought she found the perfect spot. It was a straight line over to where Apple was based, giving her a good look at the roof. She checked her parabolic microphone disguised as lipstick, and her image enhancement relay disguised as a compact, and proceeded to have a seat on the back end of a skylight-

-sitting in the lap of another woman who hadn't been there before.

She looked at the other woman and knit her brow. Like her, this woman was dressed in some of the swingingest gear that could be worn in London, fitting her perfectly. Her dress was almost identical, in fact; if this other woman didn't have blonde hair but was instead a brunette, this other woman might have passed for her sister.

Which made the woman who nearly sat on her very cross.

"Excuse me," she said, "but I believe that's my seat there."

"Oh, I don't think so," said the blonde near-seat, "because I claimed this seat first."

"I think there's been a major misunderstanding," said the first woman. "I've come quite some distance to be here-"

"Oh, but you're not allowed up on the roof," said the blonde. "Don't you know it's an EU ruling, about running along on rooftops? You should be glad I got to you before the roofs commissioners did."

"Nice try," said the brunette, "but England doesn't join the Common Market for another four years, and the roofs commissioners don't start patrolling until at least 2074."

"Ah," was all the blonde could say.

"Now if you don't mind, I came a few hundred years to get this seat for the last Beatles concert, and I don't intend to miss this one thanks to some poor history student with rude manners who-"

"A few hundred years?" the blonde asked.

"Yes, from the year 2744. Now if you don't mind, that's my seat you're-"

"I'm from 3256."

"So?" asked the temporally wayward brunette.

"So," said the further displaced blonde, "that means I've come back farther. Which means I should have the seat."

"Of all the unmitigated gall!" the brunette replied. "You can't claim a seat just because you're from further in the future than I started!"

"Why not?" the blonde stood up, trying to use a height advantage to scare back a woman who might have been her great-grandmother (though had the blonde known for sure she was her ancestor, she still would have picked a fight). "It took me longer to get here, and maybe that means something in my time."

"But it doesn't in mine!" the brunette retorted. "Look, if I ran into a temporanaut from two hundred years before I was born, and she got here first, I would not make her move just because I was younger than her."

"So maybe people from my time have more advanced technology, huh? And maybe we have weapons that you'd never seen coming, huh? How about that, huh?"

"Oh, let's see. … If I wanted to come to a concert in the past, I'd be packing something temporally destabilizing, just so that I could threaten someone whose seat I wanted. Oh, real smart! What was I, born before the Industrial Age?"

"Hey." The two of them heard a man beneath them. When the two women turned to look for the source of the voice, they saw in their claimed seat a man with unruly orange hair wearing a BEATLES sweater. "You mind? I came back from the year 2396 and I was promised a good seat here."

"Oh no, you don't!" the two women said in unison, and battle was joined.

Unbeknownst to the three who were temporally transposed, the Beatles had by now mounted the roof to play an impromptu concert. They started to plug in their instruments when they saw the commotion three sets of roofs over.

"Aw, cor," said Paul McCartney with a sigh. "You don't think …"

"Aye," said John Lennon. "More ruddy time travelers."

"Now didn't I say," said George Harrison. "Didn't I say now, when we had to stop touring three years ago because of that lot, I did say when you suggested doing another show that they were going to find us and hound us again, Paul?"

"All right, all right," said Paul in frustration, "you were right. Now what?"

"Well," said John, "they're expecting something good from us. You see them in the stands, that's as much an omen as ravens over a battlefield."

"Honestly," said Paul. "You'd think they'd stay hidden better."

Ringo Starr finished setting up his drum set and noticed the commotion. "So how many non-time travelers you think are watching us now?"

"Not so easy to tell 'ere," said John. "Remember the party with tees that had our names on them that showed up in 'Amburg?"

"And the blokes at the side door in New York with those singles to sign, the ones we 'adn't done yet?" sighed Paul.

"Right," said George. "Let's get this started already."

The fight between the three time travelers for one seat proceeded through the first number; none of them were aware enough that Paul directed the chorus of "Get Back" straight at them.

James Ryan has published the novels *Raging Gail* and *Red Jenny and the Pirates of Buffalo*, the collection *Alt Together Now,* and monograph *The Pirates of New York*. He has appeared in other anthologies and publications, including the column "Fantasia Obscura" at *Forces of Geek*. His links are at https://linktr.ee/jdanryan. This story was originally published in *Rooftop Sessions*, December 2005.

The Legend of Wyatt Ape!
Teel James Glenn

Prologue: The Lawless Frontier

My name is Lucifer Lawless and I was hung on the horns of a dilemma. On one hand, I was cold and tired because of the job I was doing, and on the other I was excited because of where I was.

The night was October 25th of 1881 and it was cold and clear in the town of Tombstone, Arizona Territory. Me and my partner were huddled in the deep shadows of an alley beside the Oriental Saloon on Fifth Street, waiting for our target to come down the street. We had been hiding there for ten minutes and my partner was already getting bored.

"Why can't we have waited for him inside the nice warm bowling alley," my partner said.

"Because this is where the assassination is gonna happen, you hairy hominid, now shut up, just follow the plan and watch."

Tombstone boasted a bowling alley, four churches, an icehouse, a school, two banks, three newspapers, and an ice cream parlor, to announce to the world that it was growing into a world-class town and was 'civilized.' All of this grew up among and on top of a large number of dirty, hardscrabble mines.

The thing that gave lie to the illusion of sophistication were the 110 saloons, 14 gambling halls, and uncountable dance halls and brothels that catered to the wild element who worked those mines.

It was a hard town to police, with the Marshal's office and the town Sheriff doing their best to balance the need for law and order against the frontier freedoms and trail end celebrations that brought in the dollars that kept the town alive.

That night a lone Deputy Marshal was walking down Allen Street, keeping to its center. To his right was the Sampling Room Saloon and Bowling Alley and to his left was the Golden Eagle

Brewery Saloon. Both were doing a good weeknight business, raucous but not enough to require 'regulation.'

The subject of our watch came along just then, ambling with a long-legged stride, with lambent blue eyes that scanned both sides of the street, missing little. I found I was holding my breath, amazed at the sight of him.

"Just like the series," my partner whispered. He started to hum a recognizable theme tune, even whispering "brave courageous and bold" before I had to smack him on the head to quiet him.

The peace officer, dressed in a long black coat and broad, black, flat-crowned hat, was called The Deacon by many. He was about thirty-six years old and weighing in the neighborhood of one hundred and sixty pounds, all of it muscle. He stood six feet in height, and had a complexion bordering on the blond.

He had a well-groomed handlebar mustachio that gave a somberness to his handsome features and made him seem older than his years.

That night he wore two holstered hip guns, both Colt Single Action Army, 7.5", .45LC. with his long coat brushed back to give him free and easy access. Normally he just tucked a single gun in a pocket or waistband, eschewing the image of a gunfighter.

"I thought he had a twelve-inch barrel on one of his guns," my partner whispered to me with disappointment in his voice.

"That was the gun that Ned Buntline gave to him," I said quietly. "There is no evidence that he ever actually wore it; in fact, most anyone who got one of them had the barrels cut down to a usable length."

"I hate it when the history books get it wrong," he said.

"That's what we're here for, you jerk," I hissed. "Now be quiet and watch."

It was still amazing to me that I was watching one of the legends of my youth right in front of me. It made my skin tingle.

The lawman reached the end of the block and started to turn right onto Fifth Street when the killers came charging out of the Sampling Room with guns blazing.

The Deputy spun with the intent to fire at the two would-be assassins, but my partner was faster, drawing his twin six-guns and getting off four shots before the lawman could clear leather.

The two failed assassins first had the guns shot from their hands then were spun around by the impact of the bullets in their bodies, to drop and lay still on the dark street.

The Deacon whirled now to face us, but I called out. "Easy, Deputy, we're friends." I stepped from the shadows to let him see my hands raised.

"I'm Lucifer Lawless," I said when I stepped closer. "Doc Lawless is the name on my medicine wagon. My partner does a shooting exhibition and I do some magic. We saw those two hooligans stalking you and then come here to lie in wait for you."

The lawman kept his guns trained on me. "You said, 'We're friends,' so let me see who else is in there with you," he said.

"Come out, buddy," I said. "Don't be worried, little guy, the Deputy won't shoot you."

The Deputy gasped when he saw my partner amble out of the shadows; but then, I guess he had not seen a chimpanzee in a black tailcoat and flat-crowned hat before. At least not one wearing twin six-guns.

"Deputy Earp," I said, "say hello to the star of the show, Khetar, the world's only six-gun simian!"

Chapter One: The Six-Gun Simian

Let me take a moment to state a few facts. My name is Lucifer Lawless and I hail from Austin, Texas in the year 2011.

I was a Texas Ranger until I had a very strange experience; my doppleganger from another plane of existence tried to kill me! That was when a member of a group that called themselves

T.I.M.E. Cops (though the technical name is Corporal Readjustment Alternity Police. That is correct, it spells C.R.A.P. so you can see why they prefer T.I.M.E. Cops) saved my bacon and opened my eyes.

I suddenly was aware that the vastness of the universe was only the beginning. There was a multiverse out there, planes of parallel existence that all started at once with the big bang and fractured from there.

The passageways between these parallel worlds were big, blue stones we called Philosophers' Stones. There seemed to be at least one on every world that had been discovered so far.

I became a full-fledged agent and paired with Khetar Wohl from the world of Chektana, who on Earth we would have called a Chimpanzee.

"We have it on good authority," the Director-general of T.I.M.E.: Kunjar Neh Zorl had said to me and Khetar, "that a descendant of William Clanton, who was killed on October 28, 1881 has gained access to a portal stone and traveled from their own time to Universe 6, your Universe Prime, Lawless, and plans to assassinate the lawman who took Clanton's life in order to prevent that death."

"But you can't change your own history," I pointed out.

"We know that, Lawless," he said. "This crosser is from Universe 30. And about two hundred years in the future, which means they have access to transformational technology that will make detecting them very difficult."

"Why should it be easy?" Khetar said. "If it was easy you'd just send Lucy here alone."

So now we were standing in the streets of Tombstone, Arizona with a figure out of my own history and I was trying to act casually about it.

Deputy Marshal Wyatt Earp stood gape-mouthed, and stared at my primate partner who, thankfully, did not throw some quip at the frontier lawman, but instead waddled over to stand beside me with his long, hairy arms folded over his chest like the little wise guy he was.

"He's with me," I said. "And yes, he always dresses like that in our medicine show." I smiled. I pulled out a piece of paper, signed by the town mayor that allowed Khetar and me to wear guns on the streets, and showed it to the peace officer.

"I have not heard of your arrival, sir," the lawman said to me, "but I am certainly beholden to you." He moved to the two fallen gunmen and checked them over.

"They're both still breathing," he noted.

"I guess they're paid up on their prayer debts," I said glibly. In fact, Khetar's superior eyesight and coordination made him a phenomenal shot. We didn't have to worry about using mercy bullets; experience had proven we could not change our own timeline so, as long as I was here, we could never kill anyone who had not died already in my timeline. One of those time paradoxes that had been proven out.

People were pouring out from the two saloons to see what the source of the noise was.

"You," Earp called to two of the men he recognized in the gathering crowd. "Get the doc over here to clean this up." The lawman then turned to me, "As for you, I want you in my office tomorrow morning. Bring the animal; you'll need a permit." He stood and with a nod headed off down Fifth Street on his rounds as if nothing had happened.

"Nerves of steel," I said with admiration.

"Balls of brass," Khetar said with an annoyed tone. "Bring the animal?"

He showed his tongue and sent a raspberry sound into the darkness after the lawman.

"Knock it off, ya quarter-sized Konga," I said. "We are here to help keep him alive, so we follow him."

"Well, this *animal* could use a drink," Khetar said.

"He's probably heading to the Long Drink to stop in by Doc Holliday's game next. We can make it ahead of him if we go directly down this street. It is pretty obvious these two goons were just locals with a grudge. Earp's safe as long as there is no audience; this Clanton nut left a note behind saying that Earp had to die publicly."

Khetar did a fair imitation of Gary Cooper as he walked down the street, and I could almost hear little spurs jingling. "Try not to be too conspicuous," I cautioned him.

"Well, there is a chance I can smell that trans-dimensional tech, whatever form this future Clanton takes," Khetar said. "At least as long as the assassin is not down wind of you."

"Keep it up, pal," I snapped. "I'll find me an Apache who is looking for a scalp and do a wholesale deal for you!"

Chapter Two: High Plains Primate

The legendary Long Drink Saloon was everything I expected and more. There was sawdust on the floor to soak up blood and beer from fights, spittoons set strategically around the room and drunks galore all over the place.

The Tuesday night crowd was a mix of miners, drummers, cowhands, sodbusters and the gamblers who were there to fleece them. The sporting gals who worked the place all looked tired but I detected an excited giggle when my pandimensional primate partner walked in under the swinging doors.

"Aren't he the cutest thing," a mighty mite of a bar girl said. She was not much taller than Khetar. "Ain't he, Ruthie?"

"Reminds me of my ex-husband, Ann," another said. "Sure is hairy enough."

Khetar snorted at me and scampered off toward the bustiest of the bar girls, making mewing noises until she picked him up to snuggle- he had a thing for busty humans- he thought boobs were funny.

I was about to grab him when a bald-headed bravo lumbered over toward us with a wooden walking stick in hand.

"What the hell is that?" the bouncer said pointing the stick at Khetar.

"That, sir," I said in my best showman presentation, "is my partner in the greatest show to ever cross the Mississippi River!" I did a flourish and produced a rose, which I offered him.

He didn't think it was funny, but the watching crowd did. The working girls all snickered and I tossed the rose to the one called Ann.

I announced, "I've come to invite you all to see Six-gun Khetar, star of Doc Lawless' Wonder Show, tomorrow near Fly's Boarding House! And for now, a round of drinks on me."

The only people in the room who did not seem to be affected by the hirsute one's antics and the free beer were a table of card players off to one side. Five men were seated around the circular table. Two women stood by, obviously to attend to the drink needs of the gamblers.

Each seated man had a relaxed attitude in their whole body, but their eyes were all but glowing with intensity.

"Another whiskey, John?" one the women asked one of the men. Her smile was a bright spot in the dingy room.

"If you would, dearheart," he said in a soft southern drawl. "I am a bit parched."

Mary Katherine Horony Cummings, who went by the none-to-complimentary moniker of "Big Nose Kate," was not a big woman and not an unattractive one. She had a slight foreign accent that was from her birth country, Hungary. It gave her a slightly exotic appeal. You could see her affection for the seated gambler, but his intense gaze-albeit from beneath half-closed eyes so that he appeared sleepy to a casual gaze-were focused on the cards.

Doc Holliday and Big Nose Kate, I thought. No photo could convey the sheer power of their presence.

Kate looked up at me with a sharp assessment as she walked past me to the bar and her companion threw down one card and drew another to rearrange his hand.

"So, Doctor Lawless," Holliday said to me without taking his eyes off the cards. "Is your anthropoid associate the major attraction of your show or do you have any talent?"

I wanted to answer, "Ask my ex-wife," but restrained myself and said, "I am a premiere prestidigitator and I, of course trained the primordial pippin myself."

The little Chektana native jumped down from the sporting girl and knuckled over to me, looking up with plaintive eyes that were full of 'screw you' attitude.

I held out my arms and he jumped up to whisper, "Trained me?"

"It's a cover, Thing Kong!" I hissed. Then I smiled at Holliday and said in a full voice, "He's a talented little ball of fur."

"And a fast one," Wyatt Earp said as he entered the saloon. He strode across the floor to stand next to me. "I didn't expect to see you two until the morning."

"Just out promoting our show," I said. Khetar held his arms out toward Earp but the lawman ignored him, apparently immune to his chimpish charms.

Not to be put off, or ignored, Khetar jumped down from my arms and waddled over to stand next to the Marshal, imitating his stance. The gesture brought snickers from all in the saloon who noticed, including Holliday.

"Looks like you have another admirer, Wyatt," the gambler said. His laugh devolved into a hacking cough and Kate rushed back to the table to hand him a whiskey. He threw the drink into his mouth the moment he could and continued as if he had not had the fit. I noticed no one around him remarked at the coughing fit at all. "Seems the little fellow is angling for a deputy job, Deacon; you think Virgil put him up to it?"

This last remark got a smile out of the grim-faced lawman. "I'll have to write mom to see if there are any of my kin I don't know about," he said, "but as to deputies, he seems more in line with Behan's boys."

I watched the lawman and those around him for any sign of any unusual interest in him. Finding an assassin who could resemble anyone seemed an impossible task. Particularly if the object of the assassin had his own set of ready-made murderers. We had been given impossible tasks to do before and so far the multiverse was still more or less intact, but as my old dad was fond to say, "Failure is always an option when people are involved!"

Earp stopped at the bar and was given a coffee by the bartender--part of his usual routine-- then came over to the gambling table. He said hello to Kate and exchanged pleasantries with Holliday.

My partner had become bored with not being able to speak (have I mentioned he's usually a chatterbox?) so he was knuckling around the room doing his, 'I'm cute' act. I suspected he was trying to sniff out the chemical signature of the transformational device that our assassin might be using.

I took a sniff and almost choked on the thick miasma of smells and smoke. Good luck scenting out the 'crosser in this, I thought.

Just as the hairy T.I.M.E. agent got to one of the whiskered miners and took a whiff (I did not envy him that moment), one of the not-so-busty saloon gals who he had ignored pulled a Mac-10 submachine gun and pointed it at the Deputy!

Chapter Three: Hominid on the Range

I yelled "Duck, Earp!"

Many things happened simultaneously. The assassin depressed the trigger and began to spray lead, Deputy Earp dropped his coffee and drew his gun, several women screamed, Khetar spun and drew both his .32 caliber six-guns, and I dove into Earp.

My dive took the lawman out of the path of the machine gun and slammed the two of us into the table in front of Doc Holliday. The table tipped over and the two us landed on the gambler's lap.

The bullets licked wood from the heavy table and the assassin screamed in frustration.

I heard Khetar's .32s bark and then the sound of crashing glass amidst the screams and chaos.

I disentangled myself from the two men I'd fallen on as Holliday launched into a debilitating coughing fit.

"Sorry, Deputy," I said. I rose to see that the assassin had thrown a chair through a side window and escaped that way. I saw my primate partner leaping through the hole.

Khetar yelled, "Follow, Lawless!"

I complied with his shout before Earp could question me and jumped the jagged glass of the window to follow my simian sidekick. Khetar was in full all-fours chase mode, knuckling down the wooden sidewalk at an amazing speed.

The crosser-Clanton must have been a marathon runner because she was way ahead of Khetar and gaining.

I raised my gun to fire and called, "Alternity Police, freeze!"

The runner did not even break stride and was soon gone around the corner into the darkness. I pulled up short and panted for a moment as I heard a horse take off at a gallop.

In a moment my partner knuckled out of the night, and, to my secret delight, he was panting as well.

"She must have cheetah genes spliced in," the chimp said. "I couldn't even get close before she rode off."

We went back to the Long Drink. Once we were inside the chaos that the crosser-Clanton had wrought was evident.

The wall of the saloon behind the bar was peppered with bullet holes, the mirrors and bottles shattered.

There were casualties as well, though in her zeal to kill Earp the wounds to the others were minor.

Fortunately, no one had noticed that the little furball had yelled to me in the middle of the attack.

"What the hell kind of gun was that?" Earp asked.

"Some sort of European thing," I offered. Khetar offered a snide snort at my adlib.

"You know, Doctor Lawless," Earp said. "That makes the second time you've saved my life tonight. You're getting to be quite a good luck charm."

"Let's hope third time's not the charm," I muttered. My hairy better half elbowed me so I added, aloud, "Glad to be on hand, Deputy, but I'd better be getting this little fella to bed or he'll get cranky. Try to stay safe till I see you tomorrow."

My primate partner ambled at my side and waved to the room before we went to the medicine show wagon.

"You think we can leave Earp alone the rest of the night?" he asked me as he scampered up to a top shelf where he had set up a little nest.

"I think so." I sat down heavily. "This Clanton-crosser wants to make a show of Earp's death; apparently her timeline is in the middle of a retro fad that got her obsessed with seeing how things would have worked out if her ancestor had lived."

"Only for this timeline," Khetar pointed out. "It's academic for her, but if the crosser kills him you might cease to exist."

"Thanks for reminding me."

"Thanks to you yelling," he said, "now the crosser knows we are time cops!" He might annoy me like no other partner I'd ever had, but he was a smart simian.

"We didn't do anything any other simian/sapian duo wouldn't," I said. I waited for him to reply but he did something that always annoyed me, he rolled over and abruptly he was already sleeping, snoring like Paul Bunyon rip-sawing Sequoia trees.

Chapter Four: The High Chimperal

Wednesday October twenty-six was clear and even colder than the night before.

Ike Clanton had been up all-night playing cards and was drunk as a skunk with a full on mad for Doc Holliday, whom he blamed for his bad luck. He was part of a group who called themselves The Cowboys, and most of the members of the group had reason to dislike the Earps- Virgil, Morgan and Wyatt- who had clashed with them numerous times over various shady dealings on both sides.

I knew that before the day was out, there was going to be a violent explosion, a flashpoint of history that might, if we failed, literally erase me from existence. That would suck. Despite that, the fact that I was going to be at that flashpoint, a legendary moment in time, had me almost as excited as scared.

I bought food at a restaurant and brought it outside to feed my fuzzy sidekick. We sat on a tree stump and regarded Fremont Street.

"I think at this point our crosser will wait to do it near the shootout; she knows we are after her so my guess is that she has already found a spot to make her move on Earp."

"Well, we know his movements during the day, so I think we should walk his route, look for likely assassination spots."

"And let's not forget we have a noon show," Khetar pointed out. "Earp will be there, and we can shadow him from that point out."

We finished our meal then walked the route we knew that Wyatt Earp would be taking that day, spotting any potential sniper perches or ambush points. Our cover for the trip was passing out handbills for our show.

Khetar sniffed at each local, hoping to catch a whiff of our prey. His crime fighting nose came up empty though he made a number of remarks on human hygiene that were unrepeatable.

We stopped by the Marshal's office to get our performance permit and Wyatt Earp accompanied us to see the show.

Earp seemed to particularly enjoy Khetar's display of marksmanship (or was that marksapeship?). The hairball shot a series of clay plates out of the air, a clay pipe from my mouth and did a display of gun twirling using both his hands and his feet.

Khetar's six-gun skills and my elementary stage conjuring earned us healthy applause and I sold eight bottles of Doc Lawless' Cramp Remedy to the rubes. Khetar and I got to keep any profits after Corps expenses!

"Nice show," Earp said when we had concluded our last bow. He regarded my furry fellow time cop with a little bit of awe. "How did you ever get that little fella to shoot that well? Even Virgil can't slap leather and hit a target like that."

I made a show of being humble about my training ability and stared my partner to silence. I knew he wanted to take full credit but his sudden speaking might have given Earp a heart attack and done the crosser's job for her.

"Well, see you around, Doc," the lawman said with a tip of his hat. Khetar copied the gesture and Earp laughed. "I gotta bring my brothers to see your show tomorrow. They'll love it!"

"The horses are out of the gate now," I whispered to Khetar. "Better get moving."

"I'll shadow Earp from the rooftops and you head to the corral and try and spot the crosser."

He scampered off to follow the lawman and his appointment with destiny.

The actual famous shootout would take place six lots removed from the rear entrance to the O. K. Corral. It was immediately west of 312 Fremont Street, which contained Fly's 12-

room boarding house and a photography studio. The lot was near the West End Corral on 3rd Street and Fremont, where Ike Clanton and Tom McLaury's wagon and team were stabled.

I surveyed the whole area and decided that two barn buildings across and down the street offered the best sniper's perch if the crosser was going to strike from a distance. I went to the barns to check them out.

Meanwhile, Khetar was following Deputy Earp. The lawman met up with his older brother Virgil at the courthouse where Ike Clanton was being fined for having been caught earlier without turning in his gun in accordance with city law.

Wyatt almost walked into 28-year-old Tom McLaury as the two men stopped short almost nose-to-nose. Tom had only arrived in town the day before.

Earp asked, "Are you heeled or not?"

"No." McLaury lied.

Wyatt saw a revolver in plain sight in the right pocket of the arrogant McLaury's pants. Wyatt drew his revolver and with a lightning swift move buffaloed McLaury with it. He hit him on the head twice with his revolver. The outlaw went down, bleeding from the temple.

"I don't like being lied to, Tom," Earp said then walked away after taking the downed man's gun.

Khetar, watching from a roof nearby, scampered after the lawman.

I searched the barns then went to the roof of one where I could see the site of the shootout. I settled down to hide from the crosser and wait.

I concentrated on trying not to think about the possibility of being blinked out of existence with a new timeline being formed if we failed to save Earp.

I might not just cease to exist, mind you; I might not be directly affected at all, but my world could. It was impossible to know what ripples would come from Earp's death, he had lived a long time, touched the lives of many people from Texas to Alaska and beyond. Hell, he even met Tom Mix in Hollywood!

It would all change if he was not there to interact with them.

Meanwhile Khetar was still shadowing Wyatt who had gone to a gunmaker's shop to talk to some of McLaury's cohorts in an attempt to defuse the situation.

Virgil Earp met up with Doc Holliday and gave a sawed-off shotgun to the former dentist, who hid it under his overcoat. He took Holliday's walking stick in return.

Virgil Earp was told that the McLaurys and the Clantons had gathered on Fremont Street and were armed. He decided he had to act. He told his brothers Wyatt and Morgan that things had come to a head, and it was time to take the guns away from The Cowboys and, once and for all, prove to the community who was in charge.

A hidden Khetar heard them argue over whether it was the right course of action, with Wyatt arguing for letting it go. Virgil was adamant, however, that a showdown had to come.

The Earps carried revolvers in their coat pockets or in their waistbands. Holliday was wearing a pistol in a holster, concealed along with the shotgun. They moved off west, down the south side of Fremont Street.

The Earps were out of visual range of The Cowboys, but I could see them up the street. I saw Khetar pop out of a barrel and knuckle along the sidewalk, keeping to the shadows. Even at several blocks distance I could see that the hairy hero was sniffing like mad and scanning the surrounding street for any sign of the assassin.

I was about to give in to the despair of it when I looked across and spotted a gun barrel sliding out from between two boards at the next barn.

The assassin must have been hiding somewhere in the loft of that barn and had sighted in their weapon on the lot where The Cowboys were talking with Sheriff John Behan.

As the Earps approached, Sheriff Behan left the group of toughs, though he looked nervously backward several times.

"For God's sake," Behan said with an unsteady voice to the Earps. "Don't go down there or they will murder you!"

The Deacon just bit his lip and stared at the Sheriff with cold eyes. "Let's do this," he said.

The four then moved past the ineffective Behan and marched slowly across the street.

On the roof I tried to move as quietly as possible and went down the ladder to creep into the next barn, knowing that I would literally be fighting for not only my existence, but that of untold lives to come.

Epilogue: Monkey See, Monkey Shoot

Down in the narrow 18-foot alley I knew the Earps and Doc Holliday were ranged across the open side facing The Cowboys; Tom McLaury, Frank McLaury, Ike Clanton, Billy Clanton, and young Billy Claiborne.

I found a ladder in the shooter's barn and moved up it. Once up I could see out the open loft to the alley. The assassin was now lying in the open, but I could see the control panel of an electronic camouflage unit.

In the alley I heard Virgil Earp yell, "Hold it, I don't want that!"

Frank McLaury and Billy Clanton drew their guns.

Billy Clanton leveled his pistol at Wyatt, but the lawman didn't aim at him. He knew that Frank McLaury had the reputation of being a good shot and a dangerous man.

Frank McLaury jumped to one side, but Wyatt shot him in the stomach. Billy Clanton started shooting.

At that point Khetar popped out from behind a water trough and intervened, shooting Billy Clanton through the right wrist, and disarming him. He always had a hard time just watching.

The crosser screamed at seeing her cross-ancestor hit.

Tom McLaury tried to hide behind his restless horse. He fired over the horse's back then tried to grab his rifle from its scabbard.

Doc Holliday stepped back for distance and angled around McLaury's horse and shot him with the shotgun in the chest.

I yelled and jumped across the loft at the assassin.

My yell startled the shooter and her rifle fired wild.

Morgan Earp fired at Billy Clanton, hitting him so hard that he slammed against the wall of the alley with a bullet in his gut.

The crosser screamed again.

I landed on the shooter and tried to grab the rifle from her hands.

"No, Earp has to die!" the crosser screamed. She held onto the rifle with a death grip, clawing and biting at me. I may have outweighed her, but her anger (and possibly some chemical help) gave her tremendous strength.

Holliday had tossed the shotgun aside, pulled out his nickel-plated revolver, and continued to fire at the wounded Frank McLaury and Billy Clanton.

Ike Clanton ran forward and grabbed Wyatt, exclaiming, "I'm unarmed. I don't want a fight!"

"Go to fighting or get away!" The Deacon snapped.

Ike ran away unwounded. At the same moment Billy Claiborne also ran from the fight.

Virgil and Wyatt were now firing. Morgan Earp tripped but fired from the ground.

Morgan Earp was shot across the back in a wound that struck both shoulder blades; he went down for a minute before picking himself up.

The crosser heaved me off her and rolled back to aim the rifle again. I rolled to my feet and made a grab for her but she squeezed the trigger before I could stop her.

Unlike her first shot this one did not go wild, but it did not hit her intended target either. My impact on her knocked the sight enough that the bullet thudded home, not into Wyatt Earp but into the body of Billy Clanton, killing him!

Down below Virgil Earp was shot in the calf and he cursed. Frank McLaury stumbled to the street and took aim at Wyatt Earp but Khetar fired and the Cowboy went down for good. (Morgan would later take credit for that one).

Suddenly the Gunfight at the O.K. Corral was over. The street was abruptly very quiet.

The crosser was babbling sounds of frustration. She tossed me off her once again and swung the rifle like a club to slam into the side of my head. Abruptly I was counting the stars in the Milky Way Galaxy.

I must have been out for a full minute because I was suddenly looking up at Khetar's hairy kisser.

"Up and at it, Lucy," he said. "No amount of beauty sleep is going to help at all."

I sat up too quickly and my head throbbed. "The crosser!" I yelled.

"Got away on a horse she had out back," he said.

"We better get her," I said shaking off a wave of dizziness. I climbed down the ladder and jumped on Tom McLaury's horse. "Hop on!" I yelled to Khetar and we were off to the races.

"Off that way to the right," he said. We were at a full gallop and moving so fast I barely had time to hear the exclamations from the townsfolk as we whizzed past.

It didn't matter now; Earp was alive and there was no point to his murder. The only thing we had to worry about was that the crosser would get the bee in her bonnet to do it all over again in a different timeline; there were at least 45 we knew of.

"Or she could just kill Earp out of spite, you know?" Khetar said.

"You are always so inspirational and uplifting," I said. The horse was moving at a full run now.

"Look," Khetar said, "all you hairless types confuse the heck out of me with your motivations."

"You understand the boobies part of it well enough," I snarked at him. We were approaching the edge of town now and the crosser on horseback was clearly visible.

"Move it, Roy Rogers," Khetar said. "We have to catch her before she kills someone or hits her transit point out of this timeline."

"Shut it, furball or I'll team up with Gabby Hayes!"

We came up on the crosser and I moved alongside. Her features were a twisted mask of hate. When she saw me she hissed like a scalded cat.

She raised a strange weapon but before she could pull the trigger my hairy partner fired, blowing the gun out of her hand.

The crosser was so startled by the shot that she lost control of her horse. She tumbled off her mount and went headlong into the dirt.

I reined myself up and spun, but Khetar was off my back and over at her before I could even come to a full stop.

"Relax, Tex," he smiled up at me, "It's all done now. T'was beauty caught the beast!"

I almost shot him right there, I really did.

Tombstone Nugget the next day proclaimed:

The 26th of October, 1881, will always be marked as one of the crimson days in the annals of Tombstone, a day when blood flowed as water, and human life was held as a shuttle cock, a day to be remembered as witnessing the bloodiest and deadliest street fight that has ever occurred in this place, or probably in the Territory.

Not a single mention of a gun-toting chimp or a medicine show magician, which means we did our job. That and the Earps didn't want to admit that a simian six-gun artist had helped them take The Cowboys down.

Teel James Glenn has dozens of published novels, and stories printed in over 200 magazines, including *Weird Tales, Mystery, Pulp Adventures, Mad, Black Cat Weekly, Cirsova, Heroic Fantasy,* and *Sherlock Holmes Mystery*. His novel *A Cowboy in Carpathia: A Bob Howard Adventure* won Best Novel 2021 in the Pulp Factory Award. You can find him at TheUrbanSwashbuckler.com. This story originally appeared in *Tales of Weird West # 4* (2015).

Buried Beneath the Gallows
David C. Strickler

Auguste Catron was about to see his final days. He was infected with a new kind of influenza, almost the whole world was. Most believed that it spread through sneezing and coughing. No one survived long enough to find out.

The Ernest O. Lawrence Institute where Auguste worked had shrunk from five hundred and twenty-two employees down to a skeletal crew in a matter of nine months. The Physics Department building itself was large—eight major research facilities, which included an electron storage ring accelerator, a center for materials research, and a whole wing dedicated to X-ray diffraction.

"Hey, hey, wuddya' say?" Auguste said in his usual friendly demeanor. It was how he greeted most of his coworkers, even though some of them were pompous and boring.

Auguste's assistant, Dr. Leo Chadwick, had arrived to help where he could, bringing boxes of canned foods. Just enough to keep Auguste's energy level up.

"You have enough to get by? I brought you more baked beans."

Once the grocery stores shut down, Leo had to get creative when it came to finding their next meal. FEMA had done most of the work of finding safe homes for him, spray-painting 4-part X-codes on every house. Each of the quadrants had a meaning, using shorthand letters and numbers to ID the rescue squad and the date of their arrival. The bottom quadrant indicated the horrors inside. If it had a "1" followed by a "2," for example, it meant there was one survivor left and two dead in the house. Looters typically broke into the homes with "0" as the first digit. It was easier that way.

Leo didn't mind taking care of his mentor. Auguste was all he had left. He no longer had any friends or family, because they all had died. Besides, where else could he go that would be less lonely than here?

The old man spent all of his time focusing on his computer, manipulating mathematical equations that Leo still had trouble keeping up with. No matter how hot the equipment got in those labs, Auguste spent his remaining time toiling away in a hazmat suit. In his mind, he believed it would prevent further spread. When his body was fit to collapse, he often slept on the break-room couch.

"Herr Catron … Auguste. Take off that ridiculous outfit. If I'm not infected by now, I probably never will be."

Auguste had already scolded Leo for what he called his excessive stupidity, but finally conceded.

"You need to find someone in immunology," he said, as he peeled away the suit. "See why you're still kicking. You might have to do your own blood work, though." His response came with a heave, as if a toxic cloud of ammonia had filled his lungs. He hacked and sputtered until he was purple before putting on his wrinkled button-down shirt and tan khaki pants.

Leo had been driving to Georgia when he learned about the pandemic on his radio. What everyone took to be the common cold turned into something far more deadly. There was always that possibility of contagion, which is why he decided not to fly. Leo never liked to fly. All that recycled air. Petri dishes with wings.

At a gas station, a man approached from behind his car. The closer he got, the worse he looked. His teeth chattered, his face was covered in sweat, and he was shaking. As he fumbled to put the nozzle back into the pump, everything Leo learned in microbiology came flooding back. Leo plunged his hands into his pockets, looking for a napkin. All he could find was a long receipt from the CVS, which he pressed against his nose and mouth.

"Please help *me* …" the man gurgled, "*. . . hospital.*"

Leo shrank from his reach before the man hit the ground. Those were his last words.

A week later, Leo peeked his head into Auguste's office, with one foot still in the hallway. His boss held his phone tight to his ear, then hung up without blinking.

"Is everything okay?"

Auguste shook his head *no*. It could be something less significant than the deaths of four billion people, but Leo doubted it.

"We have some serious business to address." There was a slight shake to his head that was barely noticeable. Leo was perceptive, but not good with interpretation. He was aware that Auguste wasn't one to keep his cards close to his vest, but it would have been nice if he didn't leave him hanging with so many long dramatic pauses.

"My friend on the inside, Rao, said they found the smoking gun. All seventeen US intelligence agencies concluded it isn't just any old plague, the result of microbial variation in nature. He said human tinkering was involved."

There had been rumors. The world population had hit ten billion people, and with it came climate change, water and food shortages, rampant disease, and political unrest. What started as a joke at one of the G10 summits quickly spiraled into something far more despicable. It was a Russian oligarch—he compared the masses to drooling cattle, saying life would be far easier if they were somehow able to thin the herd.

"Those bastards ... those immoral bastards," Auguste wheezed. "The One Percenters."

As was typical, those with obscene amounts of money wasted little time on long-term solutions. Everyone had a price. They found a scientist, a Dr. Teichert, who was willing to go along with their scheme, which they nicknamed Thin the Herd. He created a highly virulent flu strain that nearly halved the world population, but before unleashing it into the environment, they secretly manufactured a vaccine that guaranteed their survival. By the time unwitting researchers could mass-produce their own vaccine, the earth's population would be down to a more manageable size. They even kicked around the idea of making it themselves, for some extra cash.

"Their decisions depend on what's best for them. They knew our insatiate hunger for resources would never cease. I scold myself for not picking up on all the signs sooner."

Leo rested his hand on Auguste's shoulder, the same kind of gesture he would use for his closest friend.

"You all right?"

"One last thing I want you to do before you're dismissed," he mumbled. "Even though it wasn't listed in your job description."

"Yes?"

"When I die, stick me out back with a bone up my ass. Let the dogs carry me away."

"Oh, come on," Leo replied with a catch in his throat, "You'll bury us all."

He always reran in his head what he had already said out loud, wondering whether or not it was appropriate. He was weighed down by PC culture. Was it gallows humor? People were overly sensitive these days. Guess it didn't really matter anymore.

"What can be done? Now that we know … they can be arrested."

Auguste knitted his eyebrows together.

"Are you kidding? We're to the point where these pigs have so much wealth they can stand above the law."

"…and the wheels of justice turn slowly as it is. I wish there was something we could do."

Auguste looked at him dead in the eyes. Another drawn-out pause. He then shuffled over to a storage room with sliding racks, picked out a black body suit, then hung it back up just as quickly, his hands doing all the thinking. Most of the researchers knew what the suit was to be used for, knew it at first sight. The thought of activating it caused him to take a step back, as if he were the pilot on the Enola Gay, buckling under pressure to drop his payload. He wasn't its inventor; it was the work of many men and women over the last one hundred-and-fifty years. The project had been around so long, it was barely top secret.

"There is something we can do. Something *you* can do: the Leap."

Leo shook his head in disbelief. No human being had ever made the Leap, but similar, smaller outfits were utilized on animals with mixed results. Lesser creatures, like chipmunks and mice, rodents with not a lot of mass.

"We can make Teichert disappear."

Leo pressed his forehead against the table. He held his breath and closed his eyes. His hands rolled back and forth over his knees, and he thought about all the animals that returned dead. Three out of ten. Nobody ever liked those odds. The larger the test subjects, the worse their chances. Not one was ever bigger than a cat or a dog. They came back as bags of mash. Gray-brown in color. Homogenized throughout. Amorphous. Not one ligament, no muscle tissue, not even one tuft of fur was recognizable.

"So if I'm to believe we're on the same page, you're saying I'm supposed to go back in time and take out Teichert. You want me to take him out before he becomes a genocidal lunatic?"

Auguste nodded.

"No. No. I don't want anybody's blood on my hands. I'm sorry. I'm not a murderer."

"No, you're not a murderer. You're a savior. You're going to save billions of people."

"I don't know. I don't think it would be the right thing to do."

"The right thing to do?" Auguste hobbled over to his touchscreen and tapped in P-L-A-G-U-E and B-U-R-I-A-L and hit "enter." A video opened of a bulldozer pushing piles of dead bodies into a mass grave.

"Think of all the pain and misery Teichert caused."

Leo took a deep breath and clasped his hands together. The cadavers rolled over top of one another, like rubbery mannequins into a landfill.

"Can you tell me why I'm the one you're volunteering for this job?"

"Why does anyone do the things they do? Why do I collect *Mad* magazines?"

Auguste buckled over into a coughing fit. He plucked a tissue and pressed it to his mouth, hacking up green-brown phlegm.

"Okay, good. Looks like I have a bacterial infection as well."

He closed his eyes and let out a few residual hacks.

"Don't worry. I'll do everything to ensure your safety. Matter is finite. You're not meant to be there. All the forces in the cosmos of the past will boomerang you back."

Leo rubbed the oils on his forehead with nervous agitation. Sure, he would come back, but would he come back alive? And that's after killing someone. Could he live with himself?

What did they talk about in college over the occasional bong hit? Killing Hitler that one time, its ethical implications, the anti-Semitism already set in motion that might have put someone else in his place. Erasing Hitler was no guarantee that World War II and the Holocaust would've never occurred.

"What happens if I set off another reality? How do I know that my actions will remain in our timeline?"

Auguste bent down and gathered up all his three-ring binders with a smirk.

"All the non-falsifiable statements we'll have the pleasure of discussing upon your return will make your trip all the more memorable, now won't it?"

Leo stood in the tunnel, staring into the control console. His skin was warm and slick against the suit; his feet slid in his footies. His stomach hurt, like he had eaten a bag of cement.

He sniffed the air. The scent of hot metal hung in his throat—an odor that was pleasant. It clung to his lab coat and trousers whenever he got on the train after work. He would pull his collar up to his nose and inhale deeply. It smelled like science. It smelled like progress.

"I forget how the stopwatch works."

Auguste pointed toward his wrist.

"Slide from left to right up your forearm. The digital display should blink on."

Leo mimicked the gesture for a couple of swipes until a box of red dots appeared.

"Again, by my calculations, you should have fourteen minutes and seven seconds before you bounce back. Set it for fourteen minutes, to be on the safe side."

Leo loathed having to figure out technology on the spot, but managed.

14:00

"Come back to me alive, okay?"

Leo shook his head.

"I certainly hope to."

"Leo?"

"Yes?"

"I'm sorry about what I said in last year's evaluation. I was unusually cruel."

"You were, Herr Professor, but I generally keep that opinion to myself."

"You're definitely getting a better evaluation this year, I promise."

Without a conscious effort, both men gave each other warm smiles.

Wires of every color ran along the ceiling over Catron's head, like vessels in an extraterrestrial robot, a giant invader from some distant planet. A computer screen cast a cold, blue light across his glasses.

"Is it worth it? Is it worth risking everything?"

Auguste flicked some switches and activated the software patch he wrote to make up for the lack of staff. He shook his head, thinking of all the possibilities, pausing to scratch his scalp.

"I'll let you know when you get back. Or at least some version of me will. See you real …"

Long waves of electrical shock vibrated through his bones, making him unsure of his footing. When his eyes finally focused, he realized he was on a street. The name TEICHERT was glued in crisp plastic letters down the wooden post of a mailbox. He was in the suburbs of Toronto. Census data and Catron's calculations out to the nineteenth place — along with the perfectly timed bursts of dark matter — all converged on the right x-y-z coordinates. In the past.

It was night. He was so far from home. His parents were still alive and he wanted to contact them. Give them a warning about what was to come. He looked at his watch.

13:21

There wasn't enough time.

Leo ran along the side of the house — and pushed open a window. Leave it to the Canadians to never lock up their homes. He thought about what he would do if he were caught. He didn't have to. He was in the nursery, before the crib, clenching a pillow he found on a nearby chair. It should do.

Except the young Teichert wasn't a he. Teichert was a girl, a baby girl. The sight of her gave him an immediate stab of sadness. He stared at the delicate hair on the baby's scalp, and tried to imagine all those faces, four billion dead, an image he couldn't even see in his mind. The future of the world was etched upon her cold heart.

He wasn't going to do it. It wasn't right. It was easy to release his hands from the pillow.

Maybe it would be easier if he treated her like a wounded bird, a poor, delicate creature that had fallen prey to the whims of a local cat. Put her out of her misery, except it wasn't her misery he was dealing with. It was the misery of all those who had to suffer, choke, breathe their last. It was there in his hands, the power to make the dead walk again.

Auguste was deemed by *Time* as the Einstein of his day. The journal he kept as a child included the quote, "If science is to ever evolve, we must no longer stand on the shoulders of giants, but instead illuminate new ideas from the ground on up." By the time he was thirteen, his paper on wormholes and general relativity was long regarded as "radical" until the experiments backed him up. Not so long ago, the subatomic particles behind dark matter were only a theory, until Auguste came along and unlocked their mystery.

Teichert.

If Auguste hadn't gotten ill, he probably would have produced another twenty years of advances. *Fucking Teichert.* She will not rob humanity of Auguste's genius.

In that moment he filled his lungs with air. He wished he had on black leather gloves, but then he realized he was being ridiculous. No one would be able to make sense of his fingerprints. In the silence that followed, he heard the faint squeak of mattress springs in the next room. He looked at his watch and knew his time was limited.

Forgive me.

The vertebrae cracked between his fingers.

He gritted his teeth. He saw the red behind his eyes. He couldn't stand the silver-clear strands of snot pouring from his nose and wiped it on his shoulder. *What a horrible fucking life.* Tears rolled down his cheeks. He bit his tongue to keep from whimpering.

He straightened up, studying the room. Was she dead? The black-purple color of the child's face made the white sheet underneath much whiter. He held the railing and waited for the feeling of nausea to pass.

And then he saw it. The bassinet. Something moved under a pink blanket covered in white stars. It was another baby.

A twin.

Auguste made no mention of there being a twin. What if he killed the wrong Teichert?

Leo was beyond the point of regret, and he was ready. The die was cast.

0:00

Space-time shifted his direction, as if gale-force winds pushed upon every molecule in his body.

"… soon. Hey, hey, wuddya' say?" Auguste said. He was feeble now, barely able to keep his head up. Already, Leo was getting teary eyed. Only a second had passed and Leo wasn't sure if anything had changed.

He got his friend to his feet and heaved an arm over his shoulder.

Auguste felt better not opening his mouth, instead conserving his energy for the brief walk to the break room. He was sorry to be a hassle and felt a wave of relief when his body gave way onto the couch, his deathbed.

Leo said nothing about the twin. He sat on the edge of a plastic chair, holding Auguste's fingers in his closed hand. His boss had the pleasure of knowing and befriending many people, but when he took his final breath, it was Leo who was closest. So it was Leo's face that he could see, turning into a white static apparition, as his life, and his life's work, drained away. …

David C. Strickler is a writer who lives in the suburbs of Philadelphia. Since 2018, he's had a handful of stories published in magazines and competition anthologies. The scripts he co-wrote with his friend, Tisha Garcia, have garnered Screenplays of the Month on Triggerstreet.com. When not writing, he is thinking about writing. And, as would be expected, he would be happy to tell you about his cats, but he doesn't have any. Visit him on Facebook. This story originally appeared in *The Twofer Compendium*, Celestial Echo Press's first anthology, in 2020.

A Thorne in Time
Phil Giunta

Captain Garrett McNally straightened his tie as he marched along the concrete walkway that led from the driveway to the front of the sprawling Thorne Mansion. The weed-infested gardens and overgrown lawn clashed with his memory of the last time he stepped foot on this property, twelve years ago. Every inch of the place had been immaculate then—a paradise at the edge of the city.

Its luster had since faded and McNally couldn't help but wonder if that began the moment he informed Robert and Emily Thorne that their daughter, Tanya, had been the latest victim of a serial killer at the tender age of twenty-two. Robert suffered a fatal stroke a few days later and Emily lost her battle with cancer six years after that. As far as McNally knew, Tanya's twin sister Noreen still lived here, alone.

He jogged up the steps to the portico where two dead plants in mold-covered cement pots flanked a weathered mahogany door in dire need of a cleaning and new finish. He rang the camera doorbell. A few seconds later, a form undulated in the frosted privacy glass before the door swung open. McNally had expected to be greeted by a woman in her mid-thirties, but Noreen's salt and pepper hair, tired eyes, and drawn complexion lent her the appearance of someone much older.

"Ms. Thorne. It's been a long time."

"So long in fact that it's *Doctor* Thorne now. Nice to see you again, Captain. Please, come in. I appreciate you driving all the way out here so soon after I called. Can I get you anything? Water, coffee …?"

"No, thank you. I'm good. When you said you had new information regarding the Westside Slasher case, I cleared the rest of my day."

"Well, I hope to make it worth your time." She closed the door behind him. "Let's go to my office. So, how's your daughter these days?"

"Darla's doing well. Joined a new law firm not too far from here. Still misses Tanya. Talks about her once in a while."

"They were closer than anyone realized back then."

She led him down a short hallway to a room with four large monitors mounted in a square formation above a cluttered desk. They were connected to a single laptop by a tangle of cables and adapters.

Thorne tapped the space bar. Every screen lit up, each with a video file ready to play. "I must ask you to indulge me, Captain. Twelve years ago, the first victim of the Westside Slasher was Sarah Peretti. Do you recall his sixth and final victim?"

"Of course." McNally cocked his head. "It was your sister."

"Are you sure about that?" She grabbed the mouse and clicked the play button on the first screen. An anchorman with Channel 14 News shifted in his seat. "The sixth victim of the Westside Slasher has been identified as twenty-eight-year-old Mae Kaplan of Roycetown. Kaplan worked for MacHale Medical Center, just three blocks from where she was attacked and stabbed seven times. Police are—"

Thorne stopped the video.

"That's not right." McNally frowned. "I don't recognize that name and as the detective on the case, I remember every victim."

"What about this one?" Thorne launched the video on the second monitor.

"The sixth victim of the Westside Slasher has been identified as twenty-one-year-old Hailey Mahlberg of Bartlett Village," the same anchorman reported. "Mahlberg was a senior at Declan University—"

"Hailey Mahlberg was the third victim not the last one," McNally said. "What is this?"

"As I said, Captain, indulge me." Thorne slid the mouse to the third screen and clicked play.

"The sixth victim of the Westside Slasher has been identified as thirty-year-old Deb Webb, a mother of three and math teacher at Upper Carlton Middle School. Police are —"

"Are these deepfakes? Did you use AI to fabricate them?"

"I don't have access to that kind of technology." Thorne folded her arms and leaned against the desk. "Even if I did, I wouldn't use it to disrespect these women, especially since my sister was one of them. What you watched are three videos from three different timelines."

"Come again?"

"I don't have the tools to make deepfakes, Captain, but what if I had something that could help you stop the Westside Slasher before he claimed his first victim?"

McNally snickered. "Like what, a time machine?"

"A more accurate term would be time portal. Beautiful, isn't it?"

In the center of Thorne's sub-basement lab, McNally gaped at the gray metal arch that stood floor to ceiling. Several pairs of colored cables wrapped around its thick metal framework, terminating in scattered sockets where small green and amber lights pulsed and flashed. A shimmering, translucent field of pale blue filled the span beneath the arch. Across the room, four monitors were mounted on the wall above a long white counter, reminiscent of the office upstairs.

McNally paced around the arch, examining every detail, before shooting a sidelong glance at Thorne. "You gotta be kiddin' me."

"It's no joke, Captain. Those videos I showed you were the result of my three failed attempts to save Tanya's life in the past, which spawned three alternate timelines. Originally, she was the slasher's second victim. Each time I traveled back, I managed to steer her out of harm's way only for her to be murdered somewhere else a few days later. In the process, the list of victims always changed."

McNally rubbed his forehead as the reality of Thorne's words set in. "So every move you made had a kind of butterfly effect."

"Right, but where you and everyone else remembers only the final sequence of murders—the *current* timeline—I remember all four timelines, perhaps because I was tethered to the time portal. The computers in the house are all connected to the arch, which allowed me to save the videos I showed you from each timeline."

"How long did it take you to build this?"

"It was my father's invention. He spent two decades designing it and working out the math before constructing the arch. All he wanted to do was explore history, but he died before the portal was finished. So, I dedicated the past twelve years to learning the science behind it and making a few upgrades."

"How does it work?"

"I could show you fifty-five pages of equations." From the pocket of her cardigan, Thorne produced a small device with a screen displaying several rows of icons, similar to a phone. Its edges glowed with the same blue light as the arch. "Or we could just take a trip."

"You control your time travels with that?"

"Correct again. I leave through the arch and when I need to return, this handheld controller generates a portal back to it. I have two of these devices, should you decide to help me."

"I'm listening."

"Regardless of the changes in the timelines, a few things remained the same. The first victim was always Sarah Peretti, you were the detective assigned to the case, the murders stopped after six, and the killer was never caught. Now we have the perfect opportunity to stop this bastard before he even gets started."

"You want me to go with you twelve years into the past and catch the Westside Slasher before he becomes the Westside Slasher?"

"That about sums it up."

McNally laughed. "This is insane."

"Captain, when you came here twelve years ago to tell us that my sister had been murdered, I peppered you with questions about whether you had any suspects or witnesses or any leads at all. Do you remember what you told me?"

"I couldn't say much. It was an open investigation. Technically, it still is. But I believe I said I wouldn't give up until I found the killer."

"I'm offering you that chance now, Captain. Please help me save my sister."

Dried leaves crunched underfoot as McNally and Thorne emerged from the arch into darkness. A short distance ahead, through a cluster of pine trees, lampposts illuminated a paved trail lined with the occasional park bench.

McNally whirled in time to watch the arch and the lab fade into the night as if they had been nothing more than a mirage. He flexed his hands and shook his arms until the tingling subsided.

"Sorry. Should've warned you about that," Thorne said. "I got used to it by the third trip."

"Where are we ... or should I say *when*?"

"Cannon Park. October 11, 2012." Thorne glanced at the controller. "It's 9:03 p.m. Sarah Peretti will be killed nearby in about ten minutes. Let's get to the trail. She should be here soon."

When they reached the edge of the tree line, McNally held up a hand. He waved Thorne back into the shadows as four chatty teens sauntered by. No sooner were they out of sight than Sarah hurried into view from the opposite direction. Once she passed, Thorne started after her.

"Wait." McNally gripped her hand. "Slow down. We're a couple on an evening stroll."

After looking both ways, they crept onto the trail unseen and maintained a casual pace behind Sarah. The distant cacophony of city traffic, car horns, and street music meant that the park's entrance was about a quarter mile around the next bend.

"This is surreal," McNally whispered. "Seeing her alive."

"Tell me about it. Stay sharp. Should be any second now."

McNally slid a hand inside his jacket, fingertips brushing the grip of his gun. Minutes passed as they rounded the bend. The park entrance was now in sight. Sarah quickened her pace and jogged up the short flight of steps to the street where she joined a group of people waiting at the corner bus stop. Thorne and McNally ambled out of the park and turned left.

"Let's hang out here and make sure she gets on the bus," McNally said.

"Do you think we scared the killer off by following her?"

Thorne's question was answered by a scream from the park.

"Stay here." McNally dashed back to the entrance and down the steps. He rounded the bend to find three people standing over a woman lying prone on the trail. Two others knelt beside her, hands pressing a jacket against her abdomen.

"What's going on here?" he called.

"Some guy came out of the woods and jumped her." A middle-aged man pointed toward the same tree line from which McNally and Thorne had emerged earlier. "Stabbed her a few times then took off that way. We called for an ambulance."

McNally reached for his badge, but hesitated. "Did you get a good look at him?"

"Skinny dude, about six foot. Couldn't see his face. He was wearing a dark hoodie."

"Goddammit! Okay. I'll meet the ambulance crew at the entrance and direct them this way. Keep pressure on her wounds."

Thorne met him at the bottom of the steps. "Sarah got on the bus. What happened?"

"I think you were right. We scared him off long enough to save Sarah's life, so he waited for the next lone woman to come along. Some people are helping her now. Ambulance is on the way. Her name is Kelly something... Kelly... Mueller. Shit. I see what you mean about parallel memories. Now, I recall both Sarah *and* Kelly as his first victims. The good news is that Kelly will survive, but nobody saw the guy's face."

Thorne dropped onto a park bench. "I changed history again."

"No, *we* changed history. Question is, what do we do now?"

"In the current timeline, his second victim was Abby LaRuthe."

"Right. She'll be killed three days from now in the Harrison Street parking garage around 10:30 pm."

"Then that's where we go next."

On the third level of the Harrison Street garage, Abby LaRuthe backed her SUV out of a parking space and turned out of sight down the exit ramp.

McNally searched the area but found no hooded figures lurking between the cars or watching from the stairwell. "We didn't scare him off this time, because he ain't here."

"By saving Sarah, we altered the timeline," Thorne said. "And his choice of victims is changing again. Abby was spared, but who's next?"

On the street below, whooping sirens and blaring horns drew near, echoing through the garage. Flashing red and blue lights reflected off darkened windows of the nearby buildings. McNally and Thorne hurried to the edge of the parking deck as three police cars and an ambulance pushed through traffic.

"Looks like they're stopping near Declan University." McNally nodded toward the exit. "Let's get down there and see what's happening."

No sooner had they emerged from the stairwell onto the street than McNally gasped. "Darla …"

"Oh no, Captain. Your daughter—"

"She's dead. He killed her instead of Abby. I remember now. Darla's his new second victim!"

He bolted down the street toward the campus. Thorne caught up with him weaving his way through a throng of onlookers gathered along the fence outside Declan's administration building. In the adjacent parking lot, two men unloaded a gurney from an ambulance and rolled it up the walkway.

"God, no. Please." McNally turned away and slumped against the wrought iron fence. "Not my little girl. She's all I have."

Thorne squeezed in beside him and spoke in a low voice. "Captain, listen to me. There's nothing you can do for her here, but—"

"She was walking back from the gym to meet your sister. I remember her lying up there on top of the hill covered in blood after being stabbed seven times just like Abby LaRuthe in the parking garage before we changed history."

"I know, but if we could save Sarah, we can do the same for Darla."

McNally slammed the heel of his hand against the wrought iron picket. "Every time you try to save one, another dies." He leaned toward her, his voice simmering. "All you've done with that damn time portal is leave a trail of bodies in your wake and now my daughter's one of them."

"I never meant for that to happen and among your new memories you'll note that my sister will be murdered two days from now, but we can stop all of this." Thorne produced the handheld controller from her pocket. "The past isn't written in stone."

McNally sighed. "I'd love to tell you where to shove that fuckin' thing, but I don't have a choice now. What's your plan this time?"

"We travel back a few hours. You call Darla and tell her whatever you can think of to keep her from leaving the gym. We'll give this asshole a different target."

"Who?"

Thorne cocked her head.

"Hell no. I can't let you do that. You're a civilian." McNally fixed his gaze on an unmarked sedan pulling into the parking lot. "I have a better idea. We go back and call in an anonymous tip that there's a guy on campus with a knife, stalking women, but we're gonna need backup, and I know just the guy who can help."

A moment later, Lieutenant Garrett McNally climbed out of the driver's seat of the sedan and approached two uniformed cops chatting beside the ambulance. After a brief conversation, he charged off toward the administration building with the officers in tow.

"Captain, we should minimize contact with our younger selves. That could lead to severe complications."

"Look, you might have figured out time travel, but when it comes to police work, we do things my way. You called me for help, so trust me to do my job—in the present *and* the past."

In the women's locker room, Darla McNally pulled her buzzing phone from the side pocket of her gym bag and pressed the speaker button. "What's up, Dad?"

"So good to hear your voice, kiddo. Where are you now?"

She finished buttoning her shirt and slipped on her jacket. "Heading out of the gym to meet Tanya. You okay, Dad? You sound upset."

"I need you to stay there. Do not leave the building."

"What's going on?"

"We're putting the campus on lockdown. I'll explain later. Just hang tight until you hear from me, okay?"

"Will do. Be careful, Dad. Love you."

"Always. Love you, too."

Darla ended the call and started another. "Hey, babe. I'm gonna be late. My dad just called. The campus is going on lockdown. There's some kind of security problem over here and I'm stuck in the gym until it's over. So wherever you are, you might want to stay there for now."

"I'm walking across campus on my way to you," Tanya said. "The closest building is Student Services. I'll duck in there until—"

"Tanya, you broke up. Can you hear me? Tanya?"

The only response was a muffled scream.

In the security office at Declan University, Lieutenant McNally addressed four campus guards and six plainclothes officers. The latter looked young enough to pass as students.

"We got an anonymous tip about a guy armed with a knife stalking women on campus," McNally began. "From the description, we believe it's the same guy who stabbed a woman multiple times in Cannon Park last week. Tall, thin, wearing a dark hoodie. That's all we have to go on. We have some uniformed officers on the way to help with the search—excuse me."

He reached into his coat pocket and pulled out his buzzing phone. "Darla, you okay?"

"Dad, I was just speaking with Tanya. She was walking across campus to meet me. I told her about the lockdown. She was going to wait it out in Student Services but then she screamed and the call cut off."

"We're on our way there."

"That scream came from back here." With Thorne by his side, Captain McNally charged around the corner of the Student Services Building. He leveled his gun at a hooded figure kneeling over a woman lying prone on the grass. The beam from Thorne's flashlight glinted off the blade in the man's raised hand.

"Don't do it!" McNally inched closer. "Toss the knife and put your hands on your head."

"Just another fuckin' bitch that thinks she's too good to talk to me."

"I don't care. Toss the knife or I will put you down. You're wanted on one count of attempted murder. Don't make it two."

"The fuck you talkin' about?"

"We know you attacked a woman in Cannon Park last week."

"Fuck you both." With that, the man leapt to his feet and bolted around the opposite corner of the building.

"He's getting away again!" Thorne started forward.

McNally gripped her arm. "No, he isn't. Eddie Merko, drug addict and psychopath, is about to collide with eight cops led by a young and dashing Lieutenant McNally. Wait for it … Wait for it."

"Stop!" A familiar voice shouted. "Drop the knife and get on your knees!"

"It's finally over." McNally opened his jacket and tucked his gun back into its holster before turning his attention to the woman who was now curled up on her side, clutching her stomach. "Ma'am, are you okay? We'll have an ambulance here soon."

Thorne knelt beside her, holding the flashlight at an angle that allowed her to see the woman's face without blinding her. "Tanya! Oh my God. Are you —"

"I'm fine. Just… got the wind knocked out of me when he … slammed me to the ground." She sat up with help from

McNally. "Noreen? You look … different. What are you doing here?"

"That's a complicated story for another time." She slipped an arm around her sister. "I'm just glad you're alive."

"You and me both. That was the creep who tried to chat up Darla and me at the bar down the street a few nights ago. He got pissed when we asked him to leave us alone. Never imagined he'd stalk me here." Tanya glanced up at McNally. "Do we know each other?"

"Not yet, but we will soon." He pulled the handheld controller from his jacket pocket. "Doctor, I shouldn't be here when those cops show up, but I imagine you want to stay with your sister for a while?"

"I'll meet you back at the lab."

"What lab?" Tanya asked. "And when did you become a doctor?"

"Which of these icons do I tap to get back to the arch?"

"I locked your controller so only the blue button works," Noreen said. "You'll get back one hour after we left."

"Got it. I'm goin' down the street to grab a beer first. See you two later." No sooner had Captain McNally trudged off into the darkness than Lieutenant McNally arrived from the opposite direction with four cops in tow. "Are you ladies okay?"

"Wait, you were just …" Tanya gaped at her sister. "Would someone please tell me what the hell is happening?"

One Month Later

With a bouquet of flowers in one hand and a gift bag in the other, McNally rang the doorbell at Thorne Mansion. On either side of the polished mahogany door, potted tiger lilies leaned toward the sun's rays stretching across the portico. Surrounding the home, pristine gardens and a sprawling, manicured lawn completed the image of an estate restored to its former glory. A paradise at the edge of the city.

McNally smiled at the sound of light music and laughter. Darla and Tanya's fifth anniversary party was in full swing.

Noreen Thorne stood in the open doorway, wine glass in hand. "About time you got here."

"Was that supposed to be a pun?" He held up the flowers. "These are for you."

"Thank you, Captain. They're lovely. Come in and join the festivities. Would you like a beer?"

"Just what the doctor ordered."

"Follow me, *mon capitain*."

"After what we've been through, you can call me Garrett."

"Only if you call me Noreen."

"Done. So, I'm curious." Garrett lowered his voice as they stepped into the kitchen. Outside on the patio, Tanya and Darla sat with their backs to the house holding hands and chatting with friends. "Now that you saved your sister, what are your plans for the time portal?"

"Not sure yet." Noreen retrieved a bottle of beer from the fridge and handed it to him. "I'll probably explore some interesting points in history. Why, you have something in mind?"

"As it happens, I've been considering retirement," McNally said. "But I ain't one for sitting around. You and I make a good team, and there are plenty of other past murders we could prevent in this town, including several unsolved cases."

"So many lives to save," Noreen tapped her wine glass against his bottle. "So *much* time."

Phil Giunta's novels include the paranormal mysteries *Testing the Prisoner, By Your Side,* and *Like Mother, Like Daughters.* His short stories appear in such anthologies as *A Plague of Shadows, Space Opera Digest 2022, Love on the Edge,* the *Middle of Eternity* series, and more. Visit Phil's website at www.philgiunta.com.

Way, Way Out of the Building
Joanne McLaughlin

The white jumpsuit fits perfectly again. No worry that I'll split a sequined seam when I sink to my knees mid-number. Treadmill action, weights three days a week, some core work, and I am back in my fighting form. Down twenty pounds all together. Trim, unlike the man himself when he died, that's for sure.

I'm feeling the power, that pure adrenaline rush. I ease from "Unchained Melody" into the emotion-packed finale, as big as you can get with two guitars, a bass, drums, and a couple violins. As big as you can go so the folks who came for the rocking first half, the "Burning Love" portion of the show, get their money's worth despite the always indigestion-inducing intermission buffet.

I purr the first eight bars of "Can't Help Falling in Love with You," and the ladies go wild. Some of the men, too. My audiences tend toward inclusive. Who am I to say what makes them beg me to bring the goods.

The frenzy builds through the second verse. The chorus and reprise score big, and then I segue into "The Wonder of You." The music swells behind me. I drop and slide toward the crowd, right on cue.

Footlights can be blinding down here, but I know my mark. I never miss it.

Never miss it.

Never miss—

"BRIAN! Wake up! Look at you, you're half-asleep in your cereal, you'll miss the bus again!

"And what's that you're wearing?"

Mom?

Why is my mother screaming at me?

I pretend not to hear. Try to ignore the fact that I'm sprawled face down on a smooth cold surface that feels like …Formica? I squint one eye open. The arm closest to it is wearing black leather.

"BRIAN!"

What the hell is going on? Did I crack my skull? Am I having a stroke?

Maybe I'm dead, dressed in my opening-set stage wardrobe and sitting on the tarmac to the Great Beyond. Is that a pearly gate I see?

"BRIAN!"

"Jesus, Mom, what the fuck do you want?"

Crap, did I just say that out loud? Like, really loud out loud?

"Don't you dare use foul language with me, young man. Get your butt out of that chair and get to school. And don't even think you're leaving with your father's leather jacket on, not unless you want the fires of hell to rise when he finds out."

Something crashes to the floor. A bowl bounces and lands milk up, saturated sugared squares splashing everywhere.

"BRIAN! I've had it. Just get to the bus now. I am *not* driving you."

She shoves an army-green bookbag at me, hands over three one-dollar bills, and closes the door on my behind. The school bus pulls up to the corner. I run for it and stumble aboard.

"Check. It. Out! Here comes the Fonz," someone shouts. Guys lean into the aisle singing the theme from that TV show *Happy Days*.

The bus jerks, and I fall into the nearest seat available, behind the driver, next to a brunette who looks familiar.

"Going to the tryouts for *Grease* today, Brian? Cool! You're dressed for the lead part already. Me, I'd be okay with the chorus. I just hope I get picked."

What is this chick's name? Something with an "ee" sound.

Susie? Sandy? Cindy. Cindy Snyder. She asked me to the junior prom. And I went, but only because when I turned her down cold, her mother called my mother, and my mother swore to me no son of Irene Darocha would behave so callously to a woman ever again. She vowed she and Dad would *never* take me for my driver's license test unless I apologized to Cindy and accepted her invitation. My mother despised Cindy's mother, had hated her since high school. But did that matter? Nooo.

Holy shit, that was back in 1975.

How can it be 1975 again?

Shake it off, jackass, you're hallucinating. Close your eyes, click your heels, do what it takes to get you out of Oz *right this minute.*

My name is Brian McPhelan, and I'm a sixty-five-year-old Elvis impersonator working in a nightclub in Reno, Nevada.

My name is Brian McPhelan, and I'm a sixty-five-year-old Elvis impersonator working in a nightclub in Reno, Nevada.

My name is Brian Mc —

"Whoa, Bri, nice jacket, man. Your dad's gonna be so pissed, you know he loves that thing. How many times has he told us the story about how your mom just swooooned the first time she saw him in it?"

Terry Osinski. I'd know that voice anywhere. He leans over the seat behind me, karate-chopping my shoulders. Play along, Brian, play along.

"Shut up, Osinski. I thought I'd try out for the spring musical. You know, the biker guy the girls all swooooon over. Black leather jacket, white T-shirt, just like Elvis."

"Like James Dean, you mean. Does anybody still give a crap about Elvis except bored old ladies stuck in Vegas while their husbands play blackjack?"

In a couple years, after he dies, people will give a crap all right. I've made a good living off how much of a crap they give. Helped me put two kids through college. Better not mention that, though, since I'm supposed to be, what, sixteen years old?

"When my dad pitches a fit over his precious jacket, I'll tell him what you just said, Osinski. James Dean? Whatever."

"Whatever what?

Gotta remember, nobody says that yet, not until that movie *Clueless* comes out.

Gotta keep my mouth shut.

The school bus stops at good old Abe Lincoln High. I grab my books and follow Terry through the door and along the halls, toward the locker we used to share. Still share, I guess. Thank God we still share this locker, because I forgot the combination the day after graduation.

"Man, I'm so glad we have a short day today." Terry pumps his fist. "Give the teachers an in-service thing every Friday, that would be great. Come play hoops with us after class, Bri. Oh, wait, you have to go audition so Cindy Snyder can drool all over you. You know she's gonna ask you to the prom, right?"

Yeah, yeah, I know. Been there. Done that.

"Hold up a sec, it's a short day? Crap—"

"Are you nuts, McPhelan? We take that Algebra II test, then we snore through more garbage about the Revolutionary War. We have lunch and homeroom, the bell rings at 1:30, and just like that, it's the weekend. Can you taste the freedom?"

The weekend. Two shows a day, big Saturday and Sunday audiences in Reno. If I'm not dead, I am so screwed.

I hustle to keep up with Terry. Gotta get my bearings, remember what's where in this school, who's who. Gotta get through until I wake up and all this turns out to be a coma, or an LSD trip, or some crazy scientist's scheme like in *Back to the Future*.

Another movie that hasn't been made yet.

Somebody save me.

By the time Terry's liberty bell rings, I'm burping up a bologna sandwich from lunch, and my head is pounding, and I'm pretty sure I flunked the same test on quadratic equations I failed almost fifty years ago. Don't change anything, that's Time Travel Rule Number One, right? So far, so good.

I never had a part in *Grease* in high school. I'm not sure high schools even did *Grease* back in 1975, and there's no way I hung out with the drama geeks. So I am absolutely positive I won't get picked at this audition, but I've sort of committed myself because of the black leather jacket. I follow Cindy Snyder and a sea of lemon-juice blondes to the auditorium, past what seem like 700 trophy cases.

Standing at the doors, waving us in, is Mr. Traylor, the drama teacher. Old pervert that he is, probably was until the day he died, he separates the girls from the boys. Makes the girls line up on the stage while he sits in the front row, so he can watch their boobs bounce as they sing and dance. Makes the guys sit on the stage facing the seats. No jiggling for us, no sir.

"Serious work, this theater business," Traylor intones. "Everyone has a part to play in this production, and we will get only one chance to cast it appropriately. Now, select your best songs, girls, and let me hear those voices."

Unleashed upon my already terrible day is some of the worst singing ever, and I've heard truly lousy stuff in Reno. Turns out, Cindy Snyder has a good voice, but she has zero chance of getting an actual role. Not perky enough up top to meet Traylor's, ahem, standards. She gives it her all, though, with a version of "To Sir, With Love" that sounds pretty great. Who knew?

When the stage clears of aspiring Olivia Newton-Johns — she was already popular in 1975, right? — the guys get their shot. Traylor lines us up by height like we're in phys ed class, which puts me next to last. Which gives me time to reflect on my sins and when I might finally regain consciousness as an old guy singing to chain-smoking gamblers and the typically tipsy wives of same.

"McPhelan, you moron, snap out of it. You're up."

Traylor snorts when he laughs, like the pervert he is. "I bet you're just a pretty face in a black leather jacket. Let's hear what you got, handsome. Prove me wrong."

No sweat, sleazebag.

Elvis *a capella* is risky; this I know. Croon to just one woman, you got intimacy going for you. But the repertoire is all about slaying the audience with the music — sometimes pounding rhythms, sometimes lush orchestration. This is no "All Shook Up" moment, no "Blue Suede Shoes" moment, not unless I want to go for laughs, twisting like the sixteen-year-old sexagenarian I am.

Only one song will do: "Suspicious Minds."

A hush descends as I seize their souls. Cindy Snyder faints. Traylor's jaw drops.

"And there's my male lead," he announces.

"No!" I protest. "Give it to somebody else. I was joking."

"Tough luck, McPhelan. Careful what you wish for."

I never wished for this, not ever.

Cross my heart and hope to die.

My father is reading the paper and drinking a beer at the kitchen table when I walk in. Why isn't he at work? Did tryouts go that late?

"Brian, why is *that* jacket on *your* back? You know the rules."

"I borrowed it to audition for the school play. Naturally, looking this cool, I scored the lead in *Grease*."

Can I shovel it or what?

From around the sports section, he gives me the once-over. "Good. A rebel without a cause, just like your old man. James Dean was no Elvis, but still —"

Dad folds the newspaper and points to the chair next to his for me to sit. No sign Mom is around. Maybe he worked the early shift at the plant today?

He takes a long pull of his Budweiser. "Remember when we went to a Saturday matinee of *Viva Las Vegas*, just you and me, and we stayed through three showings before they kicked us out?"

"I threw up near the popcorn counter. How could I forget?" Plus, my father entertained folks with this tale at least four times a year until I left for college.

"What were you, about eight years old?"

"More like five, I think. Mom says you just wanted to watch Ann-Margret shimmy."

"Never could fool Irene, not from the second we met. She sure cursed me out when you wanted to be Elvis for Halloween, but she found someone to sew you a little black jacket and blue jeans. We bought you a plastic guitar, and you swiveled your hips to an enormous haul of candy."

Job skills learned early. If you ever saw me on stage, you'd be proud, Dad.

Mom walks into the kitchen and opens the refrigerator, searching, I hope, for whatever it is she intends to feed us. "Frankly, Pete, I'm surprised we didn't warp the boy for life. I know he learned to read by staring at movie magazine covers and gossip headlines."

She takes out something that looks like tuna noodle casserole. I won't swear to it because I haven't seen one in, oh, forty years.

"I know we told you that you were conceived after we'd had a fight and made up while 'Love Me Tender' was playing on the radio. Your dad sang along, and I just swooned."

Yeah, I've heard the "Pete and Irene Make a Baby" story. Only like 10,000 times.

Which for some reason reminds me of Cindy Snyder and the still-to-come prom and the disturbance of the time continuum I've caused by getting the stupid part in the stupid school play. I beg off dinner, claiming post-audition stomach trouble. Plus the thought of tuna casserole … it's not a complete lie.

To be honest, I'm exhausted. Lots of excitement today for an older guy like me. I was minding my own business, doing my job in a sparkly jumpsuit, and the next thing I know I'm cussing at my mother amid avocado-green appliances and knocking over a bowl of Cap'n Crunch.

I fall asleep instantly in the bedroom I saw just last summer, when Mom died. And I have the strangest dream.

"Hey, aren't you already living the strangest dream ever?" I ask myself in my dream. Except there I am, about three years old and trying to climb out of a shopping cart at the supermarket checkout to get to the *Life* magazines. Mom gently settles me back into the cart and gives me some animal crackers from a box dangling from my wrist. But I keep reaching for the magazines while Mom deposits items onto the conveyor belt, and she has to pry my sticky fingers from the metal display rack.

"Mommy, who? Who?" I ask.

"Who what, baby?"

I jab the air between me and the cover. "Who that man?" I demand, cookie crumbs congealing on either side of my mouth.

"That's Elvis, sweetie. He sings pretty songs."

The cashier chuckles as she rings up our groceries. "He's *my* sweetie, Irene," she confides. "When my husband and I make love, little does he know who's really on my mind."

The dream cycles repeatedly, and when I wake up, I'm still 16 years old. In the dark, I trip over discarded clothes and slide on sketch pads and comic books as I negotiate my way out of my bedroom.

The sun is just rising on whatever Saturday morning this is. I wander, famished, into the kitchen and take a pitcher of orange juice from the refrigerator. Freshly squeezed, I remember Mom refused to buy frozen. There are doughnuts on the counter. I grab a couple and swallow them almost whole, I'm so hungry. I haven't had this much sugar at breakfast in years, though. Quite a buzz kicks in, a good thing since there's no coffee to be had.

I bring a glass of juice into the wood-paneled rec room, where my parents' stereo is set up. Their old vinyl stands in an album rack in the corner, including not one, but two copies of the *Kissin' Cousins* soundtrack. There was a story behind that, something about a church white elephant sale and each of them buying the record without the other knowing. My parents were such huge Elvis fans, I'm surprised I don't find more duplicates in their stash.

Artifacts of my boyhood litter this space. A shoebox full of baseball cards on one of the shelves. A stack of Hardy Boys books Dad insisted I read, though I was more into superheroes and space aliens than junior detectives. When I told my parents I wanted to be a comic book artist, they smiled indulgently and said they'd prefer to pay for a bachelor's degree that might help me support myself someday. So I majored in art education, then taught mostly and worked in advertising some, always trying to stay close to New York City in hopes of landing even freelance hours with Marvel or DC, which did not happen.

After Michelle and I had kids, I started doing gigs at retirement complexes and nursing homes to supplement our income. Elvis is big in those places—he was a show business fixture for so long, the musical background of so many people's lives. It was the ideal side hustle: I had every song memorized, played passable guitar, and had been doing a dead-on impersonation ever since my voice changed.

Our nest had already emptied when Michelle and I divorced. Why not go West and hit the nightclub circuit? Worked a year and change in Vegas, in small venues the recession had somehow spared. Struggled through some lean months, too, but I jazzed up the act and shopped it at a club in Reno. The seats kept filling, so the management kept paying me. And there I stayed, until whatever happened yesterday happened.

Like Dad, Mom never saw me perform professionally. I think she would have appreciated the nuance I bring to the part.

My son and daughter come to my shows occasionally. They boast to their spouses that they have the "fun" father. Their spouses laugh, though I think they have their doubts about me.

What would Pete and Irene say if they knew I had hopscotched backward through decades?

Their grandson would crack wise, I know it. "Dad's having his Michael J Fox moment, Brian McPhelan as Marty McFly."

I shower, dress in whatever smells clean, and cram a sketchbook and colored pencils into that olive-drab bookbag, tiptoeing so I can escape without waking my parents. The less said to them about anything right now, the better.

Some internal teenage compass guides me, and before I realize it I've walked the two miles down to the high school ballfield. I played shortstop on the ninth-grade JV baseball team but was never good enough to make varsity, so I spent a lot of time in these stands watching Terry and my other friends play. I climb a dozen rows behind home plate and settle in.

It's peaceful here, green and quiet. Can't remember the last time I did something like this. I zone out, become one with paper and pencils, sketching, contouring, shading. I don't notice Cindy Snyder sitting on the bleacher near me, studying my drawing.

"Wildflowers sprouting from the baseball diamond. It's beautiful, Brian. You're a good artist *and* an amazing singer."

She catches me off guard, and I respond before remembering that I should ignore her, the way I always did. "You have a good voice too. Maybe we'll team up someday, like Sonny and Cher, the Captain and Tenille. You never know."

"You'd have to marry me first," she says. "Imagine that happening."

Cindy laughs, which lights up her face. She followed me around like a puppy all through high school, but I didn't pay much attention. Can't start now. Better shut this down.

"Don't waste your time, Snyder. The two of us won't be getting married, no offense."

The light vanishes. I've hurt her feelings, the way I always did, I suppose. But the puppy snarls in retaliation.

"So glad your crystal ball agrees with mine, Brian, no offense. I'm going to medical school to become an eye doctor or some specialty like that where you're not on call all the time, so I can have a career and raise a family also. I don't need to be famous. I just want to help others and make the people around me happy."

Fair enough. If anyone had let *me* choose my destination through time, I would have picked the days when our kids were small and Michelle and I were balancing our teaching schedules and earning barely enough to pay our mortgage in suburban New York. Hectic for sure, but we had a blast.

My ex-wife and I are still friends; our children are doing well. I like my life. Not this life—what I mean is, I like the sixty-five-year-old me just fine, though, yeah, there are things and people I miss. Things I might do over if I could.

Oh, what the hell do I mean?

"So, Snyder, you ever wonder what it would be like to live that future you have planned, then end up rocketing back to your past?"

She pulls her hair into a *Grease*-era ponytail, wraps a rubber band around it, and whips it.

"What makes you think I'm not doing that right this very minute?" She winks, acting all coy and flirtatious. But the way she says those words freaks me out.

"Yeah, right," I reply, and roll my eyes so I don't let on.

Not the time to be bullshitting me about this stuff, Cindy Snyder. It's hard enough remembering whether I had more than one pre-prom conversation with you in 1975, let alone two in less than two days, let alone figuring out why I'm on this bench with you now and suddenly spooked that this weirdness might be happening to both of us simultaneously.

She scoots closer, leans in, and kisses me hard on the lips. Like if she could, she'd go for more. My adolescent hormones stomp my adult impulse control, and I kiss her back. I wrap my arm around her waist, I want us both to go for it, and I slip my tongue between her lips. She sighs, then pulls away and races down the steps. But she waits at the bottom, staring up at me, and I feel like Juliet to her Romeo, as if something that was fated to happen just did.

That can't possibly be true, can it?

If time hiccups and hurtles people backward, I would have heard about it, right? It would be on the news. Social media would be full of idiots posting about their relived lives in ancient Babylon.

This thing, my 49-year ricochet, has to be random, doesn't it?

Thunder rumbles overhead, and fat drops splash me back to reality, or wherever I am. I gather up my art gear, humming "Early Morning Rain" while obsessing about ways to extract myself from a) this retro-existential crisis and b) the distressing presence of this girl who has been crushing on me since freshman year, without further altering my cosmic trajectory.

"See you later?" Cindy shouts, smiling at me from twelve rows below.

I pretend not to hear.

"First rehearsal is eleven o'clock today, cast and crew. I didn't get a part, but I'm building sets."

That sucks. Traylor is such a pig.

"Okay, see you later."

As soon as she's out of sight and hearing, I hum louder, as if that will beam me back where I'm meant to be. "In the Ghetto" and "Return to Sender," the whole freaking greatest-hits catalog fills my head as I dodge the drizzle and run nonstop from the ballfield to the Greyhound station downtown.

Schedules I find in the racks there list sightseeing excursions to Memphis and Graceland on Mondays, and buses to Reno via two connections every Friday. I have no cash on me, of course. The fares probably cost more than I have in my savings account anyway, assuming the passbook is still in my underwear drawer.

Better check when I get to my parents' house. See how much money I have to burn in case I keep screwing up and this delusion continues indefinitely, and I never go out of town for college, never meet Michelle there, never marry her and have two kids with her. What if I've erased my entire post-1975 existence?

Don't panic, I warn myself. Maybe this is a blip, a reversible chronological misadventure.

Don't be a fool. Don't rush in.

Just knowing what the getaway options might be makes me feel better. Less lonesome today. Maybe tonight as well.

Joanne McLaughlin writes sharp mysteries, sexy vampire tales, and sweeter short fiction, including the novels *Chasing Ashes*, *Never Before Noon*, *Never Until Now*, and *Never More Human*, and the stories *Peppina's Sweetheart* and *Grass and Granite*. She is a longtime editor of prize-winning pieces for newspapers and public media. You can find her at Joannemclaughlin.net.

Privileged Inca Nations
Gordon Linzner

Huascar's soldiers stared in bemusement at the three oddly dressed strangers who tramped through the Peruvian landscape.

The troops had prepared that morning for another attack from Atahualpa, brother and rival of their own emperor. They hardly expected to see this motley crew heading toward the city of Cuzco.

The trio's leader towered over both the soldiers and his two companions by half a foot. He projected a military bearing, although his polished leather armor, oddly shaped sword, and lack of a traditional sling indicated no affiliation. Being accompanied by a short, middle-aged woman and a boy who relied heavily on an ebony cane for support underscored his lack of hostile intent.

The woman wore a broad-brimmed hat and a long, thickly embroidered leather skirt. A small bag dangled from her left shoulder. In place of a sword, she carried what looked like an oddly shaped metal rod. The boy appeared the frailest of the three in his thin linen kilt. A bow hung over his right shoulder; a quiver of arrows was strapped to his waist.

Those two were definitely not warrior material.

Soldiers shuffled aside as Emperor Huascar came forward with his entourage to examine the newcomers personally. His gold-trimmed helmet stood out; otherwise, his llama-skin tunic and cotton-padded armor did not much differ from that of his subjects. They were, after all, going to war.

The three strangers nodded solemnly, acknowledging his status. Abruptly, the woman gave a wide grin, then swung her misshapen rod upward, toward a passing cormorant.

A thunderous boom ripped through the coastal air. The bird crashed to the ground several yards from the woman. Those soldiers nearest to it backed away, fearful of being blamed for the fowl's death. By royal decree, whoever slew one of these sacred creatures, or even disturbed its nest, without explicit permission, should be executed, possibly on the spot.

Huascar made a slight hand wave. Half his entourage stepped forward to form a semicircle around the strangers, close enough to prevent their fleeing.

Annie Oakley — the stage name under which she'd earned her fame — lowered her rifle and scanned the Incan soldiers gawking at her. Save for their crude uniforms, and the slings many of them brandished, they appeared little different from the impromptu crowds for whom she performed when not working Buffalo Bill's Wild West Show.

Huascar's appearance even reminded Oakley of her friend and fellow showman, Sitting Bull. The emperor's face seemed to hold the same subtle awe that the former chieftain's did when he first observed her shooting skills.

At least, she hoped she was reading his expression correctly.

General Sun Tzu stepped back to stand beside her. He was less pleased, his ears still ringing from the rifle blast. "Was that necessary, Mrs. Butler?" he whispered as he eyed the soldiers surrounding them.

To Oakley's left, twelve-year-old Tutankhamun tapped his cane against the ground in an ambiguous gesture. He maintained his normal fixed, stoic look, though with his inherited overbite he often appeared ready to grin. The glint in his dark eyes said that things were about to get interesting.

"I thought we should offer their leader a gift of fresh meat, to break the ice," Oakley responded. "We're only here because of those birds, aren't we? That's what the Gray One said. And standing around, doing nothing, is harder than any kind of work."

The Chinese general grunted. "These men know as little about your rifle as Tut and I did when the Gray One brought us together. They may see you as a mistress of some dark art."

"Or one of their goddesses," Tut chipped in. "The Gray One implied the Inca pantheon could give my own people's a run for its money."

Oakley blinked, fingering the thin chain around her neck. These universal translating devices used some odd idioms at times. She would have loved to hear a clearer translation of the Egyptian youth's words.

Instead, she said, "Might they not simply assume my weapon a more advanced version of their slings?"

"You should teach them how it works," Tut suggested. "I'd love to learn more about your rifle myself."

General Sun Tzu raised a hand for silence, slowly, so as not to startle their audience. "That is not a good idea, Your Majesty. We were instructed to leave as little imprint from our own timelines as possible."

"You don't need to know everything, Tut." Oakley again tapped her neck chain, identical to those of her companions. "After all, I have no idea how these translators work."

A careful observer could see their speech didn't quite match their lip movements. A minor distraction, but it reminded the sharpshooter these devices were not one hundred percent effective; they could still misinterpret concepts. Such issues arose even while she was traveling with Buffalo Bill through different areas of late nineteenth century America. It had taken the three of them hours, once they'd been brought to the year 1530 AD, to fully comprehend one another's words. During that awkward period, they revealed more about themselves than perhaps they should have. How much more complicated would it prove to communicate with the Inca, a people from centuries before her birth, let alone thousands of years in her companions' futures?

Tzu agreed. "I know these devices haven't yet picked up enough local speech to translate adequately. We must allow their leader to carry the conversation for now." The general turned to Tut, raising an eyebrow. "Are we agreed, Your Majesty?"

Tut snorted. "Do I agree with the man who ordered his own emperor's two favorite concubines to be executed because they did not take your military orders seriously? I'm good."

"Answer me! Someone must have sent you! Who? Why?" Huascar focused his interrogation on the swordsman, ignoring both woman and child.

"Sent," Tzu replied, nodding. "Yes."

"I already guessed as much! Again, why? What is your mission? Why risk coming to our land in this time of war?"

"Mission. War. Risk." Tzu shook his head, slashing his right hand downward to emphasize his negative tone.

Huascar's scowl deepened. He had no time to waste on this nonsense. Atahualpa was intent on annexing Huascar's part of the Inca Empire, even if it meant killing his own brother.

Especially if he could kill his own brother. The man's latest attack, according to Huascar's spies, would happen within the next few hours. These blank-eyed strangers barely responded to his questions and demands, beyond an occasional grunt. He doubted they even understood the Incan language, until the swordsman started dropping a word here and there.

There was also the more serious issue of their defying a prime edict of the empire. That cormorant was one of their most sacred birds, along with the pelican and the booby. Slaying one without royal permission was punishable by death. Worse, the blasphemer was a mere woman!

And yet ...

Something about these visitors intrigued Huascar, enough to curb his usually hot temper. The swordsman, obviously their leader, had yet to make an overtly hostile move. His tone, when he finally began speaking coherently, seemed conciliatory. For him to travel through the empire's shorelines and mountains and, yes, even the jungles in which few of his own people dared to venture, accompanied only by a slip of a woman and a deformed boy, was hardly the act of a dangerous enemy.

As Huascar's questioning continued, the swordsman gradually grew more conversational, identifying himself as General Sun Tzu. His companions began contributing to the discussion as well—surprisingly, without reprimand from their leader.

Strange peoples indeed, the emperor mused.

Huascar was still pondering how best to deal with the trio and getting little useful help from his advisers, when a runner pushed his way through the crowd. Approaching the emperor thus meant urgency indeed, and so there was. Atahualpa's soldiers would arrive within the hour.

"Take these strangers to my palace," Huascar ordered two of his entourage. "We shall continue this discussion afterward."

"If you will permit me, Emperor," Tzu offered humbly, "I might be able to help deal with your enemies."

Huascar blinked, looking up to meet Tzu's placid eyes. "You wish to join in our battle?"

"I might try to convince them not to attack you in the first place. The most supreme art of war is the ability to subdue the enemy without bloodshed."

Oakley stepped forward. "The general wrote a book about wartime negotiating. Its wisdom has been passed on for ... well, for a very long time."

"I refuse to empower some bizarre stranger to speak on behalf of myself and my kingdom," Huascar snapped.

"Nor would I presume to do so," Tzu replied, bowing slightly. "I only wish an opportunity to explain to your enemy why their actions are ill-advised."

"And if you fail?" *As you undoubtedly will*, Huascar thought. He was well familiar with his brother's stubbornness, having endured it personally for years.

Naturally, Atahualpa often said the same of him.

Tzu reached toward his sword hilt, but did not draw it, reluctant to alarm the emperor's entourage. "I have other methods to fall back on."

Huascar took a deep breath, considering the offer. His soldiers could use the extra help. These conflicts had not been going favorably for his people.

"Very well, General, if you think you can dissuade them. I'll have the woman and child escorted to my palace, for their safety."

Tzu nodded, turned, and strode off in the direction of the oncoming army before Huascar changed his mind.

Oakley's brown eyes fixed on the emperor's. She raised her rifle, shaking it like a sword. "I believe you need all the help you can get."

"He does, indeed," Tut confirmed. The boy unshouldered his bow and shifted the arrow quiver into a more accessible position. "I notice a definite shortage of women soldiers, for instance."

Huascar was unused to being spoken to in such condescending tones, but once more, in a rare display of control, he held his temper in check. Should he allow these two to join the battle, they would likely perish. That, at least, would resolve the issue of the woman's execution.

He found it ironically satisfying that both boy and woman seemed readier to fight than their general.

"Soldiering is not a job fit for a woman, but ..."

An adviser tugged the sleeve of the emperor's tunic, interrupting his speech, to whisper in his ear.

Huascar scanned the area. After a moment's reflection, he addressed the two strangers again. "That hilltop behind you is a key vantage point. It needs to be protected."

Tut and Oakley nodded, accepting the task.

"I cannot spare any troops to aid you," the emperor added in an almost-convincing rueful tone. "My numbers are already thin."

"Yet you would have ordered two or more of them to escort us to safety," Oakley observed.

Huascar ignored her comment. "Should you hold that position, if only for a short time, it will greatly assist our cause."

Huascar abruptly turned away from the pair. Bloodcurdling cries from Atahualpa's army were already echoing through the valley.

Tut perched uncomfortably on the lopsided boulder, easing the discomfort in his club foot. Each time the score of Atahualpa's soldiers assigned to take them out moved forward, the boy grew more impressed with the sharpshooter's skill. Her taking down that seabird, in flight, initially seemed a lucky fluke to the Egyptian boy king. Now, though, at every approach of their assailants, a bullet from Oakley's rifle discouraged them, made them pause, tore away bits of their tunics and padding, glanced off their bronze swords, scored deep bloody marks along their jowls. Her left hand blurred, so quickly did she reload ammunition from her side pouch.

"How is it you continue to miss those targets by so narrow a margin?" Tut asked, eyes widening.

"I don't miss," Oakley countered. "I do not wish to undercut Tzu's attempts for a peaceful resolution. I'm only trying to discourage these men."

"I doubt Emperor Huascar will show such restraint on his end," Tut observed. "I also cannot help noticing, although these soldiers take cover at your every shot, their pauses grow shorter, and they inch still closer."

"They will regret that soon, if they don't retreat."

Though but a youngster, the Egyptian king had learned much from his mentors in the two years since taking the throne. Obviously, the woman was reluctant to kill.

"My turn now, I think. This may be the closest I get to participating in a real battle!"

Oakley hesitated a moment, then silently moved aside. Both she and the boy were in peril, after all, and her ammunition was running low.

Tut took up his bow, threaded an arrow, and licked his lips, anticipating the next moment one of Atahualpa's men should raise his head.

Long minutes passed.

Tut's arm trembled from the strain of holding his position.

But it did not tremble badly enough to spoil his aim. He took out the eye of the next soldier who looked up.

The enemy at last started to retreat. They might not understand the power of Oakley's rifle, but a precisely aimed arrow was a different story.

Tut took down three more soldiers before Oakley joined in the rout again.

Tzu deeply cherished his Longquan sword. The weapon had been forged in iron with the greatest care and patience, by one of the finest smiths in China. It was without doubt stronger and keener and more durable than any of the bronze blades belonging to the Inca soldiers.

Still, for the moment, he kept the weapon sheathed, his hands outstretched. He even crouched, as if in uneasy fear, though in reality to avoid towering over Atahualpa's soldiers in an intimidating manner as he approached.

He stopped just beyond what he judged was the range of this group's slings, but close enough to be heard.

In his humblest tone, Tzu called out, "I wish only to talk to your commander. Nothing more."

The troop muttered briefly among themselves. A single soldier then stepped forward, as spokesman. "General Pacari is busy at the moment."

"I meant the Emperor Atahualpa."

The soldier laughed. "Our emperor had some urgent royal business to deal with this morning. We expect him to join us later, to celebrate our victory."

"I can advise your general, then, while you await your emperor."

The soldier laughed again, louder, joined by several others. "Wait? The emperor sent us here for one purpose: to do battle. We are loyal subjects. Even were we not, many of us hold personal grudges against Huascar for his cruel, petty acts. My own sister was one of his victims. She escaped his cruelty only by taking her own life."

"He had my brother executed!" shouted another soldier.

"Both my parents ...!"

Further complaints were drowned out by the ensuing uproar. Tzu felt a rock glance off his hardened leather armor, above the knee. Other such missiles hurtled toward him, all falling short.

There was to be no discussion, then.

Quickness was the essence of war.

The last thing these men expected was for Tzu to charge into the heart of the troop.

Their thick cotton armor might be sufficient protection from their own bronze swords. Against General Tzu's sharp, perfectly forged blade, not so much.

To the emperor's surprise, all three strangers survived. They now reunited in Huascar's palace, following the rout of Atahualpa's men.

Oakley rested a motherly hand on Tut's shoulder. "I'm proud of this lad. He saved me much stress today. At his age, I'd been hunting game for years, in support of my mother and siblings, but that was out of a greater need, and I had nowhere near his disabilities to contend with. Each arrow he fired this day hit its mark. It's made me again regret I am unable to bear children of my own."

Huascar shrugged, only half-listening. Today's battle was the closest to a victory he had yet achieved over his brother's forces. Whether that was due to the strangers' unusual skills and weaponry, or simply a whim of the gods, he felt justified, even compelled, to forgive the trespass of the cormorant's death.

Nonetheless, he could not allow them to stay. If he would not execute the woman, he must at least exile her and her companions. To do otherwise would have him seen in certain quarters as weak. His position was already tenuous.

Nor was he entirely convinced the three would remain on his side in the future.

"In gratitude for your aid, however, we offer a small compensation." Huascar ordered a treasure chest to be brought forward and laid before them. "Take what you wish."

Tut was immediately entranced by the gold llama statuette. He paraded it about the room, his own status as a king temporarily forgotten. General Tzu raised a golden bowl for a better view of its intricate workmanship. Oakley, too, was impressed by the fine artistic detail of the artifacts before her.

She also recalled why, the Gray One told them, the trio had been brought to this time period.

"We thank you for your generosity, Emperor," she replied, "but dare request one thing above all else."

Huascar blinked. He would never get used to women speaking up in this manner.

"Which is?"

"It would be fitting," Oakley continued, "for us to honor the memory of your sacred bird, that cormorant whose life was taken by myself, unjustly, in unwitting offense to your goddess Urpi Huáchac. As a reminder of its importance, and my error, I beg of you one thing."

"Name it."

"Guano."

General Tzu glanced toward her, impressed. *You are also quite the negotiator*, he mused. *When your friend Sitting Bull named you 'Little Sure Shot,' he referred to more than your prowess with a rifle.*

"We are aware," Tzu added, "of the importance of that substance to your agriculture, among other things. We request but a small sample. Half a kilo should suffice."

Once the time travelers returned to the cave where they'd first arrived in sixteenth century Peru, General Tzu pushed forward. He wished to hand over the guano personally. More importantly, he wished to confront the faceless Gray One, an opportunity he'd not had earlier.

"You pulled the three of us hundreds, thousands of years out of our timelines," he argued. "You put our lives at risk, and all for a bag of—?"

"Watch your language, General," Oakley chided. "There's a youth present."

Tut smirked. "I've heard worse language from my mentors. But I agree with General Tzu's point." Tut moved alongside Tzu to address the Gray One directly. "Before you return us to our proper times, explain why you had us go through all this. Why couldn't you or your people collect guano on your own, or have us, or anyone really, collect it in secret, without getting involved in that stupid war?"

"And why we three, specifically?" Oakley added.

The Gray One shook its head. "Timeline interference. A specific chemical mixture. Events in your far future. No matter how much I simplified my explanation, the rationale would be impossible for people of your time—your times—to comprehend."

"Try us," Tut responded imperially.

The Gray One remained silent.

"Huascar doesn't survive this war with his brother, does he?" asked General Tzu, breaking the uncomfortable stillness. "Our participation in that battle was wasted effort."

The Gray One shrugged. "Huascar started the war. If it's any consolation, Atahualpa falls victim to the invading Spanish a year later. Do not obsess over it, General. Once back in your own time, you'll remember little of what happened here. At most, a few images from a half-forgotten dream."

"Any chance you'd need our help again?" asked Oakley. "I've grown fond of these two. They're like an extended family. Not as fond as I am of my husband, Frank, of course."

The Gray One shrugged again. "Perhaps."

The sharpshooter couldn't resist the cue. She'd been in show business her entire career. "When? When shall we three meet again?"

The Gray One chuckled.

Tut and Tzu stared at the two blankly.

"I forgot," Oakley apologized. "Shakespeare's work is long after your times."

She tried to think of a more appropriate quip when the Gray One announced, "Now!"

The cavern filled with the same dim blue light as it had when the time travelers first arrived.

Tutankhamun, ruler of Egypt, vanished first. His translator's thin chain clattered to the stone floor. The boy king had the farthest to travel, back to the fourteenth century BC.

General Sun Tzu was next, returning to the Wu Dynasty of fifth century BC China.

Mrs. Frank Butler, Annie Oakley, only had to travel a few hundred years into the future.

All three would arrive home seconds after they'd left. Annie struggled, even as the translator slid off her neck and she herself faded into the time stream, to at least remember the names and faces of her new friends.

She almost succeeded.

Gordon Linzner, founder and former editor of *Space and Time Magazine*, author of five published novels and scores of short stories in numerous magazines and anthologies, is a full member of the Horror Writers Association and a lifetime member of the Science Fiction & Fantasy Writers Association. He can be found on Facebook.

Somewhere, Somewhen
Judith Field

'I wish I'd known Dad,' Chloe said. She pulled out a photo from the middle of the pile on the kitchen table and held it up to the morning light that was shoving its way past the rain. 'Here's one of him. I suppose this is the nearest we get to time travel into the past.'

'He'd have been crazy about you.' Dawn hugged her. It'd been hard to find a black maternity dress. She glanced at another photo. Her, Jim and his parents standing outside the register office, her pregnancy just starting to show, looking like they had all the time in the world. So much for planning.

'It's going to take you hours to scan these,' Chloe said. 'If you want to make a family archive, we should set up a Kindeo. I downloaded the app onto your iPad last night. All we have to do is record videos and upload them. They save it to their server. It's as near as we can get to time travel into the future. People can look at them forever.'

'Or as long as they're in business. I'll think about it.'

'Cool. The iPad's in my room.' She grabbed her bag. 'I've got to go, now. I've got a computer science workshop at half nine. Can I borrow the car?'

Dawn shook her head. 'I've got patients to see. If you'd asked me yesterday, I could've rearranged things.' She looked at her watch. 'Chloe, it's nearly nine now. You need to plan things, not leave it all to the last minute. And when are you going to start your A level revision? Talking about time travel doesn't count as Physics.'

'I've got bags of time for that.' Chloe shrugged. 'Motorbike in the rain it is, then.'

'Drive carefully.'

She picked her helmet from where she'd left it, on the floor. 'I will. But I've got bags of time to get there as well, especially seeing as I don't drive granny-style like you.'

'It's *careful* driving that's kept that car in perfect condition.'

'Doesn't mean some tosser won't hit it. Can't plan for everything. And I might be going out with Abi after college, so don't lock the door.'

'Where are you going?' Dawn shouted to her retreating back. 'Dunno yet.'

'Text me as soon as you ...' the front door slammed '... know.' Dawn's throat tightened. Why did she have to go to school on a motorbike?

Her mobile rang from somewhere in Chloe's bedroom. Why didn't she say she'd borrowed that as well as the iPad? *Don't ring off.* She flung her bedroom door open. As she staggered through the gloom, kicking aside a pair of discarded jeans with one leg inside out, the ringing stopped. Multiple computer screens blinked, some displaying the same thing, others not. Was Chloe studying computer science, or teaching it? Dawn didn't dare think of the electricity bill. Lights flashed from grey and black electronic components.

She made her way to the window, moved a cup, half-filled with mould-covered liquid, from the ledge and dragged the curtain open. The ringing started again from under a pile of magazines. She grabbed the phone. The display read 'Caller Unknown'. 'Chloe?' she gasped.

Office sounds in the background. A second's pause. 'Is that Nurse Dawn Kay?' A man's voice, echoing and tinny. 'How are you today, Ma'am? May I call you Dawn?'

'No, you may not. And I don't have a problem with my computer, there's nothing wrong with my bank account and I didn't have PPI on a bank loan.'

'I'm Paulie from Retroprotect Insurance, Dawn. I'm calling about your car accident.'

Dawn sighed. 'I haven't had one.'

'Wanna bet? Shame about the car. How will you get to work, Dawn?'

Had Chloe taken it? She cut off the call and looked out of the window. Her Smart Car was where she'd left it the night before. She went outside and found it still in one piece. Must have been a wrong number. Must be loads of women called Dawn. There'd been loads of them in her class at school. *Calm down. At least the rain's stopped. Less dangerous for bikers.*

The phone rang again. She answered it. 'Just get lost.'

'Keep looking, Dawn.'

Bright lights flashed in front of her eyes. *Great, a migraine.* The air flickered silver as, opposite the car, a man's head emerged through the wet pavement. Just the head, sitting there like a discarded beach ball, but with orange hair sticking out like an auburn chrysanthemum, about a foot in each direction. The head looked around and smiled. The rest of him followed, wearing a top and trousers like pyjamas made of shimmering fabric. He nodded at her.

'Hello, Dawn'.

Migraines didn't usually start like this.

He held an object like a baseball bat, made of matte white metal. Joe, six foot and about eighteen stone of muscle and shaven head, came out the house next door. He walked towards the man, and through him.

'Only you can see me, Dawn.' The man's voice lagged behind the movements of his face, like a badly dubbed film. 'I'm Paulie.' He ran his finger down the car bonnet. 'Nice paint, Dawn. Shame about *this.*' He pointed the bat thing towards the car. A piece of the wing flew off with a crack like a breaking bone, leaving a jagged edge.

Dawn screamed and grabbed at his arm. Her hand went right through.

He wagged his finger at her. 'Uh-uh-uh, Dawn. You can look, but not touch.' He peered at the car. 'Well, you live and learn. I was expecting a dent, but this is better. Smart Cars must've been made of plastic.'

'Police ...' she fumbled for her phone.

'They won't believe you, Dawn. In your time I don't exist, and I won't for a hundred years. Five hundred sovereigns will stop me doing any more. Five for every year between my time and yours.' He walked towards her, slapping the bat against the palm of his other hand.

She backed away. 'Where am I going to get gold sovereigns? I haven't got that sort of money, anyway.'

'Ah yes, pre-Brexit. I forgot, Dawn. Okay, five hundred quid. Cheaper than taking it to the body shop. Especially with this, as well.' He pointed the bat at the nearside headlamp. The glass shattered into a spider-web of cracks. She lunged at him and grabbed at his arm. Her hand went straight through.

'What you're seeing is a projection, from my time to yours. Think about it, Dawn. You don't want any more, do you? I'll text you my bank details – we set an account up in your time. Some things last. A thousand quid, now. Shoulda said yes in the first place. You can't fight me.' He spoke to someone only he could see. 'Right, Tavia. Reverse the projector. Bring me back.' He sank into the pavement, stopping when he was waist deep.

'This switch, is it?' A woman's voice, coming from empty space.

'No! The one at the end!' The air shimmered and he disappeared.

The police said there was nothing they could do without witnesses. Dawn couldn't neglect her patients, so going back to bed and pulling the duvet over her head wasn't an option. Dragging her feet, she trudged to the bus stop to get to the first call of the day.

She arrived home hours later, sheets of rain battering against her umbrella like they were trying to break through. She draped her coat over the banisters, kicked off her sodden shoes and dropped into a kitchen chair. All the garages would be shut now. She'd have to try in the morning.

The front door closed and Chloe came into the kitchen. 'What's wrong? You look like you peed yourself last week but only found out yesterday. Oh, don't cry ...' she knelt and put her arm round Dawn's shoulder. 'Mums aren't meant to cry. What happened?' She passed her a crumpled tissue from inside her sleeve and sat down opposite.

'Didn't you see the car? What a mess. A man ...' She blew her nose '...smashed it. Just after you left. Nobody believes me. Take a look when it's light, if you can stand it. Headlamp, wing, ruined.'

'What are you on about? Did you have a crash and bang your head?'

'No. There's nothing wrong with me.'

'Mum, we'd better get you to hospital.'

'I said no. A man appeared out of nowhere, said he was from the future, and smashed the car. And don't stare at me like that. I'm not mad. I wasn't even in the car at the time. I told you. A-man-came-from-the-future-and-smashed-it.' She banged her fist on the table, a blow for each word.

Chloe stood up. 'Stop it, Mum. I mean it. You're freaking me out. You must've fallen asleep when you got home and had a dream. I can't deal with this now.' She backed away into the hall. Her bedroom door slammed.

Dawn slumped. Maybe she was right, and it hadn't happened. Maybe it was migraine, or something worse. She thought of all the things that caused hallucinations.

Next day, she rang round for the local bodywork shops for repair quotes and booked the car in with the cheapest, or rather the one asking the least. They'd have to come and tow it, and couldn't till the following week. All her savings, eaten up.

Paulie texted his bank details to her. So, not a brain tumour. She was almost relieved, except that she couldn't pay him.

Chloe went off to college. Dawn didn't need to get to her first patient till eleven. She ran a bath, thinking of a picture in a magazine with lit candles all around a bathtub. How could that be relaxing? Not being able to see properly. Worrying sick you'd set the bathroom on fire.

She dropped one of Chloe's bath bombs into the water, sank in, and closed her eyes. Here was where she'd first learned to bath Chloe, all fingers and thumbs, wrestling with the slippery, wriggling baby on her own. Being on duty all the time. Having to make all the decisions. But also, not having to consult anyone else, till Chloe got old enough to argue- more or less as soon as she could talk. Nobody to help.

Her phone rang from the pocket of her dressing gown, hanging on the back of the door. Please be Chloe. Don't be anyone else calling about Chloe. She climbed out of the bath and grabbed the phone. Caller Unknown. She answered. Silence. The emergency services would speak right away, wouldn't they? She shivered as water dripped from her onto the floor. Don't be Paulie. 'What do you want?'

Paulie spoke. 'Is that Nurse Dawn Kay? How are you today, Ma'am? May I call you Dawn?'

'Go away.'

'Don't ring off, Dawn. I'm outside your house.'

She flung open the bathroom window and stuck her head out. Paulie, standing next to her car, looked up and waved. The second headlamp – smashed. Four flat tyres.

'Thousand quid, Dawn.' Paulie said.

Dawn pushed Chloe's bedroom door open and stepped inside.

'Mum! Knock first!' She switched off one of the computer screens and span round.

'Sorry, love,' Dawn said. 'But there's something you might just be able to help me with. Remember how you found Mr Henderson's address, and sent him all that manure?'

She grinned. 'Serves him right for giving me that bullshit mark.'

'If you had someone's bank details, could you get their address?' If she could tell the police where to find Retroprotect, maybe they'd do something.

'No problem.' Chloe put out her hand, jerking the fingers inwards. 'Give.'

Dawn showed her Paulie's text.

'Who are they?'

Here we go. She'd think she was off her head again. 'Er ... I want to write to them and complain about something. I've got no contact details.'

Chloe cracked her knuckles and raised her hands over the keyboard like a concert pianist. Dawn peered over her shoulder. 'Mum, you're putting me off. Go and plan next week's menus or something. I'll call you when I've finished. Close the door behind you.'

Half an hour later, she joined Dawn in the kitchen.

Dawn grabbed the piece of paper she handed her. '*Retroprotect. 23 Prospect Way, Rastidge PE23 6YY.* I've never heard of it, but the police will have. You're a genius.'

Chloe shook her head. 'Don't smile yet. I looked it up. There's no such place.'

Dawn felt sick. 'What do you mean? Don't banks check, when people set up an account?'

Chloe shrugged. 'Dunno. It's a Peterborough postcode. But when you look on the map, it's just marked "Future new town development". I can't find where they really are.'

Or when.

A few weeks passed. Dawn worked enough overtime to get the car fixed. One Sunday afternoon, as she sat sorting through the last few photos, her phone rang.

A woman spoke. 'Is that Nurse Dawn Kay? How are you today, Ma'am? May I call you Dawn?'

'Yes,' she whispered, her heart sinking till it felt like it had melted into the carpet.

'My name is Tavia. Paulie's outside your house. We've been doing a transaction with your neighbours, Dawn, but we haven't had your payment.'

'I can't-'

'We've had to add interest. And, we've noticed Chloe drives kinda fast. Better tell her to take care. Just saying.'

Dawn's mouth dried. She tried to swallow. She'd have to start giving Chloe lifts everywhere. She stuck her head out of the window. Joe-next-door's BMW drooped on four slashed tyres. The front passenger door hung on its hinges.

Paulie stood on the pavement, Dawn's car visible through his body. 'Nice repair job,' he called up to her. His head jerked to his left. 'Who the hell are you?' he shouted, to someone she couldn't see, a hundred years in the future.

A man spoke from somewhere, somewhen. 'I'm ...' a crackle, like a badly tuned radio interrupted him '...Kay, you ginger tosser.'

'Get away from that switch!' He pointed the baseball bat gadget at the car and pressed a button. Nothing happened. Dawn could no longer see through him.

Joe flung his front door back on its hinges with a crash, and he and his son Matt came thudding out of their house.

'Tavia!' Paulie shouted, jerking his head from side to side. 'I can't see the lab! I'm stuck! Get me out!' No reply.

Joe and Matt lurched towards Paulie, fists raised, arms like hams. Dawn turned away and picked up her keys.

Chloe came in. 'What's going on?' She looked outside. 'Blimey, it's them next door chasing some weird guy down the street. They're gaining on him, too.' She laughed. 'Who says the 'burbs are boring?'

'I like boring. I like knowing what's going to happen.'

'Certainty is overrated. You should just go with the flow.' She picked up a photo of herself as a baby. 'We never did do that Kindeo, did we?'

A high-pitched shout came from outside. Chloe went back to the window 'Matt's little lad's come out with a baseball bat. He's chasing as well. Keeping it in the family. Wonder if I'll ever have kids?'

Dawn smiled. 'I think you will. And grandchildren.' She looked into the distance. 'Who'll be really great.'

'Don't tell me you've got that planned as well. Give me a chance – I'm only eighteen.'

Dawn joined her at the window. 'Yes. You've got bags of time.' She kissed her and went into her bedroom.

After closing the door, she settled on the bed with her iPad. No time like the present. Better do it now, in case it never happened. She started the Kindeo app and made yet another plan for the future.

She cleared her throat. 'Hello, family. I'm your ancestor. I know the world is different for you, in 2117. But some things, like greed, don't change. There's something I want you to do for me. I know you did. I mean, I know you will.'

Judith Field lives in London, UK. Her short stories, mainly speculative, have been published in the USA, Canada, UK, Australia and New Zealand. Her novel, *The Sound of Gematria*, was published in October 2023. She blogs about London parks and gardens. Find out more at judithfieldauthor.uk. This story originally appeared in *Bards and Sages Quarterly*, January 2018.

Time for Adventure
Carol Gyzander

Gary eyed the envelope—the thick, creamy white paper and beautiful script of the hand-written address stood out among the computer printouts covering his desk. When had he ever seen something like that? It was rare enough that he got physical mail these days.

He dragged his eyes away, tapping his pen on the desk as he scrolled through the list of sales calls he needed to make. The screen seemed to mock him as it produced name after name of today's contacts. Rolling his eyes, he clicked the next one and was about to initiate a call for aluminum siding that would drastically improve the target's life.

He paused, his gaze flitting back to the envelope. With a sigh, he flipped it over and opened it by carefully breaking the wax seal on the back. A single, thick card bore his name in the same beautiful script.

Dear Gary Smith,

I am writing to inform you that you are the winner of a special prize: a free fabulous getaway vacation!

Please visit the Iliad Bookshop at 436 Market Street today to claim your free reward.

It had to be some sort of scam. He dropped the card in the trash and turned back to the screen.

But what if it wasn't?

He leaned over and snagged the card from the trash bin, examining the address: 436 Market Street. *Not exactly on my way home, but not that far out of the way.*

If he timed it right, he could stop by and still get home in time for tonight's pre-season game. He needed to finish the selections for his fantasy football team. He set an alert on his phone to remind him to stop on the way home, then dove back into a series of sales calls that took him through his lunch hour and right up until the end of the day.

Gary walked along Market Street, checking the numbers of each shop he passed. He'd worked right through the alarm reminder and already headed home before remembering to go to the bookshop. Now, he was hoping to get there and back before the game started. *432 … 434 … huh, 438? Where's 436?*

He turned around and walked back toward his car, staring at the shopfronts as he passed. It wasn't until he looked away that he caught the number from the corner of his eye. An old wooden sign with 436 burned into it hung on the door of a tiny, narrow shop wedged between the adjacent buildings. He paused and blinked.

Why didn't I see it the first time? Oh well, let's get this over with.

He twisted the worn doorknob and pushed the carved wooden door into relative darkness, blinking in the shadows after the late-day sunshine. A bell tinkled overhead as the door swung closed. The dark shapes around him resolved into shelves crammed with books, running in a parallel line toward the back of the narrow shop.

"Hello?" he called tentatively. No answer. He walked toward a dim light at the rear. The bookstore seemed to go on forever and somehow got wider, with more rows of shelves looming behind the ones he followed.

As Gary approached the light, a wrinkled, white-haired man looked up from a leather-bound book on the table before him. An ornate, filigreed cash register made of brass reflected the light from the Tiffany glass desk lamp.

"Can I help you, young man?" His voice croaked as if it were not used very often. "Is there anything in particular you are looking for?"

"Uh, no, I'm not much of a reader. I'm just here because I got this in the mail." He pulled the card from his briefcase with a shrug. "I didn't picture it would be a bookstore."

"You don't love books?" The tiny clerk frowned, his bushy eyebrows bunching up.

Gary shrugged. He'd always heard people talking about getting lost in a good book, but it always seemed like so much work to him to read all the words and figure out the place they were describing and who all the people were. It was so much easier to watch TV.

"Well, books are fine, but there's just not enough time for reading. I mean, between the job and keeping up with sports on TV ..." His voice trailed off as the elderly store clerk sat back on his stool, rubbing his chin.

"I see. Yes, of course, that makes perfect sense. So, you are very busy and would like to take a break?"

"Yeah, what's the scoop? Is this like a time-share come-on where I go somewhere free, and then I'm on the hook to keep paying?"

The older gentleman shook his head. "No. Nothing like that. You've been chosen to receive a very special free getaway. Hold on just a moment, please." He looked Gary up and down, rubbed his chin, then slipped off the stool and creaked into the back room.

Various bumps and scraping noises made Gary peek toward the doorway, but he kept his place, not wanting to pry. "Everything okay?" he called.

"Yes, yes, I'll be right there. Just looking for something ..."

The shopkeeper returned carrying a carved wooden box in one hand and a book tucked under his arm. He placed the book before Gary and thumped the small box on the table. A hollow, booming sound reverberated through the store with an echo of clashing metal. "Here you go. This is for you."

Gary stared at the box, intrigued. *What made that noise?*

The shopkeeper pushed the book toward him with one gnarled finger.

Really, the prize is a book? Gary sighed, shaking his head. "Well, thank you. That's very nice, but I really don't have time to read—"

The shopkeeper held up his hand and nodded. "I suspected that you would say that. That's why I have something special for you." He opened the box and pulled out a beautiful old brass coin.

Gary blinked. He bent to look at the coin. "I've never seen anything like that before. What country is it from?"

The elderly gentleman shook his head. "It's not legal tender in any country, but it does have great value. You see, this coin will grant you enough time to read the book." He sat back on the stool, placing the coin on the table and tapping the book he'd selected for Gary with one finger.

The cover bore a muscular man with close-cropped hair like they wore in the sixties, wearing thin-legged black slacks, a black turtleneck, and holding a gun. A voluptuous woman with long blonde hair stood behind him, one hand on his shoulder. The two peered around a brick wall into an alley.

"Ha. You mean if I take this coin, I'll have time to read this book? And that's my free vacation?"

"I suspected that you were smart and would catch on quickly." The shopkeeper tilted his head to the side. "What do you say? Are you game to step into another world—another time? It's a great story, full of action, adventure, dangerous people, and romantic pairings …"

He waggled his bushy white eyebrows somewhat suggestively, which made Gary look away in a hurry.

I'll take the book just to get him to stop doing that.

"Okay, it's a deal. So what do I do? Insert the coin in a slot in the book or something?" He snickered.

The clerk shook his head. "No, just have it on your person while you're reading, and you can take a little break from your current timeline to read the book. When you return from reading, you won't have missed anything."

Gary gave an internal eye roll. *Right.* He shoved the book and coin into his briefcase and headed toward the door. "Well, thank you, I guess," he said over his shoulder, already calculating whether he would get home in time for the game.

The next day at work, Gary slogged through his sales calls, feeling somewhat fuzzy from the beers he'd enjoyed during the game the night before. Sometimes, his job seemed like a never-ending chore, like he would never get through all the sales calls. After three hang-ups in a row, he pulled off the phone headset and sat back in his chair, chin slumping to his chest. It was 2:43, and he still had hours to go in the day.

He wished he could be somewhere else, and then the idea tickled the back of his head. Be somewhere else ... Step into another world and another time. That's what the bookstore guy had been saying. If only he could.

He reached for the headset, then paused again. His fingers opened the top of the briefcase, which he hadn't even looked at once he got home. *The book is there, but where is the coin?* Somehow feeling an urgency to find it, he rooted through the bottom of the case and finally pulled the book onto his desk, finding the coin had slipped inside the front.

He ran his fingers across the picture on the cover. *What if it really works ...?*

He was surprised to see the coin somehow embedded inside the front of the book. He tried picking at it with his fingernail, but it didn't budge.

If he turned toward the corner of his cubicle, no one would see what he was doing if they happened to walk by.

Making a sudden decision, he grabbed the book and pulled it onto his lap, knocking the pen off the desk.

With a shrug, he opened the book and turned to the first page.

The brilliant overhead fluorescent light dimmed immediately, and a damp, mucky scent tickled his nostrils. Everything around him was dark. He checked himself to find he was wearing a black turtleneck sweater and straight black pants. As he felt his chest, the muscles in his arms rippled, and he grinned. *Hey, never had that before. I feel like a badass!*

A pair of voices up ahead grew louder as they approached. Gary instinctively ducked behind what he now realized was a brick wall—the corner of a building. *Okay, those are clearly the bad guys. Now, what should I do?* As his eyes grew accustomed to the darkness, Gary saw the pair about ten feet away but knew he blended into the wall thanks to his dark clothing.

His momentary indecision disappeared as they came within range. As the two passed the corner where he crouched, he leapt up behind them and grabbed one by the chin, twisting his head to the side with a satisfying crack as the neck broke. *Holy crap. Did I really just kill someone?*

The other turned with a yell. "It's Diamond!" He reached for the gun at his side, but Gary pushed the dead man into him, causing him to stagger and drop his weapon on the rough alley surface.

Two quick blows to the man's head, and he dropped like a stone.

Gary quickly rifled through their pockets, taking a small microfiche from one man and a wad of cash from the other. He stuffed these into his own pockets and stepped back to take a breath and recover from the sudden flurry of action.

What just happened?

Back at his desk, Gary looked up from the book in his lap, his pulse racing as the falling pen hit the floor. His armpits stank of sweat.

What the hell was that? Is this really what people mean when they say they get pulled into a book? He blinked in the bright office lighting. *How long have I been … involved?*

He looked at his watch again. Still 2:43. Not a moment had passed since he opened the book.

Gary wiped his face with a shaking hand and took a deep breath, trying to recover from the adrenaline letdown after the fight. Still shaken from the adventure, he stared dully at his computer screen, trying to wrap his mind around the idea of calling someone to sell aluminum siding after he just killed one man and downed the other.

What if he had just read the time wrong and had actually spent all that time reading at his desk? If the boss saw him doing that, he'd be out on his ass so fast he wouldn't know what hit him.

He chuckled. *Christ, that guy I knocked out didn't know what hit him either.*

Somehow, he managed to get his fingers to work and placed another call. His brain took over on autopilot as he called the next three people on the computer's list but got no sales. His heart wasn't in it.

While his body went through the motions of greeting the targets when they answered and launching into the sales spiel, part of his brain was busy. *What was on the microfiche?*

The question nagged at him, but he was afraid to open the book again at work.

After the third call, he looked in all his pockets for the microfiche he'd stuffed away. *Do I still have it?* They were empty. Okay, so the physical objects didn't carry over … but he sure was tired.

After a few more calls, he couldn't stand it any longer and wanted to see what his alternate persona would do with the microfiche. He turned his back again and opened the book to the spot where he'd left off reading.

Leaving the two bodies on the ground, he walked briskly down the alley and peered around the corner at the end. No one in sight. He followed the shadows and opened the door to his red Lamborghini, sliding into the low seat behind the wheel with ease and familiarity. A short trip through Newark, New Jersey's darkened streets took him to a large warehouse with security lights.

Gary parked in the shadow of an adjacent building, turned off the interior light, and slipped out of the car. He followed the edge of the building, going up a fire escape leading to a darkened side door, and made quick work of the lock using a multi-pronged lock pick he found in his pocket.

Once inside, he found himself on a balcony that ran down one side over a huge open space. He stopped to listen a moment and made out the sound of voices from the main floor below.

Creeping closer along the balcony, he peeked over the edge. Various large scientific machines and crates labeled as fish food filled the open area below. His heart lurched. The beautiful blonde woman from the book cover stood facing him, tied to one of the support posts holding up the opposite balcony.

It's Charity! Part of him questioned how he knew her name, but he just relaxed and went with it. Of course, he knew Charity.

Two men in faded work clothes sat facing her, eating peanuts from a bag and taking turns trying to toss the empty shells into the cleavage of her V-neck top.

Gary's fists tightened, and he squinted to survey the rest of the warehouse. No sign of movement and no sounds aside from the two goons. He had to get Charity out of there.

The goons had their backs to him, but with a small movement, he was able to attract Charity's attention. As he expected, she didn't give anything away. She glanced past him, then slowly closed her right eye in a wink that looked like she had just gotten some dust in it.

He thought for a moment. Her hands were tied behind her, but her legs were free. If he could get one of them near her …

He gave her a slight signal and then launched himself over the railing, landing on the ground in a three-point landing. He sprang at the jerk who had made the last toss, knocking him to the ground and kicking him in the head while shoving the second man toward Charity as he tried to stand. The oaf fell backward toward her, but she quickly pulled her legs up and wrapped them around his neck.

Tightening her thighs, she cut off his air supply. The man reached up, trying to pull her muscular legs away, but soon lost his strength. His arms fell to his sides, and he slumped to the ground. Meanwhile, Gary flipped the first man onto his stomach, twisting one arm behind his back.

"You. Tell me who you're working for. Is it Professor Webb?" When the man didn't answer, Gary leaned in, applying more torque to the arm.

The man nodded with a grimace. "How did you know?" he gasped.

"You've been following me for days and think I didn't notice? And now you had the nerve to kidnap my friend. I'm going to have to talk to your boss about your behavior."

He lifted the man partway off the floor and smashed his head into the concrete. With a sickening thud, the man's eyes rolled up into his head, and he went as limp as his partner, who now lay at Charity's feet. Gary untied her and used the rope to tie up each man, dragging them over to sit leaning against the post. He crossed the loop around their necks in case they tried to get clever.

He turned to Charity and checked her up and down. "Are you okay to move?"

She took his arm, leaning slightly on him, but nodded. "Do you think we'll have time to stop Professor Webb before he releases the monstrosity?"

His features tightened. "We have to. If Webb sets those creatures loose, it will be the end of the world as we know it." As they started to leave, he stopped with a smirk. "Just a second."

Picking up the huge bag of peanuts, Gary pulled one man's pants and underwear open at the waist, pouring in peanuts until they were full. "There you go, buddy. At least you got some real nuts now." He snickered as he guided Charity back to his car.

The pair headed out of the city to Professor Webb's huge Englewood Cliffs, New Jersey mansion. It perched on the edge of the Palisades cliffs over the Hudson River just above New York City. Gary hid the Lamborghini in some trees around a bend in the road, and the pair snuck onto the property.

After watching from the surrounding shrub garden, the pair made quick work of the patrolling guards and snuck onto the back patio hanging over the cliff's edge. To their right, the lights of the George Washington Bridge arced over the dark water. Just beyond, Manhattan glowed on the opposite side of the Hudson, the Empire State Building standing tallest among the other buildings.

One guard stood on the patio, smoking and looking over the edge. As he turned, Charity stepped into the light with a pouting expression.

"I seem to be lost. Do you think you could help me, darling?"

As the guard gaped at the curvaceous woman, Gary leaned around Charity and leveled his revolver with the silencer on, shooting him in the head and chest. The guard fell backward over the edge, making only a slight splashing sound as he hit the water three hundred feet below.

They entered the mansion but found nothing of interest on the main floor. Gary detected a humming sound, which they followed to a door off the back hallway. There, they found an industrial staircase next to an elevator. Not wanting to alert anyone by using the elevator, they started down the steps and discovered that it kept going for thirty flights.

At the bottom, a large metal door blocked their way, but the light on the wall panel glowed green. They looked at each other, then shrugged and pushed the door open.

A huge glass aquarium dominated the large, high-ceilinged room, surrounded by smaller tanks along one side. A man in a white lab coat stood silhouetted against the illuminated round tank. Something dark filled the bottom.

He turned, blinking owlishly at them, and then his face lit up. "Ah, Mister Diamond, I see you have come to visit me at the moment of my big success. I am rather busy now. To what can I attribute the nature of your call? Are you here to try and stop my plan?"

Gary's mind raced, reviewing all the clues he'd gathered in his pursuit of this madman, while trying to see what was in the tank. He made a quick decision, smiling and segueing into a friendly but cautious manner.

"On the contrary, Professor Webb. I've been trying to track you down because I am a huge admirer of your work and wanted to see it for myself. I even brought my friend."

He placed a hand on Charity's shoulder and guided her forward with him as they approached slowly. He eyed the industrial stairs leading up to a metal platform extending over the huge tank's far side.

As they got closer, Charity jumped as something moved in the tank. A long, thick arm covered with suckers flexed up along the glass, feeling its way toward the top where a metal grate stopped its progress. The rest of the creature rose up from the bottom, a huge oval blob surrounded by multiple arms.

A giant eye opened on the side facing them, and for a moment, Gary couldn't look away. He tore his attention back to the professor, who stood with his hands on his hips.

"And how do I know you are being sincere?" the professor demanded. "You have repeatedly stopped my men."

Gary smiled easily. "Well, as a gesture of good faith, I have something for you." He slowly slipped his hand into his pocket and pulled out the microfiche. "One of your men was careless enough to drop this in an alley, and I figured it must be important to you. Come on, Josh, I wouldn't give this back to you if I were trying to do something here."

The mad scientist took the proffered microfiche and headed up the metal stairs to a control console mounted on the overhanging platform. He fed it into a viewer and peered at the screen for a moment.

"This is it! The data I've been waiting for, showing the most suitable prediction of tides and river currents to release my little friends here." He gestured to the tanks along the chamber's far wall, each filled with roiling masses of small, multi-armed creatures. A mechanism extended into each tank, attached to a metal door where the tank touched the outside wall.

Charity looked at Gary, then called up to the scientist. "Professor, I'm afraid I don't get it ... could you help me understand? I mean, you're so much smarter than I am."

"Of course, my dear. Both of you come up here, and I can show you now that you're clearly on my side."

They climbed the steps to the metal platform, where a row of maps hung over the command console. The maps depicted various centers of governmental power around the world.

Professor Webb gestured to one showing New York City and the surrounding waterways. "You see, I have designed the ultimate attack creature. Most people don't realize how intelligent an octopus is or that it can travel out of the water."

"Attack? Why would they attack anyone?" Charity tilted her head, doing an excellent imitation of a dumb blonde.

"That is the genius of my plan! I have developed a small control mechanism that I embedded into each creature, which tells them what to do. Pulling this lever will release my lovelies from my other labs into London, Tokyo, Shanghai, and Moscow—all located on bodies of water. Not to mention the ones that will go into the Hudson River around New York City here."

"But why New York City? It's not the capital." Charity frowned.

Gary narrowed his eyes. "Yeah, but the United Nations is in New York City, and there's a huge summit going on now. He'll get the leaders not in their capitals at the UN complex just across the water. Genius, Professor, simply genius."

He nodded enthusiastically while stepping slightly away from the waterside edge of the narrow platform. He slid his eyes sideways when Charity turned to him, and she stepped closer to the water.

Webb raised his arms in victory, a fierce smile covering his face. "Exactly, Diamond. I will step into the ensuing chaos and take over the world!"

As Professor Webb reached for the lever, Charity dropped to all fours behind him—between the mad scientist and the platform's edge hanging over the water—and hooked her fingers into the metal grid. Gary punched the professor in the face, then shoved him backward.

Webb's arms flailed like a windmill as he toppled backward, tripping over Charity and careening over the edge. The impact dislodged the screen, and his legs went into the water—where the giant octopus latched onto him with its suckers and pulled him underwater. He slid into the tank with a scream.

Gary and Charity watched in helpless fascination as the octopus wrapped an arm around the scientist's head, covering his entire face with a single sucker. Webb convulsed and twitched, pulling at the giant fleshy arm for a full minute until his body went limp, his arms floating off to the sides.

"It's been trained to attack. Now it got its evil master." Charity leaned against Gary.

"Yeah. For dinner."

The two watched as the cephalopod tore the scientist limb from limb, devouring it with its sharp beak. It threw the head over the top of the tank, hitting the platform with a thud and rolling to their feet, gaping at them.

Charity wrapped one arm around Gary's neck, pressing against him, and whispered, "I think you deserve a reward for saving the world, darling."

He looked at her with raised eyebrows. "You don't say?" Then he smiled, picked her up in his arms, and together, on the last page, they made their way to his car.

Gary moved his arms to tighten them around Charity, and it took him a moment to realize he still sat at his desk. However, his chest felt cold after the warmness of feeling Charity against him.

Damn. That was intense. He checked his watch and discovered that no time had passed yet again. He headed to the water cooler for some much-needed hydration.

At the end of work, he went to the bookstore on his way home, smiling at the bell that tinkled when he pushed the door open. The shopkeeper sat at the table in the back as if he had not moved from the spot. The elderly gentleman looked up and raised his bushy eyebrows as Gary held out the book.

"And ...?"

"I have to confess ... it was awesome. I read the whole thing! I felt ... I don't know ... *alive!*"

A smile creased the shopkeeper's face. "I was hoping you would like it. So, you brought it back. All done with reading?"

Gary scuffed his toe on the floor. "Well … actually … I was hoping to get another one. I know the gift was just one book, but—"

The clerk cut him off. "No, son. The gift wasn't the book. It was the coin. You can use it on any book you wish, and you will experience it the same way." He reached out and took the volume from Gary, twisting the coin off with a simple flick of his wrist.

"See, it comes right off once you're finished. And I have great news for you."

Gary tilted his head. "What's that?"

The shopkeeper grinned, tapping the book's cover. "This one's just the first in a very long series."

Bram Stoker Award® finalist Carol Gyzander writes and edits horror, weird fiction, and science fiction with strong women in twisted tales that touch your heart. She's been published in *Weird Tales 367, Under Twin Suns, Discontinue If Death Ensues: Tales from the Tipping Point* (Flame Tree Publishing). MWA, SFWA, Active HWA. CarolGyzander.com / @CarolGyzander

Schrödinger's Razor
Ken Altabef

We broke time.

Okay, all right, I admit it. I broke time. I was the one. My equations. And the entire human race suffers for it. And will likely die, because of me. All because of me. I was dubbed "the new Einstein" by the scientific press but turned out to be history's greatest fool.

I step out of my apartment building into the open air. Sunny New Mexico morning, dry heat, a hint of exhaust fumes drifting over from the sunbaked highway. It's only a few blocks to my lab at NHMFL, but under the current circumstances Los Alamos seems a lifetime away. My heart sinks in my chest. I doubt I will make it there. I dare not drive. I dare not cross the street. I stand paralyzed for only a second. Just as I take my next step, the shift comes again.

A flip of the switch. The day is suddenly dark and overcast as I stand amid the wreckage of burned-out buildings and crumbled infrastructure. The burnt smell has increased a hundredfold, mercilessly attacking my senses within the stifling confines of the full-body anti-radiation suit. I find myself on the outskirts of South Valley, trying desperately to get to the shelter beneath the University of New Mexico at Albuquerque. I doubt I will make it there.

I step carefully, taking only one step above the smoking ruin, when the shift happens again.

Back on the street in front of my apartment, the air cleaner, the sky stingingly brighter. The transition is equally shocking every time the mad pendulum swings, and I fixate on the mantra I've devised to help brush off the disorientation. "TECF." I whisper the acronym into the hard-bitten wind, and it calms me as I take another step toward the road. Four pillars. Each representing key vestiges of the past.

"T" is for time travel. Sounds like a page out of some demented grade school reading primer. Time travel, I had discovered, was indeed possible, though only in the forward direction. The unidirectionality of it came as no surprise. The rotation of the earth, the orbits of the planets, the galactic spin, are all unidirectional. Special relativity, the crowning achievement of the real Einstein, posited that at vast speeds time slows objectively. Chronological experiments on the early space missions proved it. All that's needed for time travel is to accelerate an object to incredible speed while holding it in place. Simple, really. The power drain is enormous, but with its massive particle accelerators Los Alamos was up to the task. I didn't design the apparatus, but they *were* my equations. "The new Einstein." The World Killer.

"E" is for Edmund. Specifically, Marine Staff Sergeant Edmund Pays. Our first time-traveler, and our last. Edmund bought a one-way ticket to a week in the future. What he found there was nothing short of disastrous. Nuclear war. Devastation. All in one week's time.

We maintained contact with Edmund via a miniaturized quantum string transmitter. A piezoelectric correspondence between a matched pair of entangled string crystals. Their resonance persisted, despite vast separations in both space and time. At least that was the theory. My research assistant Jerzy, brilliant and terribly young and ambitious, had designed them. Before launch, we didn't even know if they would actually work, but Jerzy, a preening vessel overflowing with the cockiness of youth, seemed certain. Turned out they did work, at least for a few minutes until the connection broke down, for reasons unknown. Enough time for Edmund to transmit a substantial, and very dire, message back to us.

The sergeant detailed the events leading up to the disaster. It had all been an unfortunate misunderstanding, a malfunctioning DSP satellite chasing a phantom trail of infrared radiation, a perceived nuclear launch, a forced retaliation cascade, and BOOM!

The shift happens again. In the two seconds I had existed in the nuclear wasteland, the other version of myself stumbled at the curb. I'd gone down on one knee, my bad knee as it so happens, and a sharp pain ripples up my leg. Damn it all. I struggle to my feet. A simple thing like crossing the road has become an impossible obstacle.

And the shift back again to Albuquerque. The apocalypse. I had stumbled there as well. At least the suit's Nu-rubber skin is still intact, its internal fans working hard against the heat. Sweat drips into my eye. I stand up. Try to get moving. I take one more step.

Now Santa Fe. The disorientation smacks me hard. The sidewalk wavers, the sudden change in smell and light. I whisper the mantra. "TECF."

"C." Correction. The nuclear disaster had been easily avoided, given such foreknowledge as the marine sergeant provided. It seemed like a good idea at the time. What people used to call a no-brainer.

But time is nobody's plaything. Our attempt to alter what fate had in store turned out to be a very bad idea indeed.

"F" is for fracture. Unforeseen consequence. We prevented the war, but also didn't. We prevented the nuclear holocaust, but also didn't. We are all now trapped in hell. Back and forth, back and forth, careening constantly between the two timelines, existing simultaneously in both. It's completely maddening. The resultant gaps in each reality, even just for a second or two, make it impossible to get anything done, difficult even to think clearly. Airplanes fall from the skies, infrastructure grinds to a standstill, fires break out. People collapse in the street. We are all going to die.

And in the nuclear wasteland we are all subject to the same distractions. Rebuilding will be impossible.

After the sergeant's report, all contact had been lost. I don't know what became of Edmund Pays. Perhaps he's still here now, wandering among the destruction. Perhaps he made it back to whatever is left of Central Command. Who knows? As the only man who physically exited the earlier timeline, it occurs to me he might have been spared the shifts. He might be the only person living in just the one timeline, and not trapped in both. In that case, he stands as a superman among all of us other perpetually distracted human beings. Victims of my supreme folly. Meddling in time! Sergeant Pays might just wind up running the world. But I think most everyone else will have died long since. Who knows?

I reach the street corner, but crossing is a dangerous game. I must get to the lab. I have to destroy the equipment. Given what has happened, nobody would be stupid enough to use that machine ever again, but I want it destroyed. This mission is all I have left. I've made it my life's goal. I doubt I can succeed. There is still traffic on the highway. I don't quite understand that, since everybody in the world is subject to the constant shifting between realities. But of course there are many crashes as well. I decide to risk crossing the instant the light changes. I'll have a full twenty seconds to make it across, with maybe ten shifts during that time. If all the cars actually obey the stoplights, I might make it.

Albuquerque. Another disoriented step.

Santa Fe. I've somehow turned round to face the building again. Back to the street. I just have to cross this one street to reach the lab. But four lanes of traffic …

I take one more step, see the car careening toward me.

The shift again. In the wasteland, I pick aside a piece of smoldering debris. That car! That car was going to—

Santa Fe. My right hip burns in agonizing pain. The car has clipped me, flung me across the street like a rag doll. No ambulance will be coming. This is the end. Just another lonely, painful death by the side of the road.

In the wasteland, I lie huddled among the ashes, broken just the same and taking my last ragged breaths. And so the World Killer dies, soon to be followed by, well, everybody else I'm sure ...

I'm sorry. I'm so sorry ...

In his office at the National Laboratory, Jerzy Dubrovitz continues his text message to a young physicist in North Dakota. The new theoretical possibilities revealed by this schism in time are breathtaking. They have much to discuss.

Simultaneously in a bomb shelter below Albuquerque, he sits at another desk, using the same phone to text a report to CentCom in Washington. He has successfully coordinated emergency supplies to survivors living in the Great Plains area.

Two different conversations, with his consciousness switching between them second by second.

He takes a bite of his sandwich.

The world is a total mess, to be sure. And the new normal does take some getting used to. But things should improve once all the clumsy boomers are out of the way. They were never very good at multitasking anyway.

Ken Altabef's short fiction has appeared in fantasy magazines such as *F&SF*, *Interzone*, *Daily Science Fiction*, *Intergalactic Medicine Show*, *Dark Matter*, *Abyss & Apex*, and *Speculative North*. He is the author of thirteen fantasy novels including the *Alaana's Way* series and the critically acclaimed *Lady Changeling Trilogy*. Visit www.KenAltabef.com.

It Started at the Never Mind
Charles Barouch

Chapter I: The Never Mind

Another night at the Never Mind Tavern. I'm in the corner, people-watching. This one shady character catches my eye.

He sat at the end of the bar, his eyes nervously darting this way and that. The drink in front of him was his third. Whiskey, neat. Just like the other two. Seedy suit that had seen better days. Rest of the bar was mostly T-shirts and jeans but he was dressed for a different time and place.

While he's toying with that third glassful, another man arrives. This one wears the uniform of the place, something sarcastic printed on his shirt, the requisite pants … but just as out of place. He's too neat, too constructed. The clothing looks fresh-bought. The man looks unaccustomed to wearing it.

The dichotomy gets my interest. It's my job to notice the unusual. Also, it's my temperament. No, I should start off with some honesty. It *was* my job to notice things. Past tense. Over. Done. But this isn't about me.

The man play-acting like a part of the crowd sits next to suit-boy. They don't look at each other. Play-actor orders a whiskey, neat. Maybe that's a sign. Why they need a sign is beyond me. Anyone paying attention could tell neither of them was a regular here.

Bartender, Shaya Deitsch, brings the drink. I see suit-boy slip his napkin under the other guy's drink. That must be the drop, the exchange. I almost believe that. It nearly takes me in, this shadow play they've got going. Thing is, times have changed. The drop was probably an NFC exchange between two phones. Best guess would be one of the people hanging around near the bathroom. Lots of traffic. Nothing suspicious about the courier pausing while they wait for someone to wash and come out.

I've had my eye on the short girl with the bottle-blonde afro. She's not as out of place as the play-actor but there are still signs. Subtle clues. Her friends are all stoned. She's clear-eyed. She's just the tiniest bit on edge.

There. She just relaxed. Not a big change, just a subtle shift of the shoulders, a change in how she's standing. Her arms aren't folded across her chest. The drop has to have been made.

Police walk in and arrest the two at the bar. I want to scream in frustration but it won't do any good. No one listens to me anymore. The worst part is that I don't know which side I'm on. Depends on what was exchanged. On who the blonde works for. On who her co-conspirator is. They could be smuggling abused women to safety. They could be selling dangerous tech. Makes a world of difference.

Either way, they are getting away with it. The cops took the bait and missed the switch. And all I can do is watch. It's all I ever do now. The frustration overwhelms me. I would kill for a drink, but Shaya won't serve me.

I notice the woman slip into the bathroom. She comes out with different hair, heels instead of sneakers, and her T-shirt is no longer yellow with a unicorn. Now it's plain, form-fitting black with a V- neck that almost shows her cleavage. She's done blending in. I'm guessing she needs people to notice her leaving.

If I'd clocked her when she arrived, I'd know if this was a book-ends costume. You know, with her arriving and leaving as the classy brunette, with the blonde afro as just a middle piece. That would track. Get them watching you arrive, seem to disappear, and then re-appear. People who aren't me will swear she was here until after the police left.

The desire to follow her out, to see where she's going, is overwhelming. I soundlessly shadow her as she makes her way out. Big strides while looking unhurried, that's the best way to describe her walk.

Three blocks later, she stops at a corner. The light's in her favor. She doesn't cross. An older man, hat pulled down, jacket despite the warmth of the night, stops beside her. I might have heard her phone vibrate. Might be my mind playing tricks. It happens sometimes. After a short pause, he crosses the street. She doesn't. Their time together is done. Instead, she walks back to the bar. Back to be seen. I guess she needs a longer alibi.

I watch her intently. This black-shirted version is the opposite of the yellow-shirted woman she was before. No blending in, no standing off to the side. Black-shirt flirts with the bartender, he's very married. That isn't going to work. It does get her a free drink, but I can see the disapproval on Shaya's face. Black shirt clearly doesn't. She smiles suggestively. I wonder which is closer to her true self. Could be both. Most people don't fit neatly into a single box, a simple label.

Theoretically, her story should be over for me. Just an intermediary. Just a step in who knows how many. The goods, whatever they were, have changed hands. The rest is just performance. I find it ironic that being at the scene of the crime will actually be her alibi. How that works, I'm not sure but obviously that's the play she's making, that's her plan.

About an hour before closing time, she leaves. I follow her again. Unnoticed, again, I assume. Turns out I'm wrong.

"What's your name?" she asks.

We're alone on the street, moving at her efficient pace. No one else here. She has to be talking to me.

"Bob Henson. You can see and hear me?"

"Tell me, Bobby, how'd you die?"

"Took a picture of two people who weren't supposed to be together."

"And one of them took strong exception, Bobby?"

"You could say. Yeah. She took twenty-two caliber-worth of exception."

"Hard break. Happened in that bar?"

"No. No. That place wasn't built yet."

"The Never Mind Tavern's been there forty-something years. How long has it been since anyone talked to you?"

"You're the first, lady. I didn't get your name."

"That's true."

"You can tell me. Who can I blab it to?"

"I don't put certain things in the air. The universe listens."

"So, what? You spend a life never saying your name?"

"Not in long years. Don't know if I can use that phrase with you. You've been dead longer than I've been alive. Tell me, Bobby, what have you done with that time?"

"My life? I wasted most of it. Pool halls, cheap bars, too much work filling up the spaces between."

"Work? You were a detective, I assume."

"Not a real one. Just a store detective. That used to be a job back in the day. Like I said, wasted life."

"But the picture. The one that got you killed ..."

"I was taking one of this couple I knew. The other couple, the ones who shouldn't have been together, they just happened to be in the back of the shot. An accident. Fatal one."

"Fate gave you the pointy end of the stick, Bobby?"

"Something like that."

"But I didn't ask about your life. What have you done with your afterlife?"

"What I'm doing now. Finding interesting moments among the living and satisfying my curiosity. I should have been a detective. Of course, living-me wasn't nearly as good at sneaking around."

"Let me show you something, Bobby ... something you haven't seen."

Not that I've seen everything, but I've seen plenty, so I didn't have high hopes. Still, it wasn't like I had something better to do. We continued in silence until we got to a shopping mall. One of the small ones. Everything was closed. She led me around, to the rear entrance of some store. No idea which one. This area wasn't my usual haunt. I think it was a farm back in my day. There were still farms this close to the city.

She fishes around in her purse and comes up with a key. She pauses before opening the door.

"I don't know how current your knowledge is. This place is pretty high-tech."

She lets us in. Not that I couldn't have just gone through the door, but this was my first conversation in a long time. I wanted to be polite. Ladies first and all that.

Inside was pretty spare and empty. She had me expecting something mad-sciency. A real Vincent Price set-up. Instead, there were three computer stations and a closet with a glass door. I know about computers, of course, and all the rest. I have nothing but time, so I indulge my natural curiosity.

"What's all this do?"

I say it like I'm impressed. You know, trying to be polite.

"That chamber opens to the past. Well, in theory. Dr. Glass hasn't gotten it working yet."

"If you want to know about the past, you can just ask me. I've got stories."

"No doubt. I can show you his theories but unless you have advanced degrees in particle physics and engineering, I don't think you'll find it interesting."

"I'm guessing you have that sort of credentials, lady?"

"You can check out the chamber if you'd like. Most interesting thing in here. Carbon sixty over polymer steel. Glass is pretty unique, too. Can survive over a thousand millibars of pressure."

"Thousand? Isn't that hurricane-level?"

"Didn't expect you to know that, Bobby. Dr. Glass theorizes that opening the portal will create some intense air pressure differentials. Other forces may come into play. It's all theory."

"But you build for the things you expect."

She opens the glass door. I drift into the chamber. There's a solidity to it that I can sense. She closes the door. I try to leave. I can't.

The info drop she did wasn't any more real than the one suit-boy did. This was the real operation. It was all about me. And not in a good way. I'm trapped.

She puts on her lab coat. A name, Dr. Glass, is stitched over the breast pocket.

"Now, Bobby. Let's see if you're the link to the past that my theories predict you'll be."

Chapter II: The Past Comes Back

I've never been scared for myself. Certainly not as a ghost and barely ever as a man. But this dame's got me terrified. Whatever she's doing on that computer has her smiling. I don't like that smile. Not one damned bit.

I test the glass of the door, the corners of the chamber, the floor, the ceiling … I'm trapped.

My only chance is that this thingamajig of hers doesn't work. I cling to that, the hope this will all turn to a pile of hooey. I haven't experienced pain since my death. That might change. I'm not prepared for it. Been decades.

There's a hum. Not a sound. More a sensation. Vibrations usually pass through me. Not this. I can *feel* it. My dad's old Nash Rambler vibrated like this. Not pleasant but not terrible. If this was all it would be, I can weather it. Problem is, she doesn't look like she's done.

She opens a drawer and pulls out a pair of boots with wires coming out of them. Despite my situation, I keep cataloging what I see. Better than just succumbing to the fear.

The boots, they're brown, stop on the low calf. Cheap material. The wires come from the heels and are going every which way. I can see small pins soldered on the loose ends. She gathers the wires into her fist and plugs them into a spot on the baseboard right next to my cell. I have trouble clearly seeing what she does. Takes a while, pushing in one pin at a time. Not that I'm complaining. I'm in no rush.

My afterlife might be nearing its end. When she's done with the wires, she slips off her shoes and steps into the boots. This might be it. I don't want to cease. Death should be final enough. This isn't fair.

She can barely reach the keyboard now that she's connected. It would be comical if I weren't in terror of dissolution. She's got one hand on the table to steady herself, her whole body aslant, and she's flailing at the keys with the other hand.

I feel the vibration change. It's more forceful, jarring. Random memories start overwhelming me. A summer night under the stars when I was eight. Fireflies scattering when baby-me toddled among them. I didn't even know I had these. I thought I'd lost them to adulthood.

Bittersweet, gaining these glimpses of my past only to lose myself entirely.

The vibration gets worse. There's a sense of ripping, rending, that muddles the memories, makes all thought painful. And then, nothing. Not me ceasing. Not that nothing. Just the end of the vibrations. The end of my pain.

I look at my torturer. She's unplugging the boots. Whatever this was, I survived it. This time. No part of me harbored the hope this was one and done. There would be more attempts.

"Success," she said once she was barefoot.

"Says you. That nearly took me to pieces."

"Good to know. I'll have to try a shorter jump next time."

"Why? Why mess with the past?"

I'm ready to say anything. If she leaves, I'm alone here, trapped. I'm not trying for empathy. Not hoping for my freedom.

She won't do that. It's writ large all over her smug face. This, whatever this was, constituted a success. And she'll want more of that.

"The past? Try to keep up, Bobby. You set an anchor opposite the force you want to resist."

"Opposite?"

"I went to the future. That's why I needed an anchor to the past."

"I thought you were trying to travel within my lifetime."

"If that's all this was, I wouldn't have to trap a ghost. I could have made my own."

"Made your … you mean murder? You'd commit murder?"

"Of course I wouldn't. Because murder wouldn't work. I mean, it might, but the statistics against are substantial."

"Your problem with murder isn't the murder part?"

"You know, Bobby, now that you've got me thinking it over, murders could work but I'd need to do a lot of them. Inefficient."

"I don't understand."

Truth is, I don't want to understand. But crazy company is better than being alone.

"How many ghosts have you met, Bobby?"

"Not a one. I stay in a small area mostly. Even so, I always expected there'd be more. Some."

"People die. They move on. Not you Bobby," she said. "That's what makes you such a good anchor. If I made my own ghosts, I'd have to keep at it until I made one like you. That's why I resorted to found materials."

"If you keep me in here, I won't want to stay anymore."

"I have tabs on three more like you, Bobby. Don't think you're indispensable."

"But I'm here. The others will require more work. So, I'm valuable, right? Worth keeping happy?"

I don't know that I've ever lied more intently than I'm doing now. I'll tell her anything for a chance to escape.

"The math is pretty simple. If I let you out, this all ends now. If you lose your tether, well … I have until then."

"Unless I lose it while you are using me as an anchor."

"Huh. You have a point. Goodnight, Bobby."

"Don't leave me alone."

"If I make you grateful for my company, you won't dissipate while I'm using you. Problem solved."

"Dr. Glass!"

"Don't call me that. It's not my name. Goodnight, Bobby."

She grabbed her purse and left. I was alone.

When I was little, my mother locked me in my room once. I didn't know it for an hour because I was reading. I asked her why and she told me, "The difference between staying and being locked in is all about who is in charge. In this life you need to keep trying the doorknobs even when you are where you want to be."

I hadn't thought about that conversation in years. For the moment, I did have an antidote to my loneliness. The flood of recovered memories would be my company.

The door to the chamber was locked, that was true. But I had another way to leave. A permanent one. The crazy dame was in charge of the chamber door, but I was in charge of my exit. That was strangely comforting.

Chapter III: Two Days Later

How long was she gone? Might have been a day, a week … not shorter than the first and not longer than the second. I was pretty sure of that much. I spent the time reconnecting with the man I was, the boy I was, all the versions of me that drew breath.

I still didn't know what to call her. That irked me more than it should. Not as much as, say her plan to turn the damned chamber on again. I'm not prepared for those vibrations to return. It was beyond me to imagine how to prepare for that.

My only plan was to let her — I say that like I could stop her, which I can't — turn it on and then take a powder. Leave her unanchored. Don't get the idea that I'm at peace with dissolution. It's just that having no control, that's worse for me. I'm the liberty or death type. That Patrick Henry fella, he had it right.

"Morning, Bobby. Ready to change the world?"

"Why?"

I expected her to ignore the question but it brought her up short.

"What do you mean, why?"

"Satisfied people don't want to change the world. Just saying."

Good. She was thinking. That bought me time. It was, once again, a precious commodity. Yesterday morning, I had eternity to amuse myself. Today, it might only be minutes.

"So, Bobby, the question isn't 'why change the world' it's 'why do I want to change the world' is that it?"

"Exactly it, sister."

"I've never really thought about it. Do a thing, succeed. Do the next thing. That's been my pattern. Sort of a kindergarten leads to post doc sort of process for me."

"You've never asked yourself why?"

"Birds fly. Men drink. It's how things are."

"But you're a scientist. Asking why, isn't that the whole thing?"

"I'm not a scientist, Bobby. I stole all this."

"What?"

"I wear a lab coat with someone else's name on it. Wasn't that clue enough for you, detective?"

"I mean ..."

"See, you don't ask yourself good questions either. I wonder if anyone does. This was lovely, but I have a world to change."

I feel like that broad, Scheherezade. Only the reverse, I guess. I'm trying to get her to tell me stories. Still stalling, whichever way you slice it.

"How'd you steal it?"

"All this? That's not interesting. Stealing it, that's just what life has taught me to do. Having it is interesting, though."

"You? But you're the lady with three degrees. Aren't you the poster child for life working out?"

She laughed.

"Degrees made out of thesis papers I bought, copied, stole … That's what my accomplishments are, theft. Not that I'm not smart. It's because I'm smart."

She starts plugging in the boots.

"How is stealing the work smarter than doing the work?"

"Projects don't always work out, Bobby. Far more fail than succeed. Better to find something that already works. Real time saver."

She finishes with the wires.

"But you can't tell anyone."

"What was that?"

"If you stole this, how do you get credit?"

"For this? I'll never claim this as mine. That's as true as it is short-sighted."

"I don't understand."

"And you don't have to, Bobby. This is about me. You're just lucky enough to get a ringside seat. Time to change the world."

She takes off her shoes. She drags the PC keyboard a little closer so she won't have to lean. Smart. I'll give her that.

"Don't you want something that's truly yours? Honestly won?"

She laughs.

"I will miss you when you … give up the ghost."

Chapter IV: Spring Ahead, Fall Backward

The vibrations run through me. Worse this time. The memories come but … no, they aren't memories. I've never been to these places, seen these people, done these things. Whoever I am in these … whatever they are … they're on some sort of stage, and I'm performing. With a microphone in front of — us? me? them? — and a guitar in my hands. I'm experiencing it as if I were the one, the center, the person involved.

Whomever this is, they are distracted, thinking about other things. Mostly, it's food and bed. There's an exhaustion that they are hiding inside them, exposed to me but not to anyone else.

I turn my head to look back at the rest of the band. What the hell are they wearing? The instruments look modern but the clothing is like someone made medieval garb based on a movies-only level of knowledge. The drummer has on what looks like chainmail. The bass player is dressed in a pied fool's outfit. Not sure what the keyboard player is supposed to be. He's got on a woman's headgear, one of those things that looks like an unpainted children's party hat — two of those — jutting up from a turban-like cloud of blue fabric and lace. The rest of him, what I can see, is in a herald's tabard.

I'm pretty sure I'm riding a woman's memories. I wish she'd look down. She doesn't. Her left hand is in my periphery. Definitely looks female. She starts shouting at the crowd. I assume there is one. The spotlight is nearly blinding her.

"Hello San Bernadino! I am Courtly Love, these are the Troubadours, and you are the lucky ducks who get to hear us!"

English accent. Cockney. Might be genuine. The crowd starts cheering. So, yeah. There's a crowd.

I hit the first chord. The crowd doesn't quiet. So I turn up the amp and strike it again, louder. More shouting, cheering. It should be gratifying but all I feel from the woman I'm riding is rage. She wants to play, to start so she can finish.

I turn to raise the volume on the amp again. The cable between amp and guitar catches my feet. I start to fall backward, gyrate back into momentary balance, but now I'm at the edge of the stage. Crowd tries to catch me. They might even think this is intentional, crowd surfing. That's a modern thing I've learned about since dying.

Except that not enough of them catch me. My legs, my back, they are held aloft, but my head isn't. My neck snaps backward. They drop me, not expecting how my body moved. I hit the floor headfirst. It all fades to black.

Before I can fully register the pain, I'm somewhere else. Wheelchair. I wonder briefly if it's the same person but realize it isn't. Only one leg. That doesn't track with falling off a stage. I'm in pajamas and a robe. I try to shift myself, to get more comfortable. My body moves easily, as if my arms are very strong and my body is very light.

Looking at my hands, I can see that this body is wasting away, emaciated, bony. Someone calls my name. Nicky. That's who I am now, Nicky. He walks in, the one who called me. Missing a leg, like me. On crutches, seems in better health.

"Got you a sandwich. Just how you like it. Even got the crusts cut off."

His accent is foreign to me. I don't know it. A bit lyrical.

"Thanks, Mick. Any news?"

That's what I say back, what whomever I'm riding says back.

"Prosthetics guy is coming in the morning. Fit us both and six others. Unless we're last and he runs out of time. That case, gonna take a week, maybe two."

And I'm out again. Moments of nothing. Then, into another. Just for a moment. And another and another. I lose count. Some are barely longer than a blink. Most last for nearly a minute.

Then it slows down again. I spend fifteen minutes as a woman in an ice bath. Fever spiking badly. Three nurses are running about, trying to get me to a state where they can take me out of the water.

After that, I'm riding an elderly man. He's got a cake in front of him. Candles say he's one hundred and six. I can feel my left leg tremor. My right hand won't uncurl from the claw it has become. There's a pain all through my spine. It seems like it has been there for decades, dull but demanding. Decades but I've only been here for this short while.

The vibrations stop. I'm back with Dr. Not-Glass. I didn't know I was still feeling the vibrations until they stopped. I was immersed in each and every one of those people. After-images, left over thoughts, stray bits of pain, they all still cling to me.

"What was the purpose of all that?" I ask. "Why are you doing this to me?"

"I need to see the future. This is how I get to do that. If all goes well, I'll be done with you sometime tomorrow. No, I have that thing at noon and the other at three. I'll be back day after. Then you'll be done."

"Done as in free? Or done as in used up?"

"Both. Either. We'll find out, won't we?"

She leaves me alone. I have a reprieve from the pain. But that comes with isolation.

This place is like a casino. No clocks. No windows. Nothing to mark the passage of time. She comes back and I honestly don't know if it's been hours or days.

She puts on the shoes. She plugs everything in. I watch, passive. There's too much trauma to this. I can't be moved to care if I survive it. For her part, she's humming to herself. She seems happy with her work and her situation.

The vibration comes. It hurts, but more like if I had empathy for someone else who was feeling it. I'm that removed from myself. Fear is the same, remote, distant.

More people. Quick flashes, long stretches, all the same to me. My mind refuses to take it in. I remember none of it when the vibration stops. Just the odd sense that I didn't discorporate. I'm still here. She could make this all happen again.

"That settles that," she says. "I have my anchor."

"I thought I was …"

I'm not sure why I want clarity. Why I want anything.

"You were my anchor. Good job, by the way. But now you're nothing. Well, nothing to me."

She opens the door, my door. The one that keeps me trapped. Just opens it.

I slip out, wondering what sort of new trap this is. Regret going, but terrified of staying.

"Off with you, Robert. Have to make room."

"Found another ghost to torture?"

"Another ghost? No, you've covered that. Couldn't have done it without you and blah blah blah."

"I'm free?"

"Free to leave. You are free to leave. Leave, you did hear that part, right?"

I settle in on the floor opposite the place she'd held me.

"I think I deserve to see what happens next."

"Deserve? People never get what they deserve. If they did, I'd really be in for it."

Chapter V: It's Obviously Not Over

I'm free. Free!

I head out and find my way to the Never Mind Tavern. It's midday, so there's barely anyone there. I can't share in the calm. No matter how much I want to, being here is no solace.

Being dead is a sort of idle, slightly bored peace. The reward for slipping off the mortal coil. I've drifted through other people's lives with no real stake in anything that's happening.

She changed that. Now I've invested pain — been forced to invest pain — in something. That's created a need, the sort that was normal for me as a living man. I really want to know what all that suffering bought. And that wanting, needing, it … it feels wrong. Dead should be different than alive. Dr. Not-Glass took my sense of serenity from me. Made me connect.

I head back to the lab. It's empty. Lights are off. She's gone.

I'm agitated. I want answers, resolution. There are none to be found.

Despite that, I settle in, facing the chamber. I need to reconcile what being in this tiny prison did to me. Of course, just looking at it reminds me of every reason I should leave and never return. Problem is, reason is part of logic. And that's useless in the face of my emotions.

Worse yet, there's no one to discuss this with. In all these long years as a dead man, I had made peace with that, the lack of conversation. Damn her, it's another thing she broke, by talking to me. And now, when I have something to say, something I need to talk about, I am alone. My only option is my jailer, when she comes back.

Not that she would offer me that solace. Not that I would ask it of her of all people.

In death there is no sleep. No temporary release from conscious thought. So I sit with my musings, alone in the dark. After an eternity, the lights come on.

"You're still here? Why?"

She's back and she's got a wheelbarrow. There's something covered in burlap that's piled into it. And that something is moving. It's a person.

"Kidnapping the living?" I ask.

"Don't act surprised. You picked her out."

"What? Of course I didn't."

"Did too. What do you think we've been doing here?"

"Wait … you mean you kidnapped her from the future?"

"Don't be stupid, Robert. Why would I be hauling her in with a wheelbarrow? If I'd brought her here using the equipment in this room, she'd already be here."

"Then …"

"Just stop talking, Robert. Honestly, you assume the most ridiculous things. Also, and I can't emphasize this enough, you were supposed to *leave*. Go away."

She ignores me and starts dragging her victim out and onto the floor. I watch, unable to intervene, as she pushes the burlap-covered woman into the chamber. Into the prison which held me until yesterday.

The burlap slips off her face. I don't recognize her, but that's no surprise. City is full of living people. I only watch a fraction of a fraction of them. She's groggy, barely moving, but clearly still among the living. Seems to be a big woman. Heavy and tall, both.

I take a very small, very petty pleasure in seeing Dr. Not-Glass struggle. Mostly, I feel badly for the kidnapped woman. She's going to wake up in a tiny cell. However hard it was on me, I don't get hungry or sweaty or need the bathroom. Depending on how long our captor plans on holding her, all of that could matter.

I try to evaluate the victim. Looks to be thirty-five, give or take. Jeans, T-shirt, middling expensive shoes. Thinning hair. More brown than gray. I'm guessing she's near six feet tall. And, as the burlap comes the rest of the way off, I can get a better sense of her weight. Has to be nearly two hundred forty pounds. Not as large as I first thought.

Takes quite a bit of effort for Dr. Not-Glass to squeeze her into the chamber. When the doctor closes the door, she finally acknowledges me again.

"Couldn't you pick a tiny woman? Maybe a mid-sized toddler, Robert?"

"I didn't pick her, Dr. Not-Glass."

"We looked at the future together, Robert. You and me. That's why she's here. Haven't you been paying attention? It's all so obvious."

"Not one bit of this is obvious! Or moral! Or decent!"

"Don't get so dramatic. If you're too stupid to understand, just say so. Look, I have time to kill until she wakes up, so I'll explain."

She walks to the computer. I assume she's bringing something up to show me.

"Well?"

"Well what? Oh, right. Explaining what you already know. I got distracted. Robert, ask yourself, what does this system do?"

"Time travel."

"Right. Are we clear now?"

"No!"

"I'll go slower. What does this system do? Time travel. Why did I need you?"

"Because I'm an anchor. I tether you to the past."

"So I can what, Robert? So I can ..."

"Travel to the future."

"Good. So we're clear?"

"No!"

"To travel to the future I needed an anchor that's solidly connected to the past. Therefore, to travel to the past, I need ..."

"An anchor that's solidly connected to the future?"

"Right. Glad that's settled."

"Nothing's settled. Why did you kidnap this woman? You said she's not from the future."

"Of course she isn't. That would make all this much harder. Have you ever tried to pull someone out of time? It's not fun. I'm not doing that a third time."

"You haven't explained anything."

"Robert, I'm only humoring you because she's still napping."

"Then keep humoring me."

"She's a psychic. That much should be obvious."

"It isn't."

"It is to smart people, Robert. Keep up. Psychics, real ones, see the future. They are connected to the future. You might even say they are solidly connected to the future."

"Wait? So you tortured me so that you could go into the future and see which psychics were making accurate predictions?"

"See? Obvious. I needed statistics to make the decision. You picked her out."

"But you said you don't want to change the future."

"Already told you that. Keep up."

"This is about changing the past."

"Nope. Oh look, she's waking up. Goodbye, Robert. This is the part where you leave."

I exit the room and hover outside. That'll give me a chance to think. I'll duck back in when she starts the machine again.

Up until now, I've been too tied up in my pain to see how any of it works. Now that it won't be me in the chamber, this'll be my chance. I feel guilty that my knowledge will come at this new victim's expense, but seeing as how I can't stop that, I am going to watch, learn. There has to be some sense to what Not-Glass is doing. I need, deeply and truly need, to understand.

Chapter VI: The Plan Awry

I stick my head inside. I'm hoping Not-Glass won't notice me. She's heads-down at the computer, tweaking settings. Her wired-up shoes are already on. I pull my head out and go around to a better vantage point. I want to see that computer screen.

It's disappointing. I've seen people on their phones, gotten a sense of how sophisticated they can get. This isn't that. It's a blocky old app. Looks to be from the earliest days of computer graphics, primitive compared to even the earliest phones.

She's typing numbers into boxes. The labels are in Greek, so I assume they are math symbols and she's setting values into formulas. Just five inputs and a button marked "Go."

I try to memorize the numbers but when she starts it, I feel the vibration. I flee the room. The effect stops once I'm a few blocks away. I had assumed the chamber was connected to the machine directly. Seems it's just there to keep the subject imprisoned. I start back. I have to see.

Each step closer makes the pain worse. I keep walking. Rationally, I know that this won't work. I'll be at a level of agony that will make me blind to everything. I keep walking. The will to discorporate grows. I keep walking.

My head is pushed into the wall. My sight begins to fail but I can see a little. Maybe the wall shields me some, I don't know.

Not-Glass is vibrating. I can hear her scream over my own. Inside the chamber, the woman isn't screaming. She's smiling. Smug. Then she looks at me, looks directly at me, and winks.

When I look back at the computer, Not-Glass isn't there. A man walks in the door. Young-ish, muscular, dressed in black, silver chain with a big ankh on it. He shuts it all down and releases the woman from the chamber.

"I can't really see you," she says. "I just know you're here. You have questions. Follow us and I'll try to answer them."

I enter the room fully. The wired-up shoes are there, empty. The man steps outside and comes back immediately with two jerry cans of gasoline. They each take one and spread it liberally around the lab.

I leave with them as the man tosses several lit matches inside before closing the door. My only regret is that the chamber will probably survive the fire.

They get in their car. I can't join them. And I know I can't walk fast enough to keep up. I guess she didn't know that about spirits.

"Wait!" I holler.

They don't hear me. How could I expect them to?

I try to work out what I know, see if there's enough clues left for me to satisfy my curiosity without their help.

I do understand how the woman escaped. For all the genius Not-Glass thought herself, she kidnapped the best psychic. The person most likely to see it coming. That explains the man and the apparent malfunction that saved her from being harmed by the machine.

I hurry back into the lab. I have no fear of flames. Maybe I can find some not-yet-burnt notes so that I can understand what happened. My only other chance at answers is headed away at sixty miles an hour.

I find Not-Glass dead on the floor. Must be fumes, the fire hasn't touched her yet. I don't have it in me to feel pity for her. Just anger that I'm left with all my questions. That's her final act of cruelty. And I'll carry it with me forever.

"Well, well, well," Not-Glass' ghost says to me. "I guess we aren't done."

"Why you?" I yell at her. "People die every day. I never see another ghost but now, somehow, you!"

"Don't get used to it, Robert. I'm not staying."

"You know how to escape death? This was your plan?"

"Me wanting myself dead? Perish the thought. Of course this isn't the plan. Don't be stupid. This is just a phase. Not my favorite one, but necessary."

"The psychic beat you."

"Obviously."

"You lost!"

"Nope. A setback. One I allowed for. Twenty-seven percent. I counted on a different outcome but I planned for this one. Watch the fire. You'll see."

It went out. No sprinkler system. No extinguisher. The flames just vanished. Then Not-Glass vanished. The body, not the spirit. The spirit was still here, annoying me with its presence.

"Are you a Steve Miller fan?"

"They play him sometimes at bars I haunt."

"Time keeps on slipping, slipping …"

And the ghost vanishes. The psychic's back in the chamber. Not-Glass walks in, corporeal. Alive.

"Wendy, you underestimated me," Not-Glass says to her captive. "I told my younger self what you did to me. She fixed it. Time travel is better than psychic power. Once I knew what you were going to do, I undid it."

Not-Glass smiles at me.

"We have an audience, Wendy. Let's put on a good show. One worth your precious Mike dying for."

Chapter VII: Why

Not-Glass puts on her shoes. She fires up the machine. I don't get caught up in it this time. Wendy does. She's screaming and sweating in the chamber. I can feel her fear radiating off her. I know that pain.

"Why aren't I feeling it?"

"I only need one tether this time, Robert."

"But she didn't tether you last time. She was smiling."

"I tethered myself. That's why I was in pain. Keep up. You are so stupid!"

I can't parse that. But I can watch. I can get answers. Maybe get answers. I'm starting to wonder if I'll understand them when they arrive.

Not-Glass vanishes. The shoes are there, empty. The rest of her clothes went with her. Wendy, the woman in the chamber, is still there and screaming. Her whole body is shaking. I force myself to look away, to disassociate. I head for the computer.

There's a file marked Wendy on the desktop. Might as well be on the moon. I can't click it open. I can't affect anything.

Not-Glass reappears. The screaming from the chamber stops.

"All done, Robert," she says.

"If Wendy can hear you, tell her that I didn't really kill Mike. He's on his way."

"What was this all for?"

"Isn't it obvious? Think about it. I beat Wendy the second time, right?"

"So?"

"So she's wrong about seventy-three percent of the time, Robert."

"But that was enough to anchor you?"

"So long as I didn't want to go to the real past. She's an anchor to a parallel universe. One where all her predictions of the future are true."

"So you went to an alternate past?"

"Keep up. Yes. I told you I wasn't changing the past or the future. From your perspective, that's true. But now, I've re-routed my life. In a minute, Mike will come through that door. He will save Wendy as she instructed him to. And he will kill the other me that I'm replacing. The one who did none of the evil I did. It's the perfect crime."

Not-Glass shimmers out. A moment later, she's back. Not her, exactly. A different her. A little skinnier, change of hairstyle, but close, so very close. Mike charges in. He draws a gun. I try to stop him but I can't. Not-Not-Glass dies. I can't bear it. This world is too hard for me. I discorporate.

Charles Barouch has five stories on the Moon in a cultural time capsule. He also has stories available on Earth at hdwp.com/r/cdb. He's been published in SF/F/H, humor, Western, and more, by Celestial Echo Press, Canyons of the Damned, Dusty Saddle, Shebat Legion, Fantastic Books, and others.

How to Prepare for Time Travelers in the Workplace
Grigory Lukin

For over [REDACTED] years, the Organization for Time Travel Oversight (OTTO) has assisted businesses, non-profit organizations, community centers, and the occasional religious compound with identification, neutralization, and deportation of unauthorized time travelers. The 97.3% success rate speaks for itself, and the Core Accepted Timeline (CAT) remains safe from catastrophic chain reactions caused by misguided, malevolent, or charmingly charismatic time travelers. (The OTTO no longer accepts questions on the Jonestown Incident or its impact on the CAT.)

By definition, unauthorized and unexpected visitors from the future can appear at any time, whether you're running a paleolithic flint-knapping sweatshop, a pre-synthesizer fast-food joint, or a humdrum paper supply company. You've doubtlessly encountered plenty of cleverly disguised, charmingly aloof, or blackout-drunk time tourists in your life. A combination of Occam's Razor and use of level-1 amnesiac perfume generally helps them maintain their anonymity. Sometimes, however, a wily interloper will attempt to impersonate a chrono-local and infiltrate their workplace. If that happens, please follow these simple steps.

1. If the suspected time traveler doesn't know contemporary pop culture, slang, and/or sports references, first try to ensure they're not a nerd, workaholic, and/or immigrant. That will avoid awkward false alarms, level-3 mass amnesiacs, and lost work productivity.

2. If you suspect your coworker, boss, or intern/trainee/serf is a time traveler, block their every attempt at conversation. Any anachronistic memes, songs, or stock tips will result in detention of all nearby persons by the Quarantine Unit Ascertaining Contraband Knowledge (QUACK). When in doubt, start singing "Happy Birthday" at the top of your lungs until the

suspected time traveler leaves. The less you hear, the shorter your QUACK detention will be.

3. If you hear a loud "Happy Birthday" song and rush in to grab a piece of free birthday cake, you'll get the longest possible QUACK sentence, you dishonorable cake thief.

4. If your strange coworker has unusual dietary habits (eating French fries with a fork, avoiding tap water from perfectly normal lead pipes, or yelling, "Boy, howdy!" before every meal), there's a distinct possibility they're simply eccentric, desperate for attention, or deliberately disruptive. If your civilization has already invented the internet, that person might be a social media influencer. If your civilization has not yet invented the internet, imagine a brain-damaged clown obsessed with mirrors.

5. [REDACTED]

6. Most post-2089 time travelers don't know how to break an egg. Many time travelers don't eat meat or other animal byproducts. Some time travelers avoid hugs or crowded spaces; they may react wildly if somebody coughs or sneezes near them. Time travelers from the 23rd century are terrified of dogs, robots, and especially robot dogs. Time travelers from the 24th century and onward get extremely excited by dogs but don't know how to pet them. Time travelers fear the midday sun: they rarely venture outside without sunscreen.

7. After activating the OTTO beacon (see the attached pictographic assembly instructions) and deafening the suspected time traveler with a chorus of nonstop "Happy Birthday" songs, you'll need to detain them until the arrival of OTTO personnel. Tree vines, duct tape, and/or nanite cords will not help you restrain a person with sufficiently advanced technology. Fortunately, there are alternatives. Confuse the time traveler by passionately advocating the geocentric model of the universe. Annoy them by mispronouncing common words like "nuclear," or "library," or "deoxyribonucleic." Enthrall them by describing an old time capsule your grandfather buried in the backyard with

all his favorite possessions. If the time traveler still tries to flee, tell them you have a vitally important message from their future self, but you can't quite recall it. Vanity almost always gets them.

8. The time traveler in your workplace might keep their time machine nearby for easy access, out of laziness, or just to show off. While subdermal time-travel implants exist, most long-term time travelers prefer larger vehicles to carry their supplies, tools, and snacks. Be on the lookout for inconspicuous old-fashioned phone booths, suspiciously fancy office chairs, and treadmills with improbably elaborate control panels. Be extra suspicious if those devices are located in public spaces like hallways, restrooms, or next to the office ficus plant, with a "NOT a time machine!" cardboard sign attached.

You may feel as if the time machine has always been there. You may not remember when your time-traveling coworker, boss or intern/trainee/serf got hired. Seek out old photographs, drawings, or cave paintings to confirm the nature of your reality. Your memories may not be your own.

9. You may have gone through this before. What had been is no more, although it will have been, lest the temporal loop falter.

If you follow these instructions faithfully, the OTTO agents' level-3 amnesiac will wear off in just a few hours. You'll feel as if you were daydreaming. Then you'll look at the clock and wonder why you haven't accomplished anything thus far. Your strange coworker, boss, or intern/trainee/serf will be gone, with a quick note saying they hate this place and they will never return. If you were in QUACK custody, you'll awaken back at work under similar circumstances. Your hair will feel slightly longer than it should be, you'll have a fading memory of the strangest dream, and you'll experience the inexplicable sensation of ennui, of longing, of having lost something or someone special, though you can't recall why. Also, you'll develop an extreme fear of ducks. Sorry about that.

Organize frequent training drills using this manual/tablet/hologram. Make your coworkers memorize the contents. Time-traveling infiltrators are as dangerous as they are curious, and following these instructions to the letter could mean the difference between life, QUACK, and an involuntary mass expulsion from the timeline.

If these procedures are followed correctly, you will never know. You will not remember. You will not cease to be. In fact, you may have already followed them before — in which case, the CAT thanks you for your service, help, and cooperation.

(Produced by the QUACK division of the OTTO, defenders of the CAT.)

Grigory Lukin (rhymes with "story" and "scene") is a Russian-American-French-Canadian nomad and adventurer. When not hiking from Mexico to Canada, he enjoys writing. This is his first published story, to be followed by more tales and novels set in the OTTO universe. He can be found at www.grigorylukin.com.

Tadpole's Time Travel
Gary Every

Rising to his knees, his shoulder appearing above the cactus spines, Tadpole drew back on the bow string, releasing the arrow from somewhere deep inside his chest, sending it sailing. He shot too high. The twang of the bow string caused a bighorn ram to look up with alarm while the rest of the herd continued to graze.

The arrow sailed beyond the crest of the hill and out of Tadpole's sight. Tadpole waited until the large ram dropped his guard, lowering his head to nibble on the grass. Tadpole rose from behind the agave and fired, just as the wind gusted. The shaft rattled through the upper branches of a jojoba bush, scattering the leaves.

Frightened, the herd fled.

"Aaaaiyee!" Tadpole shouted as he chased the bighorn sheep on foot. The herd scampered around the north side of the peak, and Tadpole followed. His stride landed him atop a large flat rock, and his weight sent the rock sliding down the mountain. Tadpole tried to surf his way down the slope, but the grade was too steep. Screaming, he tumbled off the cliff.

Bobby Cleveland sat sipping from the canteen, dangling his legs off the rock and laughing. Edward Cheng hoped his Chinese ancestors were watching and putting a curse on the amused Black man. Bobby held the canteen out in front of him, offering it to Edward like dangling a carrot to inspire Cheng onward. Cheng approached, ripped the canteen from Bobby's hands. He drank in large gulps, water spilling off his chest onto the ground.

Bobby gestured with his arms, "This is the end of the trail."

"Looks like just another rock."

"It is," Bobby pointed out, "except for the petroglyphs you're leaning against."

Cheng looked at the four crudely etched bighorn sheep on the surface of the rock and offered his opinion.

"Pretty dull."

Bobby said, "The Hohokam must have thought this was a pretty sacred spot, or they never would have bothered to carve petroglyphs into the rock."

"Think there were any human sacrifices here?"

Bobby answered him. "There may have been ceremonies, prayers, and chants for rain, but no human sacrifices. You have them confused with the Aztecs."

Cheng shook his head. "You mean on top of all your other talents as Johnny Junior Scientist Boy Wonder, you're an amateur archaeologist too?"

Bobby laughed. "At least I'm not an amateur scientist anymore. I've been hired at the new sleep research project."

"Congratulations," Cheng said as he made himself comfortable atop the rock, closing his eyes. "You're the expert. What should I dream about?"

"Dream you're an Indian."

Once he relaxed, Edward Cheng fell asleep almost immediately. He dreamt he was an Indian, and he dreamt he was falling.

Tadpole felt very bad. His feet were cold, his head warm, his stomach unsettled, and his nose stung from the bite of smoke. He could hear Old Parrot's rough and craggy voice chanting and could see his aunt sitting back on her haunches. Her right hand was sprinkling colored sand as she tried to complete the medicine circle, afraid her nephew's spirit might depart this world.

"Turkey Neck, fetch me water!" barked the sorceress in a tone meant to be obeyed swiftly.

Turkey Neck hurried for water, her normally graceful stride stumbling. The springs were far away, although her grandfather had told her that before the years of drought the springs had not retreated quite so far back into the mountains. Her grandfather blamed the drought and the dry springs on Old Parrot, whom he said was growing feeble as a shaman.

His head hurt, his feet stunk, and deep down in his heart Cheng suspected that Jesus did not love him anymore. It was a hungover Cheng who tried to wend his way through the path of bureaucratic corridors to Bobby Cleveland's office. Flirting with the department secretary revealed that Bobby was out jogging.

Cheng made his way to the track. He stood in front of the bleachers, directly across from the mural that depicted a stern warrior and wished the Pima College Aztecs athletic success. Cheng waited for Bobby to circle the track.

"What's up?" Bobby asked.

Cheng looked down at his shoes. "I think I sold a painting, but I won't get the money till next week. I could use thirty dollars."

Bobby smiled. "Congratulations. You just volunteered to be a guinea pig."

"Sick humor, dude."

"We need subjects for the sleep research project," Bobby explained. "We pay our volunteers. All you have to do is snooze, snore, and dream."

"You know," Cheng said, crossing his arms, "I have been having the strangest dreams lately."

Bobby waited for him to elaborate.

"I keep dreaming about that canyon we were hiking in. There is this Indian falling. Heck, the guy might even be a dead ringer for the one in the mural over there."

"Depends on whether he's a Hohokam or an Aztec," Bobby reflected. "If he's an Aztec, they never came anywhere near this part of the world. They settled in Mexico City after fulfilling the prophecy of an eagle grasping a snake. How soon do you need the thirty dollars?"

"This afternoon would be nice."

"Well," Bobby patted him on the back, "we had better get you wired up before noon."

Waiting for Turkey Neck to return with the water, Old Parrot suddenly started singing. Out of the corner of her eye, she saw something, a shadow, a shape, a glimmer of light, traveling along the spirit walkway at the edge of the medicine circle.

"Aren't you going to wish me pleasant dreams?"

"No way," Bobby said as he checked the wire connections. "Weird dreams make better data."

Cheng fell asleep and quickly fell into a dream. He dreamt he was falling from a great height, descending toward a lake. The flat surface of the lake stretched from horizon to horizon, and as he fell the onrushing reflection was not his own but Tadpole's. The reflection of Tadpole grew larger and larger as he fell toward the water, and suddenly Edward Cheng realized that Tadpole was falling too. Cheng wondered if Tadpole was watching the reflection of a Chinese American man falling toward the water.

A spear of light stabbed into Tadpole's right eye, causing him to flinch.

Bobby Cleveland smiled down at him, holding a penlight and checking his pupils.

Tadpole was horrified. The Black man was the first he had ever seen. His first comparison was with the charred corpses of the funeral pyres. There was something even more frightening than the Black man. Tadpole was inside a yellow body!

"You know," the Black man spoke with his back to Tadpole, speaking in a language he didn't understand, "your readings went through the roof. Then you lost consciousness. I could tell just by the color of your urine specimen that you haven't been getting enough vitamins. I'm going to give you a booster."

The Black man wheeled around holding a needle.

Tadpole screamed and ran from the room.

Cheng awoke to the sound of an old woman chanting. He rolled over, stopping just short of rolling into the fire. Cheng stood slowly, his body stiff and sore. To say nothing of the fact that his body was an unusual brown color. Not that it was an unusual color for a human being, but it was an unusual color for Edward Cheng.

The old woman stopped her chanting and spoke to him in fast, mumbled syllables Cheng did not understand. Cheng recognized where they were—on the hill looking down on the petroglyphs. The old woman put her hand on his shoulder.

"Your body walks, but the spirit is far away."

Cheng shrugged his shoulders and wondered if this was the type of dream that gave Bobby good data.

Tadpole flew down the hall, out of the building, and into the parking lot. There, he was confronted by a demon. The demon was large, square, and metallic, looking like no animal that Tadpole had ever seen. Inside, looking back at him, Tadpole could see three devoured, lost souls. He tried to free them from inside the belly of the beast.

He leapt onto the hood of the automobile and began to pound on the windshield, trying to out-shriek the frightened occupants as well as the horrible horn of the beast itself. The car stopped with a squeal of the brakes. Tadpole rolled off the hood, spilling onto the pavement as the beast sped away.

Making his way down to the petroglyphs, Cheng tripped, skinning his knee. He watched the blood trickle down his shin, surprised that he could feel such vivid pain in a dream. Cheng yawned, and this surprised him too, wanting to sleep inside a dream.

The sun began to rise over the mountains as Tadpole fed another branch into the fire, the smoke curling upward to the bottom of the concrete bridge. To the south, Baboquivari Peak towered above the landscape. Tadpole began to pray. This strange world where horrible noises sounded throughout the night had left him unable to sleep. Clapping his hands to keep a soft steady beat, Tadpole chanted the song of creation.

The verses of the song told of the world before the world and how that time had been populated by people of many different colors. The people of the world before the world had been evil. Amongst them all there was only one good and honest person. This brown-skinned man was named Iiyotoi, and he won favor with the gods and was rewarded with gifts. Jealous, the evil multicolored people murdered Iiyotoi.

The angry gods placed Iiyotoi's ghost upon Baboquivari Peak while they destroyed the world before the world with floods. When the floods receded, the gods created a new world, one populated only with the brown-skinned children of Iiyotoi.

Tadpole could not help thinking of the Black man he had seen today and of his own yellow skin without wondering if he had not somehow stumbled into the world before the world.

A hobo stumbled down the bank of the arroyo. The white man staggered to his feet, and even the shadow he cast in the feeble morning light shrank away from his own stench. The man undid his pants and urinated into a place where water flows. Tadpole was convinced that this was indeed a vile place.

Tadpole left his fire and traveled along the bottom of the arroyo until the narrow chasm faded completely into sewer drainages and cement culverts. Tadpole climbed up the banks of the arroyo, attaining the sidewalks where he saw a most wondrous thing. It was a warrior, clad in black leather and chains. His wrists, belt, and neck were adorned with metal spikes. He was bald except for a single band of green hair cut in a strip. The most amazing thing to Tadpole was that this warrior was standing atop a wheeled board. Hohokam children had wheeled toys, but the invention had never been used for transportation. Watching the warrior glide effortlessly atop the skateboard, cruising a few inches above the ground, Tadpole could only wonder if the sensation was similar to flying.

The heavy old woman rummaged through the leather pouch she wore about her neck. With great import and a sense of ceremony, she presented Cheng with a small bone that had been hollowed out to let a leather string pass through. On one end of the soft, pliable thong was a blue seashell, and on the other was a brightly colored parrot feather. The feather was from a Sonoran parrot; a bird that would be extinct in Arizona by the time Cheng was born.

The old woman was chattering at him in the strange language. After she left, Cheng decided to deal with his hunger. He fished in the river, not recognizing the shore he was sitting on, perhaps because the Santa Cruz River of his own time ran dry except for seasons of monsoon flooding and sewage treatment plant overflows. Fish of every size and shape eluded Cheng's attempts to capture them by hand.

Cheng was forced to pursue other game. Attempts at capturing quail left him scratched from impenetrable thickets as the clumsy little birds fluttered just beyond his reach. Chasing jackrabbits on foot was both futile and humiliating. Cheng decided to try lizard catching, reasoning that he must possess some sort of evolutionary advantage. Mammals were a much more recent biological invention than reptiles, and after all hadn't his ancestors replaced their ancestors.

He set out on his lizard safari with a great deal of relish and enthusiasm, discovering that this area of evolutionary advantage was not in the realm of quicker reflexes. Zebra tails, geckos, whip tails, and even horned toads all skipped beyond Cheng's fingertips into the sanctuary of rock crevices. Cheng stopped to ponder these alleged evolutionary advantages. Size was a certainty but would not do him any good unless one of the lizards leapt off the rocks and went for his throat. It had to be intelligence; Cheng needed to rely on patience and guile instead of power and speed.

Cheng sat at the base of a sun-drenched boulder, scattering the lizards doing pushups, sitting motionless waiting for the lizards to return and enjoy the solar warmth. When they did, his right hand crept along slowly, sometimes remaining still for several seconds. His left hand also remained still except to divert attention away from his right hand. Suddenly, he swooped down and captured a zebra tail.

After the thrill of victory had worn off, Cheng was faced with the prospect of eating a writhing, squirming reptile. Gutting and cleaning his prey would not leave much meat. It seemed rather pointless to skin the lizard. Faced with the prospect of eating a live lizard whole, Cheng decided to release the reptile and remain hungry.

Tadpole sat on the ground and removed his shoes. He kept the socks and was careful to save the laces, wrapping them around his biceps. Going through the pants pockets, Tadpole discarded nearly everything — scraps of paper, loose change, pens, dice, even the billfold. Tadpole did keep the Swiss Army knife, wondering if perhaps it was a magic gift from the wheeled, green-haired warrior he had seen earlier. As soon as the pockets were empty, Tadpole tossed the pants but went back and fetched the belt, wrapping it around his waist. The shirt was left on the desert floor alongside the pants.

He resumed his march along the barren riverbed of the Santa Cruz, dressed only in his Fruit of the Looms and the socks he had kept to protect his feet from the hot sand. He followed the wash until he came to a junction where a mountain watershed flowed into it. That is, if sand can be said to flow.

Tadpole turned up the canyon, following it into the heart of the Frog Mountains. The Hohokam had named these mountains the Frogs because of the large number of amphibians that resided in the deep granite pools. If there were any traces of water to be found in this dry world before the world, then surely it must be found in the Frog Mountains, he believed.

He scrambled up the nearest granite protrusion. From the top of this high point, Tadpole could see across the edge of the Tucson valley. The horizon going up was covered with a dirt-brown haze. Everywhere the earth was scarred with the flat asphalt roads used by the metallic demon beasts. Tadpole imagined the beasts were similar to the malicious goblins that Hohokam parents threatened would come to swallow the souls of misbehaving children. The demon beasts had fouled the air with clouds of flatulence rising from every tailpipe. He thought perhaps they were also responsible for the dry riverbeds and arroyos, sucking the water from the earth.

"The red-flowered stick cactus are called ocotillo."

Tadpole's thoughts were interrupted by the amplified droning monotone of a tour guide performing the usual song-and-dance for tourists as the tram rolled along the road beneath Tadpole's perch.

"The hillsides are dotted with picturesque saguaros. Ancient Indian legends told that each saguaro contained the soul of a dead warrior and each arm represented a wife. An arm turned upward represented a faithful wife while one pointing down represented—"

"Jerry, come back here!" interrupted the shattering scream of an old woman.

From the back of the tram, a teenager shouted, "Be free, little dog, be free."

The dog ran up the slope at a speed that belied his small stature. Later in the day, feeling exhausted and worried, Jerry realized he was not so much free as lost. As he stumbled across the first human being he had seen in hours, Jerry approached with his tail between his legs.

Tadpole had just found lunch.

Relaxing by a peaceful spring, Cheng dipped his finger into a clay bowl, rapidly devouring some corn mush. The food was kind of bland, but once you got used to eating with your fingers it felt good in the belly. Besides, Cheng had his head in the lap of a beautiful young Native American woman who was lovingly running her fingers through his hair. Now this was his idea of a dream.

Turkey Neck checked his scalp for lice. Full and content, pleasantly buzzed on mesquite bean wine, Cheng leaned over and sketched in the sand with the bone-and-feather talisman Old Parrot had given him. He drew a golden eagle, taking time to sketch in detail, using techniques in shading and perspective that were not going to be invented for centuries.

Turkey Neck and Old Parrot stared at his picture, a little frightened to be in the presence of such powerful magic. They were convinced that it was an attempt by his soul to communicate something it was observing while out of his body on a spirit journey.

Noticing the attentive stares of the pretty maiden, Cheng drew her another picture. This time, it was a snake spaced a little too closely to the eagle, so that it almost looked as if the eagle were holding the snake in its talons.

Tadpole came down from the Frog Mountains, crossing down the wash, along the dry riverbed, traversing the valley, and heading to Old Parrot's favorite petroglyphs. It took hours, but at last Tadpole arrived at the opening of the canyon. He was about to make his way up the path to the sacred rocks when he heard a sound that made him stop in his tracks.

It was the bleating of a bighorn sheep.

This was the first sign of game Tadpole had found in this strange world before the world. Tadpole temporarily put aside his trip to the petroglyphs to investigate. Listening closely, he was able to draw a bead on the sheep. The bleating was coming from amidst a cluster of adobe walls down the hill.

The flags of the United States, Arizona, and Mexico waved in the breeze at the entrance to the Sonoran Desert Zoo. He avoided the place where the crowds were milling about. Instead, Tadpole scrambled over the walls and landed on the pathways with a soft plop. Once inside, he was amazed. In cages where they could be safe from the evil multicolored people of the world before the world were horned toads, antelope, tortoise, bobcat, Gila monsters, and wolves. Tadpole ran from cage to cage, his eyes wide with wonder and exhilaration. There were pools of water full with beaver and otter. There was even a colony of the little people, coatimundi. This oasis was a sharp contrast to the barren world he had seen so far.

The first people to catch a glimpse of the skinny Asian-looking man running from exhibit to exhibit dressed only in his underwear screamed loudly. The shrieking followed Tadpole everywhere he went. Tadpole was about to flee when an archaeology exhibit caught his eye.

There, behind the glass, were pottery, seashell jewelry, arrowheads, and other artifacts of his people. Tadpole nearly fainted. He was not in the world before the world, but the one after his people. A world where the Hohokam way of life had disappeared.

A posse of security guards rounded the corner with whistles shrieking and clubs waving. Tadpole ran.

Cheng marveled again at the vividness of this dream. The canyon walls were washed with sandstone reds, and the palo verde trees were covered with tiny yellow flowers. Even the sky and the petroglyphs on the rocks seemed much more vivid than Cheng remembered them.

The old woman had a rather definite stink about her. She dug her fingernails into Cheng's biceps, trying to recapture his attention. One more time the old woman led him through the dance steps. While Cheng tried to mimic what she was teaching him, a woman's voice rang out farther up the canyon.

Cheng did not need to understand Old Parrot's words to grasp the venomous intent of her insulting reply.

From farther up the canyon, an unseen hand launched a stone that flew through the air in a high arc before landing dead center in Old Parrot's chest. Old Parrot inflated with hate and charged forward with a roaring bellow. A hail of rocks was released from a hundred different hiding places up and down Temporal Canyon.

She fell to the ground beneath the onslaught, and the tone in her voice changed from vengeance to anguish. Her cries ceased, and the barrage of stones picked up fury.

Terrified, Cheng fled the canyon.

Tadpole fled. He had learned from the archaeology display that this was not the world before the world, but the one after. The gods had seen fit to destroy the world once by flood and had apparently destroyed the world of the Hohokam, Iiyotoi's children, by drought. It was Tadpole's hope that he had been sent on this spirit journey with a purpose. If he could get home, it might be in time to save his people.

When he arrived at last at the petroglyph rocks, Tadpole nearly wept. The petroglyphs were worn and faded. He wondered if his people would be forgotten entirely when the petroglyphs had finally eroded from the rocks.

The security guards had followed Tadpole up the canyon, and when they arrested him the man in his underwear was doing a dance and chanting in a strange language. The guards brought him back to the zoo, detaining him until the police arrived. To avoid offending any patrons who might be upset by the sight of a man in his underwear, they wrapped him in one of the flags at the zoo entrance. Being patriotic Americans, they made sure the flag wasn't Old Glory or the Arizona state flag, wrapping him in the Mexican colors.

Bobby Cleveland filled out the last of the release forms. The hospital freed Edward Cheng into the good doctor's custody. Bobby's friend and experimental subject was led to him, still wrapped in the Mexican flag. Having an experimental subject go bonkers might be enough to get his tenure denied. If a scandal followed, he would probably be fired.

Tadpole ran his fingers across the brightly colored cloth. The cloak was draped over his shoulders as he studied the picture in the center. If there was a lesson to be learned in this spirit journey, perhaps this was it. Tadpole studied and memorized the icon of the eagle grasping the snake.

Bobby led his friend out of the building, through the parking lot, and to his car. Tadpole followed docilely along until Bobby dug through his pockets for his keys. By the time Bobby turned around, the young man following him had disappeared.

A sticky dark stain in the sand marked where Old Parrot's body had been, but there were no other signs of where the female shaman's corpse lay. Cheng followed the coyote tracks and the drag marks until he found the body. He scooped away dirt with his bare hands and dug a shallow grave. He buried the bone-and-feather talisman alongside Old Parrot.

The wind rustled a creosote bush, and Cheng flinched. He was convinced this was not a dream. He wasn't sure what was going on, but it was not a dream.

The old saying advised, "When in Rome, do as the Romans do." Even if it meant praying to a rock.

Tadpole picked up a stick and began drawing a crude medicine circle ...

...Shuffling one foot in front of the other, Cheng hoped enthusiasm would make up for precision as he chanted the only song he knew that was long enough for a ceremony based on Indian time ...

...As he danced, Tadpole observed storm clouds gathering on the horizon, the first monsoon of the season ...

..."74,586 bottles of beer on the wall, 74,586 bottles of beer." The monotonous rhythms slowly drove Cheng into a trance-like state ...

The Sonoran Desert has its monsoon season in July and August. These violent storms bring with them half the annual rainfall during short intense cloudbursts. These storms tend to be erratic, causing flash floods, wondrous sunsets, and tremendous displays of lightning. One particular chubasco storm gathered, whipping the wind and booming

across the earth with rattles of thunder. This storm never delivered on its promise of rain, weakening itself considerably as the lightning split itself across a chasm of 800 years.

Tadpole stretched his limbs across the sand, writhing like a sidewinder. Waking up was a stiff and groggy experience for him. Turkey Neck found him and came quickly to his side. He was horrified by her explanation of what had happened to Old Parrot. He had heard of shamans being stoned for being unable to bring rain but never dreamed it would happen to his own aunt. Approaching the village, he found it full of visiting Toltec Indians.

The first thing Cheng saw was Bobby Cleveland hovering above him, shaking him by the shoulder.

"Eddie, Eddie, wake up."

As Cheng opened his eyes, Bobby began to poke and prod, checking his pupils.

Cheng pushed him away. "I'm okay now."

Bobby didn't look too sure. "Lay off those anchovy pizzas. We don't need data this weird for our experiments."

Turkey Neck showed Tadpole what his body had sketched in the sand while his soul was wandering on the spirit journey. Tadpole recognized the image of the eagle grasping the snake immediately, associating it with the flag he had been wrapped in back at the oasis in the world after the world.

Tadpole was thinking long and hard about this omen as he listened to the visiting Toltecs speak. The small group of wanderers was not the usual ragtag assortment of young males. This group included women and families. They had come because the same drought that was proving costly to the Hohokam was devastating to the Toltecs of the neighboring, drier desert of

Chihuahua. They were migrating in search of a new home and offering to recruit any Hohokam who wished to follow along. Tadpole stood and began to speak.

"I have returned from a spirit journey and been shown a future where this drought continues for many generations, until the rivers run dry. I have seen a future where the many-colored demon peoples have returned to walk the earth."

The Hohokam in the audience whispered among themselves.

"In this world," Tadpole continued, "I was shown only one oasis."

Both cultures, Toltec and Hohokam, had strong traditions of sorcery and magic. They listened closely to the prophecies of a spirit journey.

"I was shown an omen," Tadpole explained. "The oasis can be found where the eagle grasps the snake."

When the Toltec asked Tadpole which direction they should follow to find the eagle grasping the snake, he was not sure. He suggested they migrate south, following the migration routes of the parrots until they found the oasis.

Another shovelful of dirt was tossed into the sifter.

"I found something!" Cheng yelled.

Bobby Cleveland washed it carefully, still not certain of the validity of this whole operation.

"Are you sure this is the place of your dream?"

"Absolutely," Cheng replied, waiting for Bobby to clean what he had just found before continuing.

Bobby held the small circular object between his fingertips as he washed it. "You buried something right here in your dream?"

"Someone," Cheng corrected. "Look, I showed you right where the village was, didn't I?"

"Buried who?" Bobby asked.

"The shaman woman who was murdered in my dream."

Bobby stopped digging and dropped to his knees, using his fingers to sift through the dirt.

"My god!" he exclaimed as his fingers tugged on a skull from the ground. "This really is a burial site."

"Remember," Cheng admonished, "you promised no grave robbing, just notes and photographs."

Bobby stole nothing, but he did take several photographs and notes, and made Edward Cheng promise to undergo some extensive interviews for the dream research project. Then everything was reburied.

Everything except for a parrot-bone talisman that used to have a feather on the end over four centuries ago. Cheng pocketed the talisman. He could turn it into a pen, he mused. Edward Cheng had a story he wanted to write.

Gary Every is an award-winning journalist, slam poet, teacher, musician, host of the Poetry and Prose Project radio program and author of two published science fiction novellas *Inca Butterflies* and *The Saint and the Robot*. He can be found at www.garyevery.com.

Uchronia
Ef Deal

The Old Woman sat at the curve of a bar, something she hadn't done since her days at school, and wondered idly why she was here, and then *where* she was—here, and upon a third reflection, *when*.

"Incoming," called the man two barstools over, a Handsome Young Man in a heavy black military coat. He had a beaming smile and eyes that twinkled with mischief.

The men along the bar raised their mugs and glasses and sang, "Hail, hail Uchronia, land of the freed from …"

They halted before completing the line.

"Welcome," said the Handsome Young Man to the Old Woman.

The Bartender rang a ship's bell hanging above the bar as he made his way to her with a glass of pale-yellow wine. "Welcome back," he said as he set it before her.

She searched her memory, a long process at her age. She lifted her eyes to the Bartender. "I—I don't think I've been here before," she said.

"Then welcome forward," the Bartender replied with a chuckle. "Hope you enjoy."

Forestalling an answer, she spun the glass, delighting in the bouquet that arose. She didn't recognize the bistro, nor any of the others seated at the bar. Quiet music emanated from the ceiling, and in a far corner a couple danced, holding one another in a most intimate fashion that would have had them arrested for indecency in Paris. A small group of people in their twenties huddled in a booth talking quietly with a professorial-looking man over a platter of small, round sandwiches.

She sipped her wine appreciatively and swallowed a memory of evenings playing cribbage with her sister in the salon at home. Tears started as she smiled.

"Bellesfées '71," she murmured. "How …?"

"He always knows," said the Handsome Young Man. He offered his hand. "Jack," he told her.

"…"

"Don't worry." He pointed to the others. "Eventually we all lose our names."

A gentleman down the way scowled. "At least you had names," he grumbled, hoisting a foamy beer to his lips. "Even the girl had a name. Not me. The Philosopher, the Journalist, Filby. Not me."

"Well, now you have a beer, sir, which is more than you had where you were."

The Old Woman peeked over the rim of her glass at the Ancient Man with a long trailing beard who had admonished the well-dressed but Nameless Gentleman. The Ancient Man seemed to be from another era, with a homespun shirt and knickerbockers.

An Asian Woman suddenly materialized on the barstool beside her on the right. She slapped her fists and two tentacle-like appendages on the bar to steady herself. The Old Woman drew back in shock, but the song went up for her arrival, and a few of the others called, "Here's to Me!" raising their glasses or mugs.

"It's never funny, people." The newcomer settled onto her seat as the Bartender rang the bell and brought her a drink.

"Peach schnapps," he said.

She curled her lip. "Irony doesn't suit you."

Nevertheless, she swallowed a large gulp before glaring around the bar, coming finally to the Old Woman with some suspicion. Like the Old Woman, the Asian Woman was of advanced age, perhaps not a century old, but the six prosthetic tentacled legs indicated she was of another age entirely. In fact, only the Nameless Gentleman and another Elderly Gentleman at the far end of the bar gave the impression they too were of the turn of the century, like the Old Woman.

If only she could recall which century.

Another woman appeared to her left, young, small of build, bright auburn hair, popping into existence, bringing an odor of sulfur and smoke in her wake. A clang of the bell and the song, and the Bartender brought a cup of some hot beverage for the Auburn Woman.

"Damn," the Asian Woman complained. "With all the baths you take, you still can't get rid of that dragonstink?"

"Says the octopus reeking of duckweed," the Auburn Woman returned in kind.

Jack vanished.

"Hail, hail—"

"Enough already!" cried the Asian Woman, rolling her eyes.

The Old Woman emptied her glass, letting the cool vanilla and melon notes soothe her sense of utter displacement.

"He keeps busy, that one," the Asian Woman said to her. "He'll be back eventually. I haven't seen you here before or after, though."

"Bootstraps or butterflies?" a man with a voice too loud for the room called to her. At this, the bar quieted to await her answer.

She recalled that those words, spoken together as they were, meant something. It took a few moments before she recognized their implication. *Bootstraps*: An object from the future goes into the past to be conferred once again to the future, an eternalized Möbius loop. *Butterfly*: Someone from the future travels to the past and makes a change that carries forward, erasing the former future, creating a new one, or perhaps creating two different futures.

Who told her that?

Someone from her future in the past.

"Whoa," said the Auburn Woman, catching her as she swung dizzily on her barstool. "Here, have some klah." She set her hot beverage in front of the Old Woman. "Must be your first *occasion.* Seamus, you should know better."

The Bartender grinned. "Not Seamus. And I do know better."

A small, Sallow Man beside the Ancient Man snickered. "His name's Edgar."

A jumble of voices spoke at once: "I thought it was Sam." "Eckles." "Hey, that's *my* name." "Sam's the piano player." "No, I mean Sam Beckett." "He was a writer." "Rudolph." "No, the stupid plays. *Waiting for* ... somebody." "Aren't we all?" "Different Sam Beckett." "Oh, boy." "Sam's the bartender." "Can't be. Rudolph was already here." "And will be again; that's the beauty of it." "Herbert." "That's a vacuum cleaner."

"I'm telling you, it's Bart," bawled the Loud Man, quieting them all. He guffawed. "Short for Bartender, get it? Get it?"

His pun was met with the derision it deserved.

"He and I are brothers in this," bemoaned the Nameless Gentleman. "Forever nameless."

The Old Woman sipped the drink called klah and immediately slid the cup back to the Auburn Woman. She gladly accepted another glass of the Bellesfées that the Bartender brought to her. Although her thoughts moozed through a fog, a thread appeared that, when tugged, pulled several of them together into a vague concept.

"Time," she muttered.

The Bartender held up a can with an attached horn and produced a blast that nearly knocked the Old Woman off her seat. The others laughed.

"We say '*occasion*,'" the Asian Woman told her.

The Auburn Woman once again steadied her, then turned to the others. "You're all being very rude. Men!" she scoffed. She wrapped her arm around the Old Woman's thin shoulders gently. "It takes some getting used to, but now you're here, tell us how you earned passage to Uchronia."

"Hail, hail U—"

"Can it!" The Asian Woman silenced the men with a murderous glare.

The Old Woman worked at the inside of her cheek. The smell of beer and frying foods carried her to her youth, downing frites in the Quartier Latin. She settled comfortably into the odors of fires and burnt metals on the Auburn Woman beside her, as in days of old at the forge and her workshop.

Did that Asian Woman really say dragons?

"Some of us, like the Dutchman there, fell asleep and woke up to find the world had moved on, decades later," the Auburn Woman said. "Others, like that good-looking man in the gray uniform down the end of the bar, were frozen in cryostasis to awaken in a distant place, a distant era."

"Freeloaders," said the Loud Man with a sneer. "Not what I call travelers. Not like they could choose their destination. Time-Skippers, I say."

The Auburn Woman pointed to the Nameless Gentleman. "That one played with scientific approaches, sliding back and forth from his age to millennia beyond his own with a machine he built."

He nodded sadly. "Brilliant machine, still no name. Even the girl had a name."

The Asian Woman gave a dismissive *pfft*. "Give it a rest. You're not the only chronic argonaut. Not even the only chrono-mechanic."

"At least I didn't work to destroy an entire civilization," he said, an accusation.

The Asian Woman grumbled.

Whether it was the wine or the Auburn Woman's soothing voice, the Old Woman's agitation subsided as she began to build logic paths.

"I was looking for someone," she said, memories drawing her back across almost a century. She leaned her head to her trembling hands, her long, silver hair flowing around her on the bar.

"Euchronia," she repeated. "That means a beautiful—" She halted when she saw the Bartender reach for the can of noise.

"No," said the Auburn Woman, "not 'eu'; just 'u.' It means—"

"Not," the Old Woman realized. "Like Sir Thomas More's *Utopia*." She looked around again. "Oh. I see."

Jack reappeared as suddenly as he had vanished, this time with a middle-aged redheaded woman on his lap, both of them laughing and pulling excelsior and confetti from their clothes and hair. The Bartender had already set down another beer and a light drink in an inverted-cone-shaped glass with a stem, rimmed with some crystalized substance. He rang the bell twice. The Redhead with a mane of untamed curls beamed and raised her glass as the rest of the bar sang the song of Uchronia once again. She turned to the Old Woman, and her smile turned to a worried frown.

"Oh, you poor dear," she said, tenderly laying her hand on the Old Woman's worn and wrinkled hand. "You're new here, aren't you, dear? Do you know *when* you come from?"

The question made sense.

"1921," she answered, keeping an eye on the Bartender lest she violate some unspoken rule against naming the specific *occasion*. "In bed."

The Ancient Man rapped the bar. "Sleeper, like me," he declared.

"No, I was awake," she assured them all. "Looking through some photographs, some old daguerreotypes."

"Bootstraps," bellowed the Loud Man.

She ignored them, pushing herself to recall details through the muzzies. Was it her age or her circumstances? She wagged her head at the effort and smiled wryly.

"They always told me I was ahead of my ... *occasion*."

The Redhead chuckled. "Eventually we all are, but you're safe here. We're all in the same boat."

"Not me." An old man in a heavy red uniform raised a hand. "I'm—a—*captain*—of—a *starship*."

"Which wrecked an entire continuum," the Redhead pointed out with a shake of her head.

Jack grinned and jerked his thumb toward him. "That man's a menace. Talk about butterflies."

The Old Woman blinked moisture from her eyes and finished the second wine. "And now I'm here."

"Yes, now," the Auburn Woman who smelled of dragons said. "*Now* is where we are."

"Where we've always been." The Redhead nodded, her curls bouncing wildly. "No *occasion* like the present, I always say."

"Death," the Old Woman said, accepting her circumstance along with a third glass of wine.

"Oh, no, dear, not death." Again the red curls bounced.

The Old Woman straightened, again lost in half a memory. "'Where is death? Always future or past. No sooner is she present than she is no longer.'"

She gasped as the memory sharpened and she saw a beloved face before her.

The Redhead smiled wistfully. "You're not wrong, dear."

A Very Tall Man seated between the Ancient Man and the Nameless Gentleman stood. "I've seen my birth and death on many *occasions*, and I've visited other things in between."

"*Between*," the Auburn Woman said. "That's what we call it when I'm from."

The Very Tall Man suddenly disappeared, and the song went up once more.

"Someone should glue his ass on that barstool and see how unstuck he gets," said the Starship Captain.

The Old Woman struggled to swallow the lump in her throat. The beloved face faded along with the memory. Perhaps she had merely dreamed him.

"Aether," she murmured. "I came through the aether."

The Nameless Gentleman clumped his mug on the bar. "Now there's a word I understand, that ineffable substance of the fourth dimension."

The Sallow Man spoke up, his eyes glinting shrewdly. "How did you accomplish it?"

"How did *you*?" the Asian Woman countered. "Chronic argonaut, my ass."

She slid her glass away in disgust and the Bartender swapped it for wine, which she approved.

The Old Woman tapped her fingers on the bar, then, noticing a rough nail, bit at it. As she hoped, the others soon turned their interest to Jack and the Redhead's tale of a New Year's Eve celebration in a place called Duval Street.

How could one forget one's name? How could one forget one's travels through the spacetime continuum?

A sudden buzz startled them all, all but the Bartender who clanged the bell twice. They turned to observe a vortex forming in the air behind them, growing larger, more intense, until it disgorged two handsome men, one older. *Father and son?*

"Hail, hail Uchronia, land of the freed from …"

"Ah, there they are," said the Asian Woman with a fond smile. "The Tunnelers, lost in the swirling maze of past and future ages. They always manage to end up here."

She slid — or rather, slithered — from her seat and headed for the Older Man, who greeted her with a kiss as she wrapped a tentacle around his waist while the Younger Man headed to the barstool recently abandoned by the Very Tall Man and accepted a pint.

"So many?" said the Old Woman.

Her initial bewilderment at the comings and goings began to settle into acknowledgement of a comforting sort that she wasn't entirely alone, a stranger among strangers. She too was a Traveler, she recalled. Her wild youth designing, inventing, creating scientific improbabilities that clearly weren't so impossible as everyone first thought, as her current companions could testify.

A third wine always brought her to a level of acquiescence. Ada Lovelace and Michael Faraday had brought her here, with punch cards for miniaturization and binary operations, and discs and cages and excited flux for punching a way through the aether.

"Electro-magnetism," she said after a while.

The Redhead turned to her. "What's that, sweetie?"

She drew a quavering breath. "I built a machine that sent me through the aether using organic electro-magnetism. That's how I traveled." Her voice fell. "I'd forgotten."

She had forgotten much. Again she surveyed the room. How long had she been here, downing wine after wine with no inebriating headiness? How long since that pile of photographs? At the far end of the bar was an Ancient Man. Had he been young when she arrived?

"It's not just *occasion*, is it?" she asked the Redhead and Jack, who seemed to be the most comfortable within their circumstances. "It's all of it."

"Now you're getting it," Jack said.

She nodded. "We are what we are."

"Where we are."

"*Sumus ubi sumus*," offered the Professor from his booth.

As she watched, he and his students slid from the booth and vanished. The song rose up.

Jack chuckled. "Unless you don't watch *ubi* you're going."

The Redhead smiled. "Isn't that half the fun?"

"What we are, who we are, where we've been, and … " She swallowed carefully. "What we've done with it."

"I carried books forward to try to start again," said the Nameless Gentleman.

"A regular humanitarian," said the Ancient Man.

"Beats nine-pins with giants," said the Cryogenically-

Frozen Man beside him.

The Auburn Woman said, "You forgot the most important question: *Why* we've done what we've done. I went back to save my planet. I went forward for F'lar." A warm smile came to her face. "And for the rest of … *occasion*, it was always F'lar."

The Nameless Gentleman nodded. "Weena."

Tears burned the Old Woman's eyes. "I remember," she said with a tremulous sigh. "A love with a fire that would burn through the ages. My life, my heart."

The Bartender rang the bell. This *occasion*, the women joined the men in raising their glasses to sing the welcoming anthem.

Gentle hands settled on the Old Woman's shoulders. "My home," a beloved voice whispered in her ear. "Chérie."

He took her hand in his and drew her into his arms.

The Redhead murmured wistfully, "A timeless love."

As the can of noise blasted, they embraced, then vanished, freed from Time.

Composer, poet, author, editor, and video editor, Ef Deal has been publishing for over 30 years. Her novel *Esprit de Corpse*, a paranormal steampunk romp set in France 1843, is the first book in the Twins of Bellesfées collection, with book 2, *Aéros & Héroes*, due out in November 2024. She lives in Haddonfield, NJ, with her husband Jack and her chow chows Corbin and Rory. She can be found at efdeal.net.

Have We Met?
Neal Wiser

The radiant sun. Seething, roiling fury. Fiery prominences cast themselves into the void.

A shadow creeps over the star. A perfect black circle, it crawls across the surface. The circle moves silently, inexorably, as it's done for eons, and will continue for eons still.

The circle eclipses the sun.

MOMENT: 314

Charlotte, in her early twenties, wears all black. Her hair's pulled into a tight bun. Her eyes are tired. Older than her years, they've seen it all, over and over and over ...

She sits at a table in an empty coffee shop. Around her, tables, chairs, and half-eaten food are scattered about. It's as if everyone ran for their lives.

Actually, the shop's not quite empty. A terrified barista reads orders out loud from a monitor. Her voice quivers. "Coffee. B-black. Sh-shot of lemon."

And then there's Larry. Mid-twenties. Might actually be good looking if he'd hit the gym once in a while. Though not quite an incel, this moment could push him over the edge.

Larry sits across from Charlotte. He stares at her wide-eyed.

Charlotte doesn't take her eyes off him.

"I'm sorry, Larry. You really are a great guy. But as long as I'm with you, I'm stuck."

Larry shakes. He can barely keep it together.

"I— I don't understand. We only just met a few minutes ago."

Charlotte speaks with sympathy, "I know you feel that way, but you just don't remember."

"Is it because I have a science degree?"

Charlotte shushes him. "Don't say anything. This is hard enough."

Larry's desperate, "But ... *What did I do?*"

Charlotte looks at him with pity, but the gun in her hand never wavers. She keeps it pointed right between his eyes.

"Oh, Sweetie. If I've told you once, I've told you a million times. It's not you. It's me."

She pulls the trigger.

A BANG reverberates through infinity.

MOMENT: 1

On Charlotte's phone, a live video feed of the moon as it eclipses the sun. As the star dims, fiery prominences cast themselves into the void.

Charlotte watches the video while in line at the coffee shop. She dresses like a hippie. Her eyes are alert. Energized. She definitely woke up on the right side of the bed.

The barista faces her. Charlotte orders, "Mocha Frappuccino. No whip. Cinnamon powder blended in."

Charlotte glances outside. The sky grows dark and streetlights flicker to life. "Please hurry. I don't want to miss the eclipse. I've never seen one before."

The barista nods and Charlotte smiles. She steps over to the pickup line.

"Have we met?"

Charlotte turns to the man behind her. She gives him a quick glance up and down. He's kind of a dweeb. "I don't think so."

"Are you sure, because I feel like we've met."

Charlotte gives him a polite smile. The tone of her voice says it all, not interested. "I'd remember." She turns back to her phone.

The barista calls out an order, "Mocha Frap. No whip. Cinn powder, blended."

The dweeb says the order with the barista.

Charlotte rolls her eyes. "Cute," she mutters as she takes her drink.

Dweeb smiles. "Oh, I just knew what she was going to say."

Charlotte gives him a cynical smile. "Or, you heard me order and you're using that as a conversation starter."

Dweeb holds her gaze. "No, really. It's my superpower."

"Yeah?" Charlotte nods to the next customer in line. "What's that guy ordering?"

The Dweeb looks at the customer, "Black coffee with a shot of lemonade."

Charlotte cringes, "Ugh, that's gross—"

The barista calls out, "Coffee. Black. Shot of lemon."

Charlotte stares at The Dweeb.

"I know. It's crazy, right?" The Dweeb smiles. "I'm Larry."

Charlotte hesitates. Evaluates him again. Okay, he's a little charming.

They sit at a table in the middle of the café. Charlotte's animated and surprised that she's enjoying the conversation. Her drink's almost empty.

Larry speaks at the same time as the barista. "Venti caramel crunch frap. Banana. Extra caramel drizzle. Extra whip. Extra ice."

Charlotte laughs. "Okay, you *have* to know these people."

"Every one? I just did like ten of them."

Charlotte can't figure it out, but smiles. "You're weird."

Larry feigns being insulted. Charlotte laughs. "I mean, you're like this magician I saw once who knew the job of every person in the audience."

"I'm definitely not a magician. It's more like … déjà vu. Anyway, I don't believe in magic. I'm a scientist. You know, like for every action there is an equal and opposite reaction."

Charlotte nods. "Newton's Third Law."

Larry's eyebrows shoot up. Charlotte explains, "I was a physics major, then I switched to drama."

"That's quite a leap. Why'd you switch?"

Charlotte looks at Larry. "Because sometimes … I just want to believe there's still magic in the world. Science is so … calculated. It misses the beauty."

"What about the eclipse? Isn't that beautiful?"

"That's nature, not science," Charlotte says as she glances around the café. It's empty. Through the windows, she sees the employees and customers outside. They point to the dark sky in awe.

"I'm missing it." Charlotte jumps to her feet and knocks over her drink. In slow motion, it hits the floor. The contents splatter.

Charlotte rushes to the window and looks up. A deep rumble shakes the café.

Larry joins her at the window and puts on a pair of cheap cardboard and cellophane eclipse glasses.

The noise gets louder.

Larry looks around. "Is that thunder? But there aren't any clouds."

Charlotte squints. "Isn't the moon supposed to move over the sun from the side? Why's it in the middle?"

Larry takes off his glasses. "That's not the moon."

The sun broils. A black object fills the center. It makes the eclipse look like an eye. But the object isn't circular. It has wings.

It's an airliner.

The airliner's engines roar through infinity as it crashes into the café.

MOMENT: 8

On Charlotte's phone, the live video of the moon as it creeps across the sun. Solar flares leap into the void.

Charlotte's at the counter, tired and cranky. Her clothes are wrinkled. Definitely didn't wake on up the right side of the bed. She faces the barista, "Hurry up. I don't want to miss the eclipse."

"Have we met?"

Charlotte looks at Larry. She's disappointed. "Oh, you again."

"So, we *have* met."

Frustrated, Charlotte walks away. Larry follows. "Sorry, I'm not trying to hit on you and all that, but I feel like I know your name. I just … don't remember. Anyway, I'm Larry."

Charlotte stops. She surrenders to inevitability. Sighs.

"Well, since you're *not* trying to hit on me, *and all that …*"

They sit at a table. Charlotte sips her drink. Distracted by her phone, she doesn't look at Larry when he speaks.

"I'm a post-grad at the university. I work on the atomic accelerator there. It's an experiment that measures quantum fluctuations on …"

Larry trails off as Charlotte finishes his sentence, "… fluctuations on gravitational waves, right." She slurps her drink and goes back to her phone.

The barista calls out a drink order, "Grande, bone dry, five-shot ristretto cappuccino."

Again, Larry says the order with the barista but stops when he notices Charlotte mutter the order too. Her eyes never leave her phone.

"So, you excited about the eclipse?"

"I used to be."

"But didn't you ask the barista to hurry so you wouldn't miss it?"

"It's not the eclipse." She looks at Larry. "It's what comes after."

"And what's that?"

Charlotte takes a long slurp. Shrugs. "I dunno. Same shit, different day."

"Do you want to come outside and watch it with me?"

Charlotte looks at Larry but doesn't answer.

"Come on, it's a total eclipse. The next one won't hit for two hundred years. We won't be around for that."

"Says you."

Larry gets the message. Well, he gave it a shot. He stands.

"Where are you going?"

"I really want to see the eclipse, but I don't want to waste your time."

He turns.

"Wait."

Larry faces Charlotte.

She struggles to find the words. "It's not that I don't want to see it. I *can't* see it."

Larry pulls out his eclipse glasses. "It's easy, just look up."

"It's not that." She hesitates. "This is going to sound weird, but this is the eighth time I've done this, and I just can't get outside. As soon as I try, something stops me."

Curious, Larry sits.

Charlotte glances around, then leans toward him, whispers, "I might just be going crazy, but I'm working on a theory. I can't go outside, and neither can you."

"Why not?"

"Don't take this personally. You're a nice guy, but you're just an NPC."

"You mean a non-playable character? Like in a video game?"

"You know how some people say the world's a simulation? I think it's a game and I'm stuck playing over and over again. And I can't get past this level."

Larry humors her. "Sounds like you're stuck in a time loop."

"Yeah, a time loop. Why didn't I think of that?"

"You know, NPCs are kinda nothing characters. They're usually just there to provide information, or for you to kill. You planning on killing me?"

Larry smiles at his joke. Charlotte thinks while she slurps. "True, NPCs have limited behaviors and are usually there for a specific reason." She looks at Larry. "I think you're here to keep me from going outside."

Larry looks at Charlotte. He sees how tired she is. "I'm not stopping you. But let's test that. Come watch the eclipse with me. I think you need to see something beautiful."

Larry holds out a hand. She looks at it, then at him.

"The door is right there. All you have to do is walk through."

Charlotte looks into Larry's eyes. She wants to believe …

She reaches for his hand —

And knocks over what's left of her drink.

The drink falls silently, caught in gravity's embrace. It crashes to the floor and the remnants spill out.

A car horn wails. People scream. A light falls on Charlotte. She looks outside.

Customers and baristas dive out of the way as a car jumps the curb. Its headlights blaze at Charlotte and Larry as it crashes through the café window.

MOMENT: 464

"I hope I'm not interrupting, but have we met?"

Charlotte glances up at Larry. She's in a foul mood. She cracks open a mini-bottle of vodka and dumps it in her drink. She kicks a chair in his direction. "Sit. We need to talk."

Larry sits. "So, we have —"

Charlotte cuts him off. "Do you think God's a time traveler?"

Larry blinks at the sudden change of subject.

Charlotte continues. "Think about it. God's all powerful and all that, so if God made the universe, then God transcends time, right?"

Larry's confused but rolls with it. "If God created the universe, then he had to exist *before* the universe in order to be around to create it? So, if God existed before time, which is a weird oxymoron—"

"Or maybe God exists outside of time," Charlotte adds.

Larry considers it. "Either way, God being God, he could exist in the past, present, and future simultaneously, I think."

"Do you think God can loop time?"

Larry struggles to keep up. "If God is all powerful, then looping time should be within those powers. But, if God *transcends* time, if he's everywhere all at once ... I'm not sure why he would need to loop it."

Through the café windows, daylight dims. Frustrated, Charlotte drops her head into her hands – and knocks over her drink. It spills on the floor.

Charlotte stares at the spilt drink. "There goes Theory A."

Charlotte takes a breath, then looks at Larry. "Which leaves me with Theory B, but you're not going to like it."

Across the store, a delivery driver enters carrying a long, narrow box. Charlotte waves at him. "Delivery dude. Over here."

The delivery dude approaches the table. "I'm Charlotte. That's for me."

The delivery dude scans the box, hands it to Charlotte, then leaves. Charlotte sits, picks at the tape on the box.

Larry's amused. "I didn't know you could have packages delivered here. You must come here a lot."

"You have no idea."

The barista calls out another order. Larry mumbles it with her. "One pump classic. Nonfat. Six scoops matcha. No foam."

Charlotte frowns at Larry. He's embarrassed. "You were talking about your theories?"

Charlotte pulls a long strip of tape off the box. "You see, I'm stuck here. No matter how many times I come here, I can't leave. It's like that U2 song, *I'm Stuck in this Moment, with You, and I Can't Get Out.*"

Larry looks at Charlotte. "That's not quite what it's called—"

Charlotte pulls off another piece of tape. It sticks to her fingers. Annoyed, she struggles with it as she speaks. "I've been through this over and over. And the only commonality is you. Ergo, this is all your fault."

Now Larry's really confused. "What did *I* do?"

Charlotte picks at another piece of tape. "Damnit, how much tape do they have to use?" An edge comes up. Progress.

Charlotte continues. "I've been through this moment a million times. I've done this so many times I've lost track counting how many times I've lost track."

Larry does the math in his head. "But you just said a million—"

Charlotte rips off the last piece of tape. "All I know is you're keeping me from my destiny."

Larry's past confused. Now he's regretting sitting down. "I what?"

Charlotte pries the box open and reaches in. She scoops out handfuls of packing peanuts. They spill on the floor.

"At first, I didn't know what the fuck was going on. I thought I was losing my mind, and I did, for a long time. Then, I just went with it, you know? I figured if I'm going to repeat all twenty-two years of my life over and over, I should at least have some fun." Charlotte drifts off, lost in memories.

She snaps herself out of it and looks into the open end of the box. "But after a few hundred loops, you realize you're not having fun anymore. But you also realize how much you can accomplish in twenty-two years if you repeat those years over and over and over—"

Larry's not having fun anymore either. "What's this got to do with me?"

"I'm getting to that. So, in a time loop you learn a few things. Such as, there are no consequences for your actions because you just reset."

Larry's concerned. "I don't know what you're talking about."

Charlotte smiles. "No, you don't. Anyway, I started to wonder how I could change the ending. You know, break the loop. And while I haven't figured out how yet, I realized that somehow, you're the key."

"Me?"

"Yeah. I can't do this anymore. It's making me loopy, get it?"

Larry looks at the empty vodka bottle. "How much have you had to drink?"

"You mean today? Anyway, I'm going to spend every day of every twenty-two years figuring out how I'm going to get out of here, and you're going to help me."

Charlotte puts the box on the table and knocks over her drink. It crashes to the floor.

Charlotte ignores it.

"We've got to figure this out soon because Larry, if I look at your face one more time …" She laughs maniacally. "I'm just gonna die. Unless you die first."

Larry blinks. "Wait, what?"

Charlotte pulls a long, slender object from the box. It's a Samurai sword. She knocks over the table, stands, and draws the sword.

"Sorry, Larry. It's not me. It's definitely you."

Terrified, Larry jumps back as Charlotte raises the sword, "Wait. Wait—"

Charlotte swings the sword.

MOMENT: 7796

The eclipse begins.

Larry faces Charlotte. He smiles. "Have we met?"

Charlotte's dressed like a hippie; long blonde hair, bead necklace, hasn't shaved her armpits in a decade. She opens a massive box and pulls out a stuffed buffalo head. She looks at Larry who says an order with the barista, "Venti berry hibiscus refresher. Ten Equals—"

Something slams into Larry. He looks down at the buffalo head's horn that's impaled through his chest.

MOMENT: 11342

The moon's disk takes a bite out of the sun.

"You look familiar. Have we met?"

Larry and the barista say, "Venti green tea Frappuccino. One pump soy. Two scoops vanilla bean."

As Larry gazes outside at the dimming sky. Charlotte pours powder from a container into his drink. The container's label reads, "Rat Poison."

Charlotte hands Larry the drink. He smiles. *Bottom's up!*

MOMENT: 37342

The moon covers half of the sun.

"Excuse me, but have we met?"

Larry and the barista: "Grande Sumatran blend. Extra cinnamon dolce topping. Seven pumps caramel syrup."

Charlotte pulls a carbon dioxide tank out of a box.

Larry lies on the floor. A hose runs from the tank and is duct taped to his mouth.

MOMENT: 3.14 x 10⁹

The moon covers the entire sun. A ring of solar flares wraps around the star.

"Uh, have we met?"

Larry and the barista: "Grande chai tea. Four bags jade citrus mint. Two pumps peppermint. Steamed lemonade."

Charlotte faces Larry. Her pregnant belly leads the way. She wears a wedding gown and holds a pump shotgun. CLACK. She chambers a round and levels the rifle at Larry.

MOMENT AFTER MOMENT AFTER MOMENT

The moon's shadow slides over the radiant sun as it's done for eons. All that remains is a ring of fire. For a brief moment, *totality*.

LARRY'S MOMENT: REVENANT 314

An alarm clock *clicks*: 6:00AM. On the radio, a newscaster speaks, "Today's the big day. A total eclipse of the sun. Remember, don't look directly at it."

In bed, Larry opens his eyes, but he's not really awake.

Larry showers. Soaps here and there. Eyes empty. Unfocused.

He mumbles absentmindedly, "Venti caramel crunch frap. Banana. Extra whip …"

Larry drives on autopilot. The radio's on, but he's not listening. "…there won't be another total eclipse for two hundred years, so don't miss it …"

He mumbles, "Grande, five-shot ristretto, extra-whip cappuccino …"

Larry's in a meeting. Eyes vacant. Absentmindedly takes notes. On his computer's screen, *Grande black coffee. Three pumps hazelnut …*

Larry's back in his car. He hears on the radio, "Time to get to a good viewing area. The eclipse starts in a few minutes."

Larry mumbles, "One pump classic. Nonfat. Six scoops matcha …"

Larry stands in line in the café. Eyes vacant. A customer places her order. Larry says it with her, "Mocha Frappuccino. No whip. Cinnamon powder blended in."

Larry blinks. His eyes focus. In front of him is Charlotte. She wears all black. Her hair's pulled back into a bun.

Larry watches as she takes her drink and sits at a table. She takes a sip and looks right at him.

The barista hands Larry his drink and he heads for the door.

At the door, he glances back at Charlotte.

Their eyes lock.

Larry takes a breath, summons his courage, and walks to Charlotte.

Before he can speak, Charlotte says, "For a moment, I thought you were actually going to get out." She shoves a chair toward him. "Have a seat, Larry."

Confused, Larry sits. "Have we met?"

Charlotte smiles. "In a different life."

The barista announces another order. Larry says it with her, and so does Charlotte. "Trenti iced coffee, double-blended. Three pumps vanilla. Splash of soy."

Larry looks at her, amused. "How did you—"

"I've been coming to this same café for years. Same orders. Same people. Same you."

"So, we *have* met. Weird I don't remember you."

"And yet, it always ends the same. Well, not the same, same. But the end result is. A loop."

"A loop?"

"Yeah, and after all this time, after all the loops, something finally occurred to me. You *know* all those orders."

"Oh, that's just a déjà vu thing—"

"It's not. You *know* those orders, because you've heard them before, over and over and over again." Charlotte leans toward Larry. "It's memory. You remember them, because you're looping too. That's why you keep asking me if we've met."

Larry's confused. "I asked you just once, a minute ago."

"You've asked me a million times, because we've met a million times. But something's affecting your memory. To you, it's déjà vu because it's percolating in your subconscious. I think you're starting to remember, and I think I've figured out a way to bring it to the surface, for you to have total recall."

Larry sits back. This isn't going how he had hoped.

"A minute ago, you started to ask how I knew the orders. It's because I've heard them before, too. Because I'm stuck in a *time loop*."

Larry does a doubletake. "You're what?"

The delivery dude enters. Charlotte waves at him. He gives her a box and leaves. Charlotte peels the tape off.

Outside, the sky dims. Streetlights flicker on. Charlotte opens the box and looks in.

"Finally. You have no idea how hard it is to get one of these things delivered."

Larry stands. "I think I'm going to go watch the eclipse."

From the box, Charlotte pulls out a huge gun. She points it at Larry. "Sit."

Larry freezes.

A customer sees the gun and screams. "Gun! She's got a gun."

Customers and staff scream and run. They knock over tables and spill drinks.

Charlotte points the gun at the last barista behind the counter.

"You, stay. Do me a favor and read out those online orders as they come in."

The barista's petrified. Charlotte urges her on with the gun. She reads off a screen, "Trenti iced coffee, double-blend skinny mocha …"

Charlotte points the gun at Larry. He's terrified.

"For the longest time I thought you were just an NPC. But you're also a scientist working on quantum shit involving time."

"So?"

"So, you're the key. But you're useless if you can't remember, so somehow, I have to jog your memory. I've tried scaring you shitless. Humor. Sex … And I get nothing but *déjà vu*. Then it hit me."

Charlotte shows Larry her phone. On screen, the moon covers the sun.

"It's the eclipse. It ends at totality, when the moon fully covers the sun, but I can't get to it. For some reason, the universe is keeping me from it."

The barista reads another order.

Larry shakes, "What do you want from me?"

"Just sit, until totality."

The barista says another order.

"Then what?"

"Then I kill you."

Larry starts to panic. He hyperventilates.

"Shhh. Don't worry, it won't hurt. We'll reset, and the next time we meet, you'll remember, and we can get to work getting out of here."

"What am I supposed to remember?"

"Who you really are."

"But I'm just me."

"No. You're so much more."

The barista says yet another order.

Larry starts to cry. "But I didn't do anything."

Charlotte looks at him with pity. "Oh, Sweetie. If I've told you once, I've told you a million times. It's not you. It's me."

Again, the barista says another order.

Larry snaps at the barista. "*Shut the fuck up.*"

Then, without looking, Larry reaches back and grabs the gun. He twists and slams Charlotte's hand and gun to the table and pins them there.

Charlotte's drink topples over.

With his other hand, Larry catches it.

A ring of fire circles the moon. Totality.

Then, the moon continues in its orbit. It slides away from the sun and night turns back into day.

Daylight fills the café.

Charlotte notices the daylight. She looks at Larry.

Larry places Charlotte's drink back on the table. He stands tall and faces Charlotte. "Charlotte, my name is Lawrence, and I've come across endless loops to rescue you."

Charlotte smiles. A single tear slides down her cheek. "It's about time."

In this time period, Neal Wiser is a Filmmaker and Screenwriter who has won several screenwriting competitions and Fellowships. He teaches sometimes at Drexel University. Other times, he's worked at Paramount Pictures, Warner Bros., and Fox on several shows and consulted for organizations such as Comcast, MLB, and NASA on cool projects. NealWiser.com. @NealWiser on X.com (formerly Twitter) - https://x.com/NealWiser.

The Red-headed League
Brenda W. Clough

The Reverend Jack Wragsland was to preach his first sermon on Sunday, September 18, 1848. Therefore on Saturday he walked through the rain to inspect Willowgarth Church.

The building was a century old, shadowed by tall oaks, slumbering in the middle of a quiet country graveyard. Using the big brass key to unlock the front door filled Jack with quiet pride. His first sermon as a priest! Since his flock numbered barely a hundred souls, the cancel was modest. He went straight back past the ancient wooden pews to the little nook behind the lectern. This was simply furnished with a hook for his tall hat and dripping umbrella.

The low wooden door beside it led to a path at the back, which ran between the ancient gravestones to the coal store and the privy. The door should have been latched. But, strangely, today it stood ajar, letting in a crack of light. Jack frowned and pulled the door open.

What was revealed made him blink. No lichened monuments or rain-wet grass could be seen. Through the portal blazed a thoroughly un-English sunshine. A muggy tropical heat enfolded him like wet wool. Opening a door into another realm, this sort of thing only happened in dreams. He pinched himself, and when the graveyard did not reappear, he put his head through.

It was not Willowgarth village outside. Good God, were those vehicles? There were no horses, no drivers, no reins or traces. Did these glorious machines run on steam? Jack's great flaw was his distractibility. He forgot all else. Enthralled, devoured by curiosity, he stepped out, through his church's back door.

Immediately noise surrounded him, the thunder of wheels, the roar of engines, the blare of horns. Strange fumes made him sneeze. Someone yelled, "Wait for the light, you stupid fuck!"

Jack beamed up at the speaker, who perched above in a tall blue engine. "Is that an internal combustion propulsion you have there? Would you object very much to showing me how it works?"

The reply he got was another curse. Suddenly the carriages were rolling, all of them surging into motion, a herd thundering past in a haze of stench and grit down a roadway as wide as a river and edged with fringed trees. Palm trees! It came to him like a blow. He had more important questions to answer than how horseless carriages worked. He was very far from home. How had he got here? And the crucial question made him go cold in spite of the heat: could he get back?

He turned. Behind him was a high wall, the back of some vast building. There was no door, no windows, nothing but drab paint peeling from the underlying masonry. Certainly there was no portal back into Willowgarth village church. Shock made his limbs go numb, but his incorrigibly active brain continued to work.

This was somewhere on Earth, but certainly not England. Could it even be 1848? When the surging tide of vehicles halted again he leaned on a low one this time, and peered in the window. There was no one inside, neither driver nor passengers. Incomprehensible! He staggered to the next. Here was a driver, an older Asian woman. She glared at him through huge goggles. "Beg your pardon," he called. "But do you know the date?"

The window neither raised nor slid aside. It seemed to thin out at one edge. Through the stingy gap the woman snapped, "It's Thursday, ten forty-five in the morning."

The window began to thicken up again and he shouted, "The year. What is the year?"

The glass halted its progress long enough for her to say, "Holy shit, what cave did you crawl out of? It's the year 2051." And before he could ask more the vehicles roared into motion again, fast as racehorses out of the gate.

It was impossible to loiter here. Jack staggered onward, his boots skidding on the gravelly pavement. He was lost, with no way back. A thousand questions, no two even distantly alike, surged into his head. Who would preach his sermon on Sunday? Was there any hope of somewhere to sit down, perhaps get a cup of tea? He had to count on his fingers to be certain he had it right. Somehow he had stepped through almost two hundred years into the future. How had this happened, and why? Was this China? It was hot enough. Yet everyone spoke English, oddly accented but quite understandable. Some hellish future Britain? But this was no English sun, a blast furnace pouring a brutal heat down onto his bare head. He had no hat. His woolen frock coat and trousers were already damp with perspiration.

And then he looked up and saw it, the most exciting thing he had ever beheld. A vast metal spear rose slowly and majestically above the endless tangle of roadway and the fringed trees. The thing was enormous, as large as a steamship, glinting white and silver in the unrelenting sun. It balanced on a plume of fire that carried it with inexorable power up and up into the brassy sky. Perfect love casteth out fear, the apostle said. Jack forgot all his questions. He was no longer afraid. Instead he was running across the roadway, chasing the dream, calling out in incoherent joy at the fantastic sight. Were it not for the tropical heat this could be Olympus, Valhalla, some home of the gods!

By the mercy of Providence he was not struck by a vehicle and killed. He came to himself panting, drenched with sweat, far beyond the flow of indifferent traffic. He stood on a narrow street lined with sun-faded shops and buildings. Their doors were boarded over, the shop windows veiled inside with sheets of paper. There were no fringed trees and not a soul was in sight. The enthralling sky-spear was gone into the heavens beyond reach and he was here below, in Purgatory, or perhaps even Hell. Urgent issues beset from every side: thirst, the heat, this buzzing haze of questions. If he could just grasp what his true problem was he might have a hope of solving it.

The eye is always drawn to one's own name. Jack had to look twice before he could believe what he saw. He went closer. The placard was stuck to the inner side of a dingy shop window. In black letters on a white ground it proclaimed:

The Voice of

JESUS

Calls the Sinner to

REPENT!

East Miami Urban Mission

J. Wragsland, Pastor

His surname was not a common one. Without hesitation Jack pushed through the door. Within was a narrow cool corridor. A blast of delightfully icy air hit him in the face. Mechanically induced! Distracted yet once more, Jack identified the source, a rectangular machine set high up in a wall of the small front room to his right. Before rampaging curiosity could run away with him, a man rose from his seat behind a desk.

And Jack looked into a mirror. This man in summer-weight clericals was exactly his height. His own long face was here, the turn of the broad brow, the hollow cheeks and lean jaw, only its milky pallor tanned. He was perhaps thirty pounds heavier, porky around the middle. The curly red hair was frosted with gray, and there was some sort of metal brace or support strapped onto his right wrist and arm. This was no superficial similarity, but a true twinning. Here was he, himself.

He said it. "You are I. Jack. Jack Wragsland."

"You had better call me Pastor," the other Jack replied. He held out a long narrow hand, so exactly similar to Jack's that Jack almost expected a spark or explosion when he gripped it, the positive and the negative poles touching. But the other man's clasp was cool and dry, familiar and comforting in this strange place.

"Sit down, old man," Pastor Jack said. "I'd wager you could do with a drink."

"And knowledge." Jack eagerly took the proffered chair. "What is this place? What has happened to me? Who are you – are you truly I? Have you too been transported through time and space?"

The street door slammed. "Jesus H, another one. We could start a music hall troupe."

Jack looked up at the new arrival and sucked in a sharp breath. It was himself, a third Jack, younger than this older Pastor Jack but some years older than himself. "My God. How many of us are there?"

"No one knows," Pastor Jack said. "This is Mr. J, by the bye. He's been here for sixteen years. I've been here for twenty."

"And I arrived today."

Mr. J flung himself carelessly into a chair and put his strangely-shod feet up on another. From a paper sack he produced a metal cylinder. "Then you're going to need something stronger than lemonade."

"This is a teetotal mission, Mr. J," Pastor Jack protested.

In vain -- Mr. J. did something to the top of the cylinder, revealing it to be a container. He passed it over. The mysterious word 'Michelob' was emblazoned on the side, but it held perfectly ordinary beer. Jack was so thirsty he swallowed half the container in a few gulps. "And did you come as I did? From a portal at the back of Willowgarth Church?"

Pastor Jack beamed with mild pride. "So you achieved your degree and were ordained a clergyman? I congratulate you. I was just starting my second term at Cambridge, when I espied a portal between two trees near the boathouse."

Mr. J fished out another beer for himself. "I was a schoolboy on the train to Harrow and found the portal in my compartment."

Jack sucked down the last of his beer. "How is this possible, then? If you fell through at the age of fourteen, and the Pastor here at eighteen, how is it that I was available to come through at the age of twenty-three?"

"We're the same man," Mr. J said. "Born in Willowgarth, am I right?"

"Yes. An older brother Thomas, my sister Fan."

"I also," Pastor Jack said.

"Is this how you started this ministry, Pastor, to succor your other selves?"

"The Red-headed League is what we call it." The pastor chuckled. "You'll find it's a curious comfort, here in this strange far future, to read stories from our own era. No, this is a genuine mission outpost, a ministry to help the least and the lost of the greater East Miami metropolis. Rescuing duplicates of myself plucked out of their own period is an overlapping and slightly different project. I should have thought to put my own surname on the signboard years ago."

Mr. J grinned like the villain in a panto. Jack had not quite realized how all his teeth were visible when he smiled. "Now you've had a brew, mebbe you want to come see the social room."

Jack set down his empty container and followed. The narrow corridor led into a considerable chamber at the back. The low ceiling made it astonishingly noisy. On a table in the corner was food, sandwiches and fruit. Hymns blared out on one side from some invisible organ, and on the other chairs were arranged around a large flat window. Behind this glass pane colorful puppets were enacting some sort of melodrama. When Jack went close he could see the flat caricatures speaking aloud like real actors. "Curse you, Superman!" one squealed. "You'll never trap me in the Phantom Zone again!"

Fascinated, Jack pressed his hand on the glass. "Hey, chico," a man behind him complained. "Get outa the way."

Another poked him hard in the back, yelling, "Siddown. Siddown!"

Annoyed, Jack turned and gaped at yet another version of himself. But this one was reflected in a distorting mirror: degraded, dressed in rags, with black crescents of grime under the broken fingernails. The blue eyes were fixed and blank. "Oh God." Jack retreated. "How many of us do you find?"

Pastor said, "Since I began this ministry, about one a month."

"And that's just the ones we come across, or who wander in here," Mr. J added.

"One a …" Jack gulped. A dozen forcible transplants a year, for these many years. "You have enough for a squadron of identical men."

"There's attrition," Mr. J said. "Most of them come to grief."

"I was struck by a vehicle the hour that I arrived," the pastor confirmed, lifting the arm in its brace.

Jack surveyed the audience watching Superman. Four or five Jacks were here, in varying states of disintegration. All of them were visibly *non compos mentis*, drunk, lunatic, or drugged. "This is nightmarish. How can it be?"

For once his besetting distractibility stood him in good stead. Jack's mind seemed to make a sideways skip to a clue. "Fanny – my, or our, sister – she's been researching time. We've been debating how time works. Is it a river, as Heraclitus suggested? Maybe this hellish situation shows he was wrong."

"We're the same Jack Wragsland," Mr. J pointed out.

"But," Jack said, "if time is a tree, we may be from different branches. That would explain why we're slightly different versions of each other."

The other two stared at him. "Goddam," Mr. J breathed. "He's right. We're from different streams of time."

Pastor Jack clapped him on the back. "Brilliant, sir. And you're the eldest. Not in years lived, but you're the one who was furthest along in Willowgarth. You completed your degree."

"You began working with Fan," Mr. J added. "She had a brain better than mine."

"Time travel," Jack mused. "Between the versions. That would explain it. A portal from these various Victorian Englands, in 1840, 1842, 1837, to this single Miami in 2051."

"But to what purpose?" Pastor demanded. "Is this a natural phenomenon, like being sucked into a whirlpool?"

"Like fun it is." Mr. J's bright blue eyes blazed. "Of all the people in all of these Englands, just us? No, it's got to be deliberate. Someone is choosing us. For torture and damnation."

"Or salvation," Jack put in. He had been ordained only this past summer. "Perhaps we're supposed to derive some lesson, some benefit, from this. Improve our souls."

The pastor pointed at one of the junkie Jacks dully watching Superman. "Before he began doing needle drugs, he told me that he stepped through when he was seven. What crime could a seven-year-old lad commit to merit this?"

"It's in Dante," Jack said. "We are born in sin. Even children must atone. The only sinless ones die right after their baptism."

"You got that bit right," Mr. J. agreed. "Yeah, we have to work our way out. But fuck that churchy stuff. Don't you see? This is war. Some bastard has done this to us. An enemy's imprisoning us here. All of us." He glared at Jack. "You're the oldest. You must have made a mortal enemy. Who hated you, hates us, that much?"

"I'm a clergyman," Jack protested. "A follower of Christ. I hate nobody, and no one hates me."

"You namby-pamby!"

But at that moment the hymns, which had been blaring in the background, concluded with a chime of bells. "Ah, lunch time."

The pastor raised his voice to address the entire room. "Come, gentlemen. Let us gather around the meal that our Great Shepherd has provided for His lambs."

Superman and the Phantom Zone vanished from the pane of glass, leaving it black and blank. The congregation raggedly joined in to mutter some formulaic grace.

When the meal began the images returned, but they were different. The flat colorful fictions were replaced by thrilling images of the fiery sky spear. Jack sank into an empty chair and watched intently. It was a simple presentation, probably addressed to children, and he happily absorbed it: sky boats that carried people to the Moon, to Mars! The one he had seen had taken off from a port quite near this Miami city, on the coast of Florida. In the 1960s the Americans had partnered with some new nation, a USSR, to achieve domes and buildings, human settlements on the other planets!

Mr. J sat down beside him. "That's where the action is, pal."

"This?"

Mr. J passed him half a sandwich and nodded at the flat display panel. "Down here, it's losers and servants. Peasants and the lower orders, like back in England. In this future, in 2051, everyone who has any get-up and go has got up and gone. Into space. Strugatsky Base. The Mars Clarke Dome. Verne City, on the Moon. That's where everything is nowadays."

"Heaven." Jack spoke the obvious and undebatable fact: "I have to get there."

"Exactly what I said. Yeah, we're the same man." Mr. J grinned that predatory grimace. "The padre and me, we've been chewing on what this is about for years. And you step in and figure it out. I knew you were a right one. Not one of these rummies and Bedlamites. This future, it's ground them down and spat them out. But it won't grind up you 'n' me."

Jack bit into his sandwich without tasting it. "How do we do it? Buy a ticket, like getting on a train?"

"Nothing like. We need ID. An identity."

"A what?"

"They don't let just any bloke up into space," Mr. J said impatiently. "You have to be healthy – that's why the pastor'll never go, with that busted wing. You and I, we have the health but not the qualifications. The degrees in engineering, the astrogator certifications, the tech training. We don't have 'em and can never get 'em. Even people born in this era, only one in a thousand can do it. It's impossible."

"All things are possible with God," Jack said shrewdly. "You have a plan."

"I sure do. C'mon."

The repast was more or less over, and the congregants were dispersing. Some waited their turn for the bath, a few wandered out, and others settled to doze in front of the image panel again. Mr. J neatly scooped up one of these dozers before he quite nodded off. "Hey, Diego. Wanna beer?"

This Diego was not of the Red-headed League. He had a sheaf of straight black hair tied in back with a piece of string, and a brown weathered face. He seemed unable to speak. Jack followed as Mr. J jockeyed him around into the quiet front room. "Shut the door."

Jack obeyed. Mr. J lowered the other man into a chair by the desk and produced another cylinder from his paper bag. Diego sat up, recognizing it. In moments he had popped it open and drunk it down. Mr. J passed him a second, and then a third.

"I say," Jack protested. "Ought he to drink them so rapidly? The beer here is alcoholic, is it not?"

"It sure is. You know how IDs work, here in the 21st century?"

"Not like they did in Victoria's day," Jack surmised. "No papers or passports."

"No shit. This is how they do it." The other man now was limp, his black eyes closed. He made no protest as Mr. J picked up his limp left hand and pushed the tattered shirt cuff back. Mr. J pointed at the brown skin of the forearm. "Here, under the skin. Can you feel it?"

Jack probed the slack skin gingerly with his fingertips. "A pellet. From a shotgun?"

"It's a pellet all right. But not lead. It's data. The chip has his entire life on it. Name, medical records, certifications, degrees, the whole ball of wax. Look." He turned the limp arm and pressed the place to a glass panel set in a desk console. A small window bloomed into light beside it.

Jack forced himself not to become distracted by questions about how it worked. Instead he blinked at the words that scrolled by on the glass. "Diego José Rafael Suarez," he read. "Born in 1999. Graduate of Rochester Polytech in 2021 with a degree in mechanical engineering …"

"I've been keeping an eye on all the intake here at the Mission," Mr. J said. "I knew sooner or later that we'd net a techie. A guy who could be led to Jesus by Pastor Jack and turn over a new leaf so as to be eligible for the space colonies again. Only it'll be me, with his chip in my arm."

"You can do that?"

"I can cut the thing out, nothing to it. The chips are tiny, only skin deep. But to insert it into my own left arm can't be done with only my right hand. And no use asking the pastor. I was going to get one of the junkie Jacks to do it. But you'd be better. I have a blade right here." He reached into a pocket and produced a scalpel-like instrument. The short, pointed blade was set into a silvery handle and protected by a clear sleeve.

Jack goggled in horror. "J, is this not rather rackety in conception? You'll present yourself at the door of a spaceship, claiming you're Diego Suarez, mechanical engineer. What do engineers do, do you even know? And what happens to the real Diego, here?"

"Nobody'll miss him." Mr. J's grin was terrifying. "He's not supposed to have alcohol."

"Well, of course not, if this is a Mission --" But at that moment Diego began to wheeze. He sounded like a concertina, fighting a shrill battle for air. Jack quickly dragged him out of the chair and laid him flat on the floor to see if that would help him breathe. "What's wrong with him?"

"Chemically-induced allergy to alcohol," Mr. J said. "They do it to drunkards in this era. One beer makes him sick. Three should kill him."

"What? J, that's murder!"

"Someone is murdering us, pal," Mr. J said, unmoved. "Tossing us here on a Florida trash heap to die. It's a dog-eat-dog world here in 2051. And I'm not going to be eaten." He slid the protective sleeve off the scalpel and squatted down beside the supine man. When he began to cut into the forearm Diego writhed, wheezing dreadfully.

And then his breath stopped. The brown face went the color of lead. He shuddered and went still. Jack cried, "J, you mustn't do this. Stop!"

Mr. J ignored him, digging with bloody fingers into the flesh of Diego's forearm. "Aha, here we are. It's subcutaneous, do you see it? Just under the skin, keep that in mind. You can't go too deep. Here, take this. We can sit at the desk. You damn well better not nick any tendons or major vessels." He dropped the gory knife into Jack's left hand.

"I'll have no part of it," Jack shouted.

"You dumb fuck. I am you. You're me. We are going to do this." With bored efficiency Mr. J backhanded Jack across the face. Something in him seemed to snap. Jack returned the blow in full measure. Suddenly they were battering each other like pugilists. Mr. J locked his arm under Jack's and pounded his head from close range. Gasping, Jack pummeled back.

He had forgotten he was holding the knife. Suddenly the little blade sank in, way in. Mr. J bellowed at the top of his lungs, "You fucker! Oh Jesus, my eye!"

Mr. J slumped against the wall. The gleaming metal handle protruded from his eye socket. Jack spat blood from a cut lip. No thought of restraint, no impulse to mercy crossed his mind. A huge fury shook him. The seeping bastard! With deliberate venom Jack gripped the bloody metal and pushed hard. The needle-sharp point grated on bone as it went in. And then Mr. J gave at the knees. His head thumped on the floor. Blood slowly pooled under it.

His pulse slowed, and a scarlet fog seemed to clear from Jack's vision. "Oh my God. Oh my God, I've killed him. Me." Was it suicide? Or murder?

When Pastor Jack spoke from the doorway Jack startled like a Victorian maiden. "You damned young idiot," he said. "What have you done?"

Jack's tongue did not seem to be working properly. "He was, he said he was … I didn't mean to stab him but once it went in … Murdering another, stealing his identity, in hopes of some chimerical self-gain … Oh God, but I'm no better."

"You certainly are not." Pastor Jack pushed the body over. The silvery knife handle was plain to see, sticking out of the dead man's left eye. "Dash it, two of them to dispose of. But Mr. J had the right pig by the ear, lad. It's on you now. You must take on the identity of Diego Suarez. We know it's something to do with time travel. Get up there and get your hands on this future knowledge. Find out who did this to us, and why. You've shown yourself to be smart enough and hard enough." He picked a gory gobbet up from the floor – the identity chip.

Jack's stomach turned over with a queasy flop. "It was you. The one who runs the mission and keeps track of the congregation. You picked this poor fellow out for Mr. J to kill."

"This is important, Jack," the pastor said, with fatherly patience. "Someone is attacking us, each and every Jack Wragsland across the branches of creation. That's more important than a single life, even two."

"Or three, or four."

Pastor Jack prodded Diego's lifeless form with a toe. "They're not us, Jack. He wasn't in the Red-headed League."

Slowly Jack reasoned it out. The terrifying truths fell into his hands one by one, like black leaden fruits dropping from a contorted tree in Dante. "I killed Mr. J. I deliberately stabbed him in the eye with a knife. I, we – we're all the same. This isn't Purgatory, where you can work your way out. This is Hell. You, me, him – we're equally violent, equal in amorality. We were transported here like lepers, to be quarantined. In some mysterious futuristic prison."

"Mr. J never would have it," the pastor replied. "But you see it as I do. Yes. This whole world, as you postulated, this whole branch of time – it's a prison. You're like me, like him, an amoral killer. And you're the one who's going to break us out. Get out, get up. Track down who's killing us. And serve them with a double helping of their own sauce."

"Kill them."

"Exactly. Now sit down, old chap. It won't be easy to insert this ID chip into your arm, but between us we have two hands." He pushed another chair forward.

Jack stood, staring down at the other man. That unknown omnipotent enemy knew him – knew all the Jacks, across many timelines. Knew him well enough to easily trap him. A new and inexplicable thing was like catnip, irresistible. And each and every Jack had instantly risen to the bait. And if someone knew him that well, it must be someone he knew in turn. Who?

Could Pastor Jack be right? He could do it. If he could just take apart the cooling machine, the flat window of images, the rushing vehicles, he could understand them. He had the ability, the power. He could encompass it all, even that giant sky spear, or the colony on Mars. He could, yes, invent – or reinvent – a time machine. He could – but should he? He had been searching for the question that he had to answer, and here it was. Like every vital question in this life, it was a moral one. For an excruciating moment Jack balanced on it, the pinpoint of the dilemma. Which way should he go?

The pastor clicked his tongue in annoyance. "Of course, you'll need the scalpel." He bent and with his good hand casually plucked the knife by the handle out of Mr. J's gory eye socket.

And suddenly Jack's decision was made. Without another word he turned and walked out, out the door and into the hot glaring streets of East Miami. The host of buzzing questions hovered almost visibly around his head, but he pushed past them. He might never find the answers. He might wind up a derelict, dirty, drunk, perhaps demented, here in Hell. But at least he wouldn't deserve it. He would not deserve his damnation. He was not a member of the Red-headed League.

Brenda W. Clough is the first female Asian-American SF writer, first appearing in print in 1984. Her latest work is "Clio's Scroll," which appeared in *Clarkesworld* in July 2023. A historical novel, *A Door In His Head*, won the 2023 Diverse Voices Award. Her novella *May Be Some Time* was a finalist for both the Hugo and the Nebula awards. Her complete bibliography is at brendaclough.net.

The Biography
Daniel Lumpkin

If you had walked into Vincent Malone's apartment right after he opened the package wrapped with simple brown paper, you would have stumbled upon the moment he determined the gift was a prank. Freed from the wrapping, the text, hardback, laid on his table like some specimen in need of dissection. *A Triumph! The Biography of Vincent Malone.* The title was what made him certain. The portrait behind the words on the front cover, while impressively done, was clearly him, though due to some photo editing, the older, stern-looking man staring at him had seemed quite authentic but not recognizable as *him* at first.

A smile stretched across Vincent's face as he slowly took in every detail of the book. He was looking for the joke itself. This prop, this farcical tome, was merely the setup. He flipped the book over, and while his smile only grew, it did so because the setup was getting more absurd. The text on the back only sang his praises.

Esteemed biographer Hershel B. Yates spent close to two decades working on his subject, the world-renowned Vincent Malone. Spanning family history and each major period of Malone's life, the Gold Seal Biography of the Year-winning volume explores the significant milestones and personal tragedies throughout Malone's life and career.

It was all so strange. Vincent couldn't help but flip the large book and run his hands over the embossed letters on the jacket before opening it. He looked up at the clock. More than an hour before he needed to leave for work. Vincent brought the book over to the small worn couch in his—their—apartment. It was in both their names. He supported her as she went to school. That was the first stage of their ten-year plan. Vincent would work while Claire studied nursing. She would finish her degree in two-and-a-half years. In that time span, Vincent would figure out what he wanted to pursue. They'd get married, Claire would start her career as a nurse, and Vincent would study X—meaning he had zero idea what he wanted to pursue as a student because he had zero idea of who he wanted to be. This was partially why they agreed Claire should go to school first. Also, her being a nurse would allow Vincent the freedom to go to whichever school or program he wanted.

That's how Claire phrased it. Vincent thought it would be more accurate to describe the schools as whichever one was foolish enough to accept him. Vincent didn't do well in school. It wasn't his work ethic; it was his interest. That's just not where he excelled.

If you needed to see proof of Vincent's work ethic, it could be found on his punch card at the Pit Stop Diner off 24. Generally, Vincent pulled a couple of doubles a week, on top of the normal five days. Recently though, he was clocking in more and more shifts. Their anniversary was coming up. Vincent wanted to do something nice for Claire. No idea what. But nice things required money, so he took more shifts and told himself the *great idea* would come to him as he scrambled his millionth egg or buttered his billionth piece of toast. You could see his work ethic on the small burns on his fingers, hands, and forearms, burns that used to hurt but were merely forgotten as soon as they happened. You could smell his work ethic, too. The onion. The grease. The burned coffee even made its way into his hair and pores. This was the day-in, day-out stuff that nobody ever talked about, but hard work did a number on a man. Even if the hard work's pay was dirt, Vincent still walked home proud of his efforts.

He wasn't a man who read much, but the temptation was great. He flipped open the cover of his biography, seeing the title page again and then a few more thin pages before reaching the table of contents: Introduction; The Malone Family; Childhood; Early Years; New York Years; California; Toronto; Washington, D.C.; The War; Peace and Recovery; Reemergence in Public Life; Death and Descendants; Additional Photos; Notes; References.

A laugh escaped him. "The War? The New York Years?" Nothing made sense. The apartment he had with Claire in Montgomery, that was their price range.

The book was too good, in a way, to be real. Too much detail. Too rich, as his uncle would say. Each early page was too rich to stand. He wanted to read it all at once, immediately, but perhaps that's when the seed of doubt really began to grow. Perhaps he pushed the doubts away through his laughter, through his disbelief, but the details made him really begin to question the reason someone would go to such great lengths for an odd joke. Where was the payoff? No one saw him open the book or watched him peruse the pages. He flipped back to the title page, and the publisher page. The copyright was more than 100 years in the future. The title itself was registered with the Library of Congress. Again, far too rich for it to be worthwhile as a joke.

The book then began to seem cruel. Whoever did this, did they see his life now as a joke, too? That somehow a diner chef would go on to become someone deserving of an award-winning biography? What was the joke? That he would ever amount to a great life?

Spurred by this notion, Vincent did something very dangerous that, while hardly anyone ever gets a chance to do it, no one ever should. He discovered the book he now read was no joke or prank. It was real, all too real and it would dawn on him only a mere twelve pages into the first section, the one about his family, when he would uncover something that he took as rude, as mean, but not true. The first dozen pages were accurate, surprisingly accurate. They had names and even letters and descriptions down. Then he stumbled upon something that made him angry and made him want to throw the entire thing out the window.

"Hello, Vincent," his grandmother said when she answered his phone call. "I'm surprised you aren't working today."

"I clock-in in about a half-hour," he said to the woman who raised him, looking at the clock on his microwave. "Listen, I've got a weird question for you."

She could hear that always-playful tone in his voice, but there was something behind it. Something more serious. Something distrusting. Not of her, but she didn't know.

"What is it?"

He didn't know how to phrase what he was going to ask in a way that—well, he just didn't know how to do it. Nobody really does. So he just asked.

"I've got this book here that says Granddad wasn't actually my dad's biological father," he said. "That can't possibly be true, can it?"

It was her silence, her struggle to deny, her guilt, even. That's what made him realize this book was no mere prank.

"Who told you?" Just three words, no *that*, and said with such pain he regretted ever opening the book in the first place. He hurt her with the question, one he thought they would laugh about, but instead a question that made him only wonder more about the book on his lap. Vincent did his best to explain. It was the book. The book knew the truth, however, one that his grandmother, choking back tears, could barely explain.

"It was a long time ago, and Charles was your dad's only father," she said. "Even if he wasn't … if he wasn't his actual father!"

As his grandmother continued, explaining without saying very much at all, Claire walked in from school. She had a bag of groceries and smiled when she saw him, happy to get home early enough to catch him before he left.

"I'm sorry, you're right, it doesn't matter," Vincent said. "I will call you tomorrow morning, when I'm off work. I've got to go in and do an all-nighter, okay? I love you. I'm really sorry."

His grandmother relented, but she was now curious about *that* book.

"What's this?" Claire asked, seeing the book upside down on the couch as she walked over to kiss him.

"I found it after I woke up from my nap," he said, dashing to grab it. She looked curiously at him, then at the book he held, and then back to him.

"Where did you find it?" she asked, thinking he was playing a joke on her.

"On the table," he said. "I thought it was from you. It's not, right?"

"I didn't buy you a book, Vincent. We can barely afford the ones I need this semester. Can I see it?"

"I'm not sure you should."

"Why? What's the book about?" She grinned a mischievous grin, like she wanted to go along with whatever game she thought he was playing.

"Me," he said plainly. Her grin grew with his next words. "It's a biography."

"The cover looks like an old man," she said with a sharp laugh. She could always tell when he was joking.

"Look," he said, holding the book up so she could see the dust jacket.

"Oh, wow," she said, eventually seeing that it was a high-quality portrait of him but aged considerably. "How much did that cost?"

"I promise I didn't buy it," he said. "I swear."

"It's a joke," she said.

"I thought so," he said. "But it's a mean one. I don't know why someone would do this to me."

"What do you mean?"

Vincent told her about the first twelve pages, the fact that the man he knew as his grandfather wasn't his dad's biological dad. He then looked at the clock. He needed to leave for work.

"I want to read it," she said.

"I don't think that's a good idea."

"You read it," she said.

"Up until I realized that it's …" but he trailed off.

"You don't think it's real, do you?"

"I don't …I don't know." He hesitated at first to admit his ignorance, and then felt a little foolish to admit that it possibly could be real. "It's real in the sense that it knew a family secret. I'm not really sure what to think. My head's spinning. I've got to go to work, though."

"Okay," she said. He kissed her, but she didn't purse her lips. The dead kiss was a signal that the conversation wasn't over. Vincent walked over to the brown paper shell still on the table and did his best to re-sheath the large book.

"I was thinking I could take it to that bookshop near work," he said. "They could determine if it was real or not. I love you."

She didn't say anything. He headed out the door with the book in his backpack.

The shift itself was uneventful besides the stress of the dinner rush. Burgers, hash, eggs. Burgers, hash, eggs. Bacon, bacon. Double fries. Can you try that patty melt again, and melt it this time? Where's my pickle? Vincent worked distracted. A line cook needed to keep his eyes on about twelve things at once and then on the clock, too. He had perfected this into a habit, a craft, even, but tonight he worked absorbed in fear. What if someone grabbed his bag? What if he opened his bag and the book was gone? How did the book find its way into his apartment in the first place? Now, he was burning the toast.

"You need to get it together, Vinnie," Kathleen said. "That's the third slice tonight you had to toss."

"Sorry," he said.

"You feeling okay?"

"Yeah," he said. "Just need more coffee."

He pounded the coffee. She made it strong for the truckers that barreled in. The diner was never empty for very long. A place that was always open drew in the weird and wild, the folks on the fringes of society, like moths to a flame, plus, everybody liked a good cheeseburger. From prince to pauper, a good cheeseburger seemed to solve most of the world's problems.

The diner sat on the outskirts of town, where truckers who used the bypass could stop for a bite and some coffee before getting back on the road, but also where the folks from the city, usually college kids, could come in during the latter parts of the evening. Vincent liked the lone college kids who entrenched themselves in booths and barricaded themselves with mounds of books and their laptops. They usually only ordered coffee. He sometimes made toast with jam on the house, dropping it at their tables without saying much. A man would lose his mind on coffee alone.

While the double patties Vincent was eating didn't solve the problem, or problems, he had with the book in his bag, they made him feel better about the idea that he would eventually figure it out. By the end of his shift, as the sun was rising and the next chef came in to take over, Vincent felt almost certain that it would somehow settle, that his entire life would fall back into being completely normal, boring even. He looked across the street. Most of the shops were still closed. Next to them, Hal's Books also had its lights off, but there was someone at the front door of the shop now, reaching for keys in a pocket to unlock the door.

"Hal! Hal!" Vincent called. Hal turned to see who was shouting his name, then waved. Vincent darted across the empty street.

"Could you take a look at a book for me?" he asked.

"When I'm open," Hal said.

"Come on," Vincent said. "I've gotta get home."

"I've got to feed my cats and do inventory," Hal said.

"I'll give you a free meal at the diner across the street. I'm a—"

"I know you work there," he said, nodding to the diner. "You make a better steak for my steak and eggs than the other two guys."

"What do you say then? A great steak and eggs on me next time I'm working."

"I said a *better* steak and eggs. Not a great one." Hal looked at Vincent over his glasses. Vincent didn't blink. The old man rolled his eyes. "Fine. Come in, but just give me a minute to set some stuff down."

Vincent followed him and, as they entered and Vincent locked the door behind them on Hal's instructions, the meowing started. There were at least two cats in the cramped little store. One of the cats, a fluffy, overweight orange cat with a collar, rubbed up against Vincent's leg.

"Milton," Hal said with a couple of snaps. "Come and get yummy."

The cat ditched Vincent's leg, following Hal through the stacks of hardbacks and paperbacks and past an Employees Only door. Vincent looked around. He got one of Claire's books here. It was used, but still over one hundred dollars. Once Milton's meowing died down, Vincent figured the cat was eating. Hal returned to the front of the shop and carefully moved around the register. It was one of those rare, glorious bookshops where the owner was a hoarder of books in all conditions and nearly every category you could think of. Finding a specific book, well, that was a quest.

"All right, where's your book?" Hal asked, sitting on a stool behind a display case of expensive volumes. Some signed. Some first editions. Vincent reached into his bag and pulled out the book, still haphazardly wrapped in the paper shell.

"A gift?"

"Something like that," Vincent said.

"I'm not buying it if it's stolen."

"It's not stolen. Somebody gave it to me. I'm just not sure who."

"How do you know it was for you?" Hal asked. Vincent's eyes fell on the portrait, on his own eyes, before responding.

"Trust me," he said, sliding the book and wrapping forward for Hal's expert evaluation.

"What would you like me to do with this?"

"Is it ...legitimate?" Vincent asked, not really knowing what the correct word was. He didn't want to explain the book. Mainly because he would sound like a crazy person, but he also just wanted a neutral opinion on what it was, and to know if maybe the bookstore owner had seen something similar before.

Hal nodded slowly and looked at the book through thick glasses that magnified his eyes slightly. He quickly snapped his fingers and smiled.

"That is a legitimate book," he said. "You want to know if it's a forgery of some kind?"

"Is there such a thing?" Vincent asked. Hal nodded.

"It's rare, usually nothing like this, however. Most forgeries attempt to look like first drafts from famous authors, rather than post-publication. I'll check."

Hal looked at the spine.

"See that? Penguin is a big name in publishing. The logo is a little different, so that's odd, but it's the name that counts. Book looks brand new. Should be easy to search."

Hal searched on his computer, first the title and then the title with the author's name, but nothing came up. He flipped to the copyright page and found the ISBN. Vincent saw his curiosity and frustration mount when the ISBN didn't pull up anything either.

"Strange," Hal mumbled as Milton hopped up on the counter. The bookstore owner rubbed behind his orange cat's ears without looking. "Down, Milton."

The cat meowed once in protest before hopping down and again rubbing against Vincent's leg. Vincent watched Hal pull out a magnifying glass wedged between his computer monitor and the wall. He held it up to the copyright page and then flipped through the pages, skimming text and even the white-space margins.

"Who gave this to you?" Hal asked, without looking up.

"I don't know," Vincent said. "It was left for me, wrapped, at my home."

"Curious upon curious …I'm going to do something to your book on a hunch, if you don't mind."

"What?"

"Just observe with me," the man said. He dipped his finger in a glass of water sitting on the desk. He moved his hand quickly and cupped it underneath to catch stray drops. Then he let the droplets fall on the book's title page. Instead of landing and being absorbed by the fibrous page, the droplets sat on top of the page intact.

"That's not normal," Vincent said.

"No, it is not," Hal said. "There are waterproof books, but not like this. I had a waterproof Bible during training in the Army up until we did full gear drills in the pool. Those pages worked like sponges. Became twenty pounds of dead weight. Nearly drowned myself in a pool exercise. This is different. Actually, the pages aren't even paper. Something that looks exactly like paper and performs like paper while turning a page but isn't. In fact, I would even wager …Do you have a light?"

Vincent pulled a lighter from his pocket. Anyone who worked at a diner learned they got better tips if they were able to help their patrons smoke—albeit outside, but still. The bookshop owner held the lighter to the book's pages but hesitated before sparking the ignition.

"I never thought I would do anything like this," Hal confessed, but then he pulled at the striker wheel and produced a flame. He held the flame to the pages, which should have curled away and blackened instantly, but they remained white. The pages had remained unaltered by the flame or the water.

"That's generally a cardinal sin for people in my profession," he said. "I'm impressed. You've got me. Are you recording me?"

"What? No," Vincent said.

"Let me see your phone."

Vincent pulled his phone out of his back pocket and showed the man that he wasn't secretly recording him.

"Damn." Hal smiled as though it was good news. "I thought I had you. I thought I had you at the copyright date, quite honestly, but I played along. But this is, well, this is something else. You didn't buy this?"

"No," Vincent said. "It was left at my house, like I said."

"Right," Hal closed the book. "I don't think you could afford it. That's not an insult. The publication quality is very high. This isn't some small-scale publishing house. Whoever put this book together used cutting-edge equipment and technology. The pages, the binding, everything. It's an exquisite book. Except it isn't. Biographies shouldn't be lies, yet this one has to be. The image on the cover kind of gives it away. At first, I thought it was just a passing resemblance, but then I thought, you know, it could be a relative, but that's not it. This is you."

He tapped on the portrait.

"I believe so," Vincent said. "Or it's supposed to be."

"Well, therein lies our predicament. We have a choice to make. Three options, really. Option one is that we're both crazy. I'm a bookshop owner that just tried to light your book on fire, so things aren't looking great, but I don't think that's the case here. The second option is we're both lying. I'm lying to you and you are lying to me simultaneously about this book. That could be possible, but what are we getting from this? You've worked all night. I can smell it on you. You're tired. You don't need to waste your time. I don't want to waste mine. So, option number three."

"That it could be real?"

"That it *is* real," he said, nodding. "So, have you read any of it yet?"

"Yes," Vincent said. "Very little, but I have."

"What did you uncover?"

"A family secret," he admitted.

Hal whistled and shook his head. "Books can be quite dangerous. The great ones usually are."

"So what do I do with it?" Vincent's voice trembled.

"Gah, I don't know," Hal said. "You could rush home and read the whole thing, but that might ruin your life. Or, you could never read another page, but it would be difficult to stand up to temptation for the rest of your life. I'm not sure a man could do such a thing. You could also destroy it, but that's proving more difficult than usual, isn't it?"

"I don't want to read it," Vincent said.

"I wouldn't either. Is there someone you could trust to read it? Maybe there is something in there that would be good to know, or terrible to know, now that I think about it. What if you put that person in a dilemma to tell you something so important that it changes the entire course of your life? Man, there's a lot of bad choices here."

"Thanks," Vincent said.

"Come on," Hal said, trying to lighten the mood a little. "You've got somebody, right?"

"My girlfriend," he said, but he wasn't sure he wanted her to read it. That was a lot to ask of anyone. As soon as Vincent said it, he felt as though that was wrong. Hal seemed to agree.

"My grandmother?"

"Only if it's a good book," Hal said.

"What do you mean?"

"Well, if you were to walk down through the rows of biographies, you will see great men. Lincoln. Churchill. Roosevelt. Washington. Newton. Plenty of biographies on great men and men that did great things, but there are also biographies of Mussolini, Mao, Hitler. Men who achieved power but wielded it in terrible ways."

"I doubt that's me," Vincent said.

"You don't know. Do you think they did? They were always hell-bent on genocide, war, absolute power? No, I don't think that's true, not a hard rule, anyway."

"Who, then?" Vincent asked. "You?"

"Let's not rush," Hal said. "You don't know me."

"I brought it to you anyway," Vincent said. "You're kind of the perfect choice. We're strangers."

"This is an enormous burden you're potentially putting on me," he said. "I don't know what I'll uncover in this book. You could be the guy who cures cancer or the next guy to knowingly give cancer to millions while making billions for himself. What if I read something where I decide the only moral good is to stop you from doing what you do in this book?"

"I mean," Vincent said, half-shrugging, "I don't think that's me."

"You don't know, though. The truth is nobody does."

"Don't you have the obligation to read it, then? Nobody can go back and stop an evil man from doing evil things, but if someone in that time *knew* what the evil man would become and they did nothing, wouldn't they be guilty of inaction?"

Hal looked down at the book and placed his hand on the cover. He stroked it the way he stroked behind Milton's ear.

"That's a lot to ask of a man, a complete stranger, too," he said. "What if you fight for a cause that is moral, but one I personally disagree with?"

"Somebody needs to read it," Vincent said, growing annoyed that this man seemed to be rolling away from a task that was so easily his own. "It's irresponsible not to."

Hal looked away, rubbing his chin.

"Leave it with me for a week," Hal ultimately said.

"You'll read it? Thank—"

"I will *consider* reading it," Hal said. "I will spend the week determining if I should or not."

"Okay," Vincent agreed. "Don't do anything to it. I want it back."

"It will remain intact," Hal said.

The men shook hands, and Vincent thanked Hal. As he walked out of the shop, the door chiming as it closed, Vincent realized he had no idea if this was the right decision.

He walked back to his apartment, several blocks through rough neighborhoods, but the morning was the safest time. Vincent realized that what this book made him do, what it had already changed about him, was how he thought as he moved through the world. He looked at problems within society, and didn't see them just as blights or misfortune, but he began brainstorming solutions. The garbage that littered the streets, perhaps there was a better way to manage human waste? He saw the cloud of pollutant emissions coming from cars and buses and trucks that drove by. Was he the man who would solve those problems? Vincent shook his head. He did not have much of a scientific or engineering mind. No, it would have to be something else. What could it be?

This was all he thought about until he walked through the front door of his apartment, surprised to see Claire waiting for him on the couch as he closed the door behind him.

"What are you doing here?" he asked, happy to see her. "Don't you have that early lab on Thursdays?"

"I can't go," she said wearily. "I couldn't sleep."

"Why? Are you sick?"

"I don't know," she said. "I'm not well, but I don't think it's an illness. I think it's that book."

"Don't let that book bother you," he said. "I've handled it."

Had he really, though?

"How?"

"The bookshop owner, he's going to determine if he should read it or what I should do with it," Vincent explained. He attempted summarizing some of Hal's philosophical arguments for reading it and against reading it, but Claire didn't appear interested in anything he was saying.

"What's wrong? I think this is the right move."

She didn't look at him. She stared straight ahead at the television that didn't work, then at the walls with the bad patchwork done to cover the previous tenant's fist-sized holes. Vincent put his hand on her cheek and gently turned her face toward his.

"What is it?" There were tears in her eyes that refused to fall.

"What if I'm not in there?" she asked. "What if I'm barely mentioned, or just a footnote and nothing else?"

"Oh, Claire, come—"

"No, this book isn't just about you. It's who you build your life with and the people who surround you. If I'm not in there, I shouldn't be here. We shouldn't be together."

"Claire." Vincent shook his head. "Don't think like that. I love you. We're going to go through this together."

"We might not," she responded, as cold and emotionally detached as he had ever heard her. She didn't even sound like herself. She sounded already hurt, already betrayed.

Despite his rationalizing and pleading, she didn't soften. Her attitude remained rigid. There was nothing he could say, surprisingly, to dissuade her. She hardly spoke to him over the next two days. They became strangers dwelling in the same place. It was as though she had already left him, yet she still stuck around. Vincent couldn't stand it. He couldn't stand the unknowing-ness of it all. He understood the blissful ignorance of their own lives, their own futures. He saw the book as a curse. The next day, he woke up hours early and headed to the bookshop. He didn't need sleep. He needed answers.

Vincent walked into the shop, the door chimed, and Hal looked up from his desk with a stern, stoic expression. He wasn't happy to see Vincent pass through his doors.

"I'm here for the book," Vincent said.

Hal looked around, making sure there weren't any customers. "You were supposed to give me a week," he said, standing and going to the door. He locked it and flipped the sign to say that Hal's Books was closed.

"I couldn't wait a week," Vincent said. "My girlfriend is going to leave me. She needs to know if we're —"

"What's her name?"

"Claire," Vincent said. Hal nodded, repeating the name to himself as though it was a fact that he had forgotten.

"Have you been reading it?" Vincent asked, but Hal didn't say anything. He reached under the counter and retrieved the shell of paper wrapping along with the book. A bookmark stuck out a little more than halfway through the book, with many little sticky slips of paper flagging the pages like confetti.

Vincent reached for the book, but Hal's hand gripped it. He hadn't looked up. He looked off, away, guilty.

"I must confess," he said. "I am reading it, but not for good reasons."

"What are you talking about?" Vincent asked.

"It dawned on me, once I got past your breaking point, the family secret about your grandfather I'm assuming, that there could be details in this book that would be financially beneficial. Think about it. A mention of a small company, that's a chance to get in at the start of something big, you know? What if we could go back in time and invest in Apple or Amazon from the very beginning? I started looking for that or hints about other sure bets. I combed through pages and pages of details. I found one. I actually *found* one. Can you believe it?"

Vincent didn't want to rip the book from the older man's grip, but he didn't like the sly grin that was spreading across his face.

"Give me my book."

"No, not yet. You need to secure one thing for me."

"What's that?"

"My future," he said, holding the book in both his hands, away from Vincent. "Secure my future."

"What are you ta—"

"Write me a check," he blurted out. "Date it for nine years from now."

"I don't have a check," Vincent said, thinking about how easy it would be to walk behind the counter and physically remove the book from the man's hands. He didn't want to do that, but Hal wasn't helping Vincent anymore. He was looking out for himself.

"Go to the bank," Hal said. "Get one. Make it out to me. I'll give you an exact date, too. Leave it blank. I'll be very fair, young man."

"No," Vincent said. "Give me my book. This is the last time I'm going to ask for it. Listen to what I'm saying. Give it to me right now."

Hal considered his options before relenting. He exhaled slowly, like a deflating balloon, and handed Vincent's book to him. Vincent quickly placed the book in his backpack.

"What the hell?" he said, shaking his head.

"I'm sorry," Hal said, sitting back down in his chair behind the counter. "You don't realize how much power is in there. Look at me. How many opportunities do you think I've had to just get a slice of something real?"

"Why do you think I wouldn't have done that for you anyway?"

Hal stared at Vincent for a few moments and then looked away.

"Money corrupts, even just the idea of getting it," he said. "I'm sorry."

The apology was pained and genuine, full of regret and humility. Vincent saw what the book was, a lifelong affliction. The idea of each page's potential destroyed the character of everyone that interacted with it. Vincent couldn't see the book as anything other than a tool for evil. Hal walked around the counter and went to the door. He unlocked it and stood there. Vincent walked over, but something made him stop. He reached into his bag and found the shell of paper around the book. He pulled it out of the bag.

"Did you think of a way we could destroy it?" Vincent asked.

"Much easier said than done," Hal said. "The pages don't even tear."

Vincent looked down at the book and flipped it open to the bookmarked page.

"Hold on," Hal said, and he reached for the book, but Vincent moved, turning away from him. The page tore loudly. Vincent looked at the fractured leaf in Hal's hand and then flipped to the title page in the book. It was a biography, but not Vincent's. Both men looked at each other.

"Please, wait," Hal pleaded.

"Give it to me," Vincent said.

"I can't!"

"Give it to me!" Vincent shouted. Hal recoiled.

"Please," he begged. "It's going to destroy you. No matter what you become, good or bad, reading it will change the course of history. That will change lives, countless lives. We can't do that.

You can't do that! You need to forget about the book. Just carry on with your life. Trust—"

"You can't be trusted," Vincent said. He grabbed Hal by the collar and stood over him. Their faces were only inches apart. "Give it to me right now."

Hal stared into Vincent's eyes, back and forth between each one, knowing some details already of what they would see in years to come.

"Yes, I see it now," he said, nodding. "I see it."

"Give it to me!" Vincent yelled, pulling his fist back, not falling for Hal's distraction.

"Is your fate already sealed? Is Claire's? Has she told you she's pregnant yet?"

Vincent crashed his knuckles into Hal's face. The punch hurt the bookstore owner, but he kept talking.

"She hasn't, has she? You'll have a daughter next year," he said, spitting out blood. "Do you want to know her name? Do you want to know how she dies?"

Vincent swung again and again. Each punch sent Hal to the floor. He would try to crawl away after he crumbled to the ground, but Vincent did not let him get far. After his fifth or sixth punch, a particularly hard one that made Hal's legs give out, Vincent flipped Hal over on his back and pressed a knee into the older man's belly.

"Give me the book," Vincent insisted.

"Don't you see?" Hal sputtered. "I'm trying to save—"

"Save me? No. Tell me where it is." Vincent demanded, pressing harder into Hal's belly now, his knee pressing hard against Hal's organs. Hal groaned in pain and tried unsuccessfully to squirm away, but Vincent held him in place.

"Not you, you fool!" Hal yelled. "The world. *From* you."

Vincent became paralyzed, unable to know which of Hal's lies was the truth, or if any of them were at all.

"Kill me," Hal said. "Go ahead. There will be a lot less blood on your hands, but enough. Enough. They put you away and …"

Vincent stood up and rubbed his knuckles.

"What are you doing?"

"Keep it," Vincent said. He reached down to help Hal up, but Hal refused.

"No!" Hal said. "You don't—don't you want it back? You want it!"

"No," Vincent said. "My life's not going to be determined by some book, or by you."

"I'll press charges," Hal threatened.

"Go ahead," Vincent said. "Your choice. It's my choice to walk away from all of this."

Vincent stood over Hal with his hand extended for a few more moments, until Hal took his help.

"I'm sorry," Vincent said, assisting him to the chair behind the counter. "I'm sorry about everything. Do you want the phone?"

Hal didn't answer. Vincent picked his bag up off the floor. He took the book jacket with him but left the false book behind. The front door closed with a ding, and Hal watched the young man stand there for a few seconds. He reached for the gun he kept under the cash register, an old revolver that had belonged to his father. He brought the pistol up, his hand shaking. Hal did his best to aim, with both hands wrapped around the wooden handle. He had a shot, but he couldn't take it. Vincent walked away.

"I can't," Hal said. "I can't do it."

Daniel Lumpkin is from Georgia. He currently teaches college English Lit and Comp courses at Shorter University. He loves being a husband and dad. You can reach him at: nonprofitstepbystep@gmail.com.

Literary Time Machine
John Bukowski

I've always been interested in time travel. No, more than interested — fascinated. Actually, obsessed, if you believe my sister Babs, who has long since eschewed that juvenile nickname in favor of her given Barbara.

Babs says two years' residence in the past is long enough. "Sarah is gone, and you need to get back to living."

"L'chaim!" as the old song goes. But what does Babs know?

Her one foray into love ended in a knock-down, drag-out over who got the TV, the dog, and the house in East Lansing. Rand left her in a leased Mercedes, not a six- by two-foot box. Hatred drove away from Babs, not love. Love so constant, you didn't know its depth until it was gone. The love I shared with Sarah.

But I was talking about time travel. About my obsession with it. And about how I discovered it was indeed possible, a discovery made while sitting on the comfy recliner in our mountain getaway.

More a cabin, really: four rooms and a sewing nook. Not much. Just a peaceful place in the country. A summer place we'd hoped to turn into a year-round dream. A dream filled with the golden years that lay between suburban hubbub and rest-home docility. A dream oft planned but never fully realized.

The cabin is empty now, except for me. I move from easy chair to kitchen to bath and back again, pausing at the quiet sewing nook, the Singer carefully covered to keep off the dust. I eat and drink by rote. I sit and read. I ponder time travel.

We've all heard the naysayers: the scientists, priests, philosophers. They tell us that time is a one-way affair. We can only move forward, never back. Well, I'm telling you they're wrong; Stephen King proved it to me.

My summers in eastern Tennessee have always involved reading a lot of Stephen King. Mostly rereading him. Usually the short stories, but even the novels during long stretches of rainy weather. Oh, there were hikes in the Smokies and dinners with our neighbors George and Jan ("she of the artificial hair and rack to match," to quote the fair Sarah). There were days splitting firewood, followed by Bengay rubs. There were nights of passion, and those spent listening to the wind and the snoring from the other side of the bed. But evenings by the fire were mostly the sound of the Singer and the comfort of old friends with names like *Four Past Midnight*, *Skeleton Crew*, and *Christine*.

A few evenings ago, I'd just finished *Joyland*, a minor King vehicle, but a real gem. Less than three hundred pages but packed with laughter, tears, gasps, and, of course, time travel. Travel to the 1970s through the eyes of an old man reminiscing about summer and being twenty-one.

When I turned the last page, I was left with a familiar sense of loss. If you're a reader, I'm sure you've felt it too. The last words are read, the journey ended. In a way, it's akin to the death of a loved one. Analogous to life itself.

We begin the first pages with great expectations. The tale is new, exciting, as exhilarating as a moonlight kiss. We grow to care about the characters. We share their dreams. Weep at their losses. We take joy in visiting them hour after hour, page after page. Yet, in the dark recess of the soul, we know that the friendship, the joy, must end. We finish the final chapter and close the book.

When Sarah's chapter finished, I closed my book. The end. No going back. Or so I thought. I was as wrong as the naysayers.

I held *Joyland* in my hand, hefting substance that was more than its two hundred-odd pages. I studied the cover, caressing the tufts of fabric creasing the title, their jagged line seeming to separate *Joy* from *land*. And I had an epiphany. I didn't know where it came from, but it arose in my mind cold and complete, as all great notions do.

I'd been born again. The book had given me life. Life by proxy. Life as a lovesick twenty-one-year-old kid from Maine working at a Carolina carnival in 1973. Ridiculous? Perhaps. But true, nonetheless. I'd never been to either Maine or North Carolina, but I'd lived there just the same. And there was more. Much more. Oddly, and at the same time, I'd relived my own 1973.

I'd been back to the summer of over fifty years ago, a twenty-one-year-old kid from Detroit cutting lawns rather than greasing bumper cars. I could almost smell the grass, its aroma green and pungent. I'd stopped to wipe sweat from my forehead and saw a girl drive up with my sister, summer sunshine dancing off golden hair. Babs introduced us with, "Oh, that's my brother, Pete." The girl smiled and said her name was Sarah. I don't remember what I said. I just remember a faint whiff of coconut as we shook hands. And I remember Sarah's smile.

The images were so clear, more than memory. They were life itself. That's when I realized that time travel didn't involve portals or wormholes or fancy devices. Those fictional gadgets were too complicated. Time machines were actually quite simple. They were lined up in front of me on a homemade bookshelf in a little cabin in Tennessee. Then the second shoe dropped with all the subtlety of a thunderclap. If a book from 2013 could do this, what about one from 2006 or 1996 — or 1986?

I didn't hesitate. I didn't go to the bathroom, or get a drink of water, call a friend, or turn on music. I walked right up and grabbed a time machine.

Without consciously thinking, my mind had it all worked out. I'd travel backward with the books. I'd live again, through the books. And so would Sarah.

Quickly checking their front matter, I arranged titles in reverse chronological order. Anything published after *Joyland* wouldn't work, that was traveling into the future, the time of cancer diagnoses and trips to the chemo center. That future didn't interest me. I wanted the past. I likewise discarded short stories. Something told me that time travel couldn't be done in dribs and drabs—it required immersion. Electronic versions were also out, time trekking called for paper. How did I know all this? I just did.

After half a harried hour, I was left with ten titles: some dog-eared paperbacks; others big, hardbound tomes with their glossy jackets still intact. I piled the books beside the chair and settled in with *Duma Key*.

For the next while, I can't say for sure how long because time had become a fluid thing, I was in the late 2000s, experiencing the life of a beach-bum artist in the Florida Keys. Also, and at the same time, I was retiring after thirty years of teaching, misting up when my students presented me with a two-foot-tall card signed by all of them. I was also guest of honor at our combination retirement and going-away party, when our Dayton friends bid Sarah and me off to happy twilight days in Tennessee, not knowing how quickly that happiness would sour. I even had an old cat named Lisey who made the trip with us, yowling for the first hour before relaxing into the car ride.

The noonday sun was streaking in the cabin window when I read "the end." The old familiar jolt of loss was there, but it was different than the usual book-end melancholia. For this was no ordinary book, it was a time machine. Now that the machine was shut down, the meddlesome present was trying to return, along with his evil and constant companion, Mr. Future. I'd need to keep them at bay, and only the time machines could do that. Ignoring the stiffness in Señor Present's aging bones and a mouth as dry as Lisey's litter, I grabbed the next novel in line.

Tempus did fugit, only now it was winging backward. I experienced a Maine autumn as a journalism intern solving a murder with two sweet old codgers, while at the same time I attended my mother's funeral. I walked the streets of Desperation, Nevada, with Collie Entragian, and walked endless hallways as vice principal at Daniel Daye Middle School, moving on feet that were starting to feel their age. I helped Dolores Claiborne knock off her husband, and I helped five relatives carry my father's casket. When the Creeds were burying Winston Churchill in the *Pet Sematary*, I was making that last visit to the vet with Klondike. And right around the time the Torrances were checking into the Overlook, I was carrying the most beautiful bride that ever lived across the threshold of a Hampton Inn.

And that was when the most amazing thing happened. I heard the Singer humming in the nook. I smiled. At least I felt like I was smiling, it was hard to tell.

Things have gone a little funny lately. My eyes have been having trouble focusing, making it difficult to read. My mind has grown cloudy, too. I've given up trying to swallow, as that kitty litter between my teeth has turned to glue. Transitory needs like eating, drinking, and sleeping have been discarded; they could break the rhythm of the time machine. My heart has been beating both quicker and quieter, taking on a kind of flutter that is odd but not unpleasant. I've tried to pick up the last book. Is it *Salem's Lot*? It doesn't really matter, as my fingers won't grasp the well-thumbed pages. I might be lying in something wet, but again it doesn't matter.

I've noticed that the Singer has stopped humming. Sarah must have gone to sleep. I think I'll close my eyes and join her.

John Bukowski was previously a researcher and medical writer with professional publications ranging from journal articles to website content to radio scripts. In fiction, he has two novels and fifteen short stories in publication. He's a native of the Midwest, but currently lives in eastern Tennessee. You can find him at www.thrillerjohnb.net.

Zach and Deke's Stumbling, Bumbling Adventure in Time
Stephen W. Chappell

Skulking through the grounds of the research facility in the dark was not the way Zach had wanted to spend his evening. But money was money, and his employer wasn't known for his patience, so what else could he do? So here he was, scurrying to the shadows any time a patrol came around while he waited for Deke to hack the hangar's badge reader.

"How long is this gonna take?" Zach hissed. "We're too exposed out here."

Deke's nose twitched in annoyance. "It'd have gone faster if you'd stolen the right badge." The badge that Zach had stolen hung loosely from a pink beaded lanyard.

"How was I supposed to know that lady didn't have access?"

Deke tapped a button on his tablet, then swiped the stolen badge. The light on the reader turned green, and the door slid open. "I gave you a list. You grabbed the one badge that wasn't on it."

The door slid shut behind them, leaving them in near darkness. "What exactly are we looking for?" Deke asked.

Their footsteps echoed through the spacious hangar. Zach stopped when he triggered a sensor and the overhead lights came on.

"That."

Before them sat an egg-shaped contraption perched on four landing struts. Covered in iridescent scales, it was at least fifteen feet tall and wide enough to comfortably hold several people inside. A ramp led to a closed hatch.

"What the hell is that?" Deke asked.

"According to the boss, it's a time machine." Zach stepped closer, examining it appraisingly, as if he had a clue what he was looking at.

Deke nodded. "Oh." He put a hand to his chin. "How are we gonna get it out of here?"

Zach shrugged. "Damned if I know. It's bigger than I thought."

Deke walked up to the contraption. "We need a truck."

A siren sounded, and red lights flashed. Deke looked down to see a red stripe circling the craft. He'd just stepped over it. "Oops."

Panic twisted Zach's face. "You idiot!"

"Me? This was *your* idea!"

Zach's head swiveled as he searched for an escape. "We have to open the hatch."

Deke ran up the ramp. "What, you want to climb in?"

"It's better than getting caught!"

"You think they're not gonna look in there?"

Zach shook his head. "I have a plan," he lied.

Next to the hatch was a featureless black plate about the size of his palm. Deke traced his fingers over it, then banged it. The hatch slid up just as the hangar door opened.

"Stop!" A guard ran into the room, plasma pistol drawn.

"Get in!"

A plasma bolt splashed against the hangar wall as they tumbled through the hatch.

"Are they shooting at us?" Deke's voice trembled.

Zach ignored him. "Shut the door!"

Deke slapped a button, and the hatch slid into place. He grabbed a lever on the inside of the door and slid it to the left, into the "locked" position.

Zach climbed into a seat and examined the darkened console. "How do you drive this thing?"

Deke settled into his own seat and threw up his hands. "How should I know?"

Urgent banging filled the cabin. "Come out of there now!" The door's motor whined, but the lock held firm.

Panic blossomed on Deke's face. "What are we gonna do?"

Zach touched the console, and it came to life, with displays, buttons, dials, and sliders. One display labeled "status" featured several red icons.

"Good evening," said a feminine voice behind them. "Welcome to the TTX-1000 Prototype Time Craft. Please state your instructions."

They turned to see a semi-transparent hologram of a woman standing behind them. Her gray hair was in a bun, and she looked down her nose at them through thin, round glasses.

"Do you know how to drive?" Zach asked.

The banging on the door became more insistent. "Exit the vehicle immediately! The police are on their way!"

"Yes," the hologram answered.

Zach exchanged a look with Deke. "Then get us out of here!"

"Of course. Caution: Spatial stabilizers are offline." Zach glanced at the status display. One of the red icons was labeled "STBL."

"This is your last warning!"

Sweat broke out on Zach's forehead and ran into his widened eyes. "We have to go *now*, doll!"

"Very well. Please engage your safety harnesses."

The machine vibrated and started to hum. Their teeth rattled as the vibrations intensified.

Vroooom!

The machine lurched. Zach dug his fingers into the arms of his chair and gritted his teeth.

"Enjoy your trip," the hologram said.

Boom!

They were thrown to one side as the vehicle rolled. It righted, then they were slammed into their seats by the craft's acceleration. It rolled again and bounced like a motorboat skipping through choppy waters.

"I'm gonna be sick!" Deke moaned, looking green.

Zach's stomach flip-flopped. "Maybe this wasn't such a good idea."

The craft bucked, rolled, and rattled. "We're not gonna fall apart, are we?"

Crack!

Their stomachs dropped out as if they were in free fall, and then there was a bone-jarring jerk as the craft rolled end over end.

Zach moaned as his head spun. Nausea threatened to upend his stomach. He gasped for breath as his eyes rolled up, and then, finally, mercifully, everything went black.

"You have arrived."

The prim voice drifted into Deke's awareness. He was exhausted and achy, slumped against his safety harness. He cracked open an eye and surveyed his surroundings. The craft's cabin was spacious, with four seats and room to walk. The hologram sat behind him, adjusting her pink shawl. Three doors adorned the back wall, one of which he hoped was a restroom. Zach stirred beside him.

"Arrived where?" Deke croaked.

The hologram smiled politely. "Philadelphia. June 7, 1897."

Zach bolted upright. "What?"

"You heard the lady," Deke chided.

The blood drained from Zach's face. "We've got to go back!" He spun to face the hologram, but immediately put a hand to his head. "Oh," he moaned.

Deke shook his head. "Lightweight." He turned to the hologram. "How do we go back?"

The hologram shook her head. "We cannot travel at this time."

"Why not?" Zach groaned.

Graphics appeared beside the hologram. "It will take thirty-six hours to recharge," she said, pointing to one of them.

Zach shrugged. "That's just a few days." Deke nodded his agreement.

She pointed to the other graphic, a schematic of the craft. "We have sustained critical damage to both the Higgs capacitor and the quantum displacement field generator. We cannot travel until repairs are completed."

Zach narrowed his eyes at Deke. "You do know how to fix those things, right?"

Deke didn't even know what those things were. "Uh, maybe?"

"Fabricators and nanobot repair factories have been engaged."

"Great!" Zach and Deke said together, relieved. "How long will repairs take?" Zach asked.

"With available materials, two hundred and forty-seven years."

Zach hid his face in his palms. Deke threw back his head to stare at the ceiling.

Why did I ever go along with this harebrained idea? Deke wondered. "Why so long?"

A holographic list appeared in the air in front of him. "Certain materials, such as tachyon-infused beryllium, are not readily fabricated and will not be developed for over two hundred years."

Zach moaned. "So, we're stuck here?"

Deke hung his head in silence, his expression a mixture of depression and disgust. How was he going to get paid if he was stuck in the past?

At a grumbling in his stomach, he unfastened his harness and reached for the hatch.

"Where are you going?" Zach asked.

"Bathroom. Then outside. I'm hungry."

Zach half-heartedly slapped his arm. "We ain't got no money." He inspected his stylish black twenty-third century clothing. "And we're going to have problems with these clothes."

"The fabricator is creating period-appropriate apparel," the hologram announced. "It will be available shortly."

They really thought of everything, Deke mused. "What about money?"

The hologram looked over her shoulder. "A small number of coins are being fabricated."

Zach's brow wrinkled in confusion. "You can print money?"

"Quantum manipulation of raw material allows me to fabricate nearly anything you may find necessary."

"Hot dog!" Deke rubbed his hands together. "You print enough of that, we'll be rich!"

Zach cuffed him. "We'll be stuck in 1897, you idiot."

Deke scrunched up his face, annoyed. "What about that tachyon-infused burny bellum stuff?"

The hologram raised an eyebrow at him. "Tachyon-infused beryllium cannot be fabricated without a supply of tachyons."

Deke shook his head. "Then I guess we're stuck." He walked to the door labeled "Fabricator Lab."

"Might as well have a look around."

Changed and refreshed, they exited the craft into a secluded grove near the banks of the Schuylkill River. It was a warm day with a clear sky, but an unpleasant haze hung in the air. Zach wrinkled his nose.

"It smells like someone is burning horse dung," he complained.

Deke pointed toward the river. A dirt road ran alongside it, carrying people, bicyclists, and mule-drawn carts to and from the city. "There's your dung." He motioned back toward their craft. "Should we cover that thing up?"

They turned toward the craft. Its scales glowed and the air around it shimmered for a moment, and then the craft was gone. In its place was a moss-covered boulder.

"Guess not," Deke said.

Zach consulted a small device as he walked down the slope to the footpath. "According to this map that stuck-up hologram gave us, Philadelphia is that way." He pointed along the river in the direction the device had shown him. "We can't stay here," he said. "If we don't find a way to deliver this thing to the boss, we're toast."

Deke slumped his shoulders. "I have a wife. We gotta get some help."

Zach threw his arms out. "Look where we're at, Deke. Where are you gonna find help? It's not like you can email the Help Desk."

Deke stopped in his tracks. His face brightened, and a smile threatened to break out on his face.

"What?"

"Maybe not an email. But if we can figure out a way to send a message, then maybe we can get some help." Deke fixed Zach with a satisfied smirk.

Zach couldn't imagine a way to send a message to someone in the future, or who that someone would be. He said as much to Deke.

"What if we sent it to ourselves?"

"No, no. We're already here. How will that help?" Zach resumed walking, carefully avoiding a pile of mule dung.

Deke spoke as if talking to a child. "If we get it before we steal the machine, then we can get everything on the list and bring it with us."

Zach scrunched his face in confusion. "But we didn't get it before we stole the machine."

"Right," Deke nodded. "We didn't send it yet."

"But if we were going to send it, wouldn't we have gotten it already?"

Deke stopped and scratched his head. He examined his shoes, then looked at Zach. "Is that how it works?"

Zach shrugged. "No idea. It's making my head hurt."

"We should send it to somebody else," Deke conceded.

Zach nodded. "Who, though? Not the boss."

"Why not? What do you even know about the boss?"

What did Zach know about the boss? Winston Emerson Fairchild, their employer, was a billionaire, at least. He had his fingers in everything but somehow managed to stay out of the public eye. The one thing that Zach did know about him, that everybody knew about him, was that he was shady. It was common knowledge that he hadn't gained his fortune by staying on the right side of the law. It was also well-known that people who got too curious about him tended to disappear.

Zach could not even say for sure what he looked like. He had met the boss once, late at night in a darkened alley. He was very tall and very thin and wore a long, flowing coat. But he also wore a hat that kept his face shadowed, and he never took his hands out of his pockets.

One other thing Zach knew about him: People who crossed him tended to end up in pieces.

"I know enough to know that we better deliver that thing," Zach replied.

Deke scratched his head. "It's a prototype, right?" Zach nodded. "It's one of a kind, then. How is he gonna get us?"

Zach shook his head. "Probably build another one out of spite just to come after us," he said. "Anyway, they built one, they can build more. He'll come for us, don't you worry." He glanced at Deke, who had resumed his slumped posture. "So who should we send a message to? And how are we gonna send it?"

Deke wrinkled his forehead in concentration. "Well, I got a cousin who helps me sometimes. Harold might help us."

Zach nodded. He knew Harold and thought he was a good choice. Someone with the right connections to get what they needed and to steal another time machine, if or when there was one to steal. "Okay. How do we send it to him?"

"I couldn't help overhearin' you fellas," said a voice behind them. "You need something delivered?"

Zach nearly jumped out of his skin. "Why are you sneakin' up on people like that?" He turned to see a dark, thin man wearing overalls and a straw hat. Behind him, a mule pulled a produce-filled cart.

"Yer makin' so much noise, ain't much that couldn't creep up on ya." He reached out a hand. "Preston Gauger. Pleased to be makin' yer acquaintance."

Zach took the proffered hand but immediately regretted it; it was sweaty and covered in grime. "Zach. My friend here is Deke. We need to send a letter to his cousin."

Preston nodded. "So you'll be wantin' to go to the post office."

"What's a post office?" Deke asked.

"Fer city folk, yer kinda dumb, ain't cha?" Preston asked.

Zach gave Deke a dirty look. "It's complicated."

Deke brightened up. "Yeah, uh, it has to be hand-delivered."

The man squinted an eye and cocked his head.

Deke glanced at Zach, then continued. "We, uh, can't really take it to him. We've got to give it to his, ah, his grandfather." Deke scratched his head. "His name is Duncan."

"That his last name?"

Deke shook his head. "Duncan Whitman." At Zach's perplexed look, Deke continued. "Studied my family tree going back to the first Civil War."

Preston's eyebrows raised in a question, but Zach cut in before he could speak. "Deke is a little addled," he explained.

Deke side-eyed him. "Thing is, we gotta find him, and I'm not sure where to look."

Preston nodded. "Well, the post office knows where most everybody lives around here."

Zach smiled. "Thank you, sir."

"You men know where the post office is, do ya?"

Zach and Deke exchanged glances, then shook their heads.

"Well, ya follow this road past the hog pens and the cattle sheds and such, and you'll get ta Market Street. Take a left over the river, and it'll be, oh, ten or so blocks."

Zach turned toward the city. "How far do you think that is?"

Preston shook his head. "Mebbe an hour's walk, mebbe more."

Deke groaned while Zach thanked the man. "We best get a move on then."

The one calling himself Winston Emerson Fairchild adjusted his disguise and stepped onto the sunlit slope above the Schuylkill. The fake beard irritated his skin but was necessary for this daytime excursion. He pulled gloves on over his slender hands, struggling to fit too many fingers into too few holes. Another necessary compromise.

He coughed as he reached the footpath. The air was thick with pollutants in this time; he would have to be careful to limit his exposure.

Fairchild tapped the side of his dark glasses. An overlay appeared in his view, showing him the direction that his employees had taken. They had failed in their task, and Winston Emerson Fairchild was not one to suffer failures.

He coughed and set off after them.

"That'll be a penny for the card and envelope," the man at the counter said as Deke put down the fountain pen. They had stopped at a general store before going to the post office, realizing that they would need an actual note to give to Deke's ancestor.

Zach dug out one of his fabricated coins. The man lifted an eyebrow. "Will you be wanting some postage for that, as well?"

Zach shook his head. "No, it, ah, needs to be hand-delivered. To his, ah, grandfather." *Great-grandfather,* Zach thought. *Times ten or so.* Deke had gone through the whole line with him.

Deke smiled at the man. "Maybe you can help us find him? Duncan Whitman?"

The man chuckled. "Good ol' Dunk? You'll probably find him over on Broad Street, next to the Odd Fellows Hall. He's in the bar there, most days." He handed them their change and gave them directions, and then they were on their way.

The Odd Fellows Hall was a beautiful, squat building constructed of marble and brick, ornamented with terra-cotta cornices and pilasters. From across the street, Zach pointed to a small door next to it. "That's where we're going," he said. A yellow sign above the door read "Hartley's Place."

"Good, I need a rest after all this walking."

Pedestrians lined each side of the street, while bicyclists shared the center with horse-pulled carriages. Deke started across but stumbled as Zach held him back. A carriage passed through where he had been about to walk.

"Watch yerself!" the driver called.

They tried again, carefully avoiding the cyclists, horses, and other obstacles, and entered the establishment. It was dimly lit and lightly attended at this time of the afternoon. A bartender stood at the far end of the bar, chatting with an older man with white, wispy hair and a young woman at his side.

"Don't know why they're 'spectin' me to go down there," the older man was saying. "Look at me, I'm all busted up! That lawyer is s'pposed to be takin' care of everythin'."

"Dad, I'm sure he's trying his best," the woman said soothingly.

Deke and Zach walked along the bar toward the group. The bartender nodded at them as they approached. "Get you fellas something?"

Zach smiled. "Just, ah, we're just—"

Deke broke in. "We were told we might find Dunk Whitman here."

The older man thumped a heavy cane on the floor. "Well, that's me," he said in a creaky voice.

Deke rubbed the back of his neck. "Pleased to meet you. I'm Deke, and this is Zach. We, ah, well, this is going to sound weird, but, ah—."

"C'mon, now, spit it out." The man scrunched up his face in impatience.

Zach looked from Deke to Dunk, a half-baked lie forming in his mind. "We saw a psychic up the road," he said, remembering a sign they had passed. "She told us to send a letter to a, uh, a descendant of yours."

"A descendant, eh?" The man looked skeptical. "I don't know nuthin' about that."

"Dad," the woman interjected. "Let's hear them out."

Deke glanced at Zach, then continued. "His name is Harold. The, ah, psychic said there's something important he has to do. She wrote it down and put it in this sealed envelope." He became more animated as he pulled the note from his pocket. "She told me to give this to you to hand down to your children, and them to their children, and so on, until it gets to Harold Stover."

The man squinted and wrinkled his nose at him. "I gots eight children."

Deke's face fell. "Oh."

The woman walked over and snatched the letter from him. "Dad, stop being difficult." She turned to Deke. "If it puts your mind at ease, sir, we'll be happy to hand your letter down and make sure it gets into the right hands."

Zach's face broke into a wide, toothy grin. "Why, thank you, ma'am, you have no idea how much it means to us."

His elation was short-lived as they heard a cough. From behind them came a raspy voice. "I believe you boys have my property."

They turned to face a tall, thin man wearing a long, flowing jacket. Dark glasses and a full beard covered his face, but there was no doubt in Zach's mind who it was.

"Mr. Fairchild, sir, we can explain," Zach started.

A coughing fit overcame Fairchild. "How can anyone breathe in this time?" he wheezed. He pointed a gloved finger at them. "You had explicit instructions."

"Yes, sir, but there were extenuating circumstances."

Dunk stood and hobbled toward the tall man, leaning heavily on his cane. Perched on his head was an ill-fitting blue cap. It had the gold emblem of a hunting horn and the number 119 in red.

"Look here," he said, poking his cane in Fairchild's chest. "These men came to see me. You leave them 'lone till I'm through with them, ya hear?"

Another fit of coughing took over Fairchild. "Argh!" He doubled over as his cough worsened. His hat, sunglasses, and beard all fell to the floor, revealing the green lumpy skin covering the back of his head.

Fairchild lifted his alien head to glare up at them with bulbous, insect-like eyes. "You were to bring the machine directly to me," he wheezed. "Humanity is not worthy of such technology." He was racked with another coughing fit. "It must be destroyed."

"I dunno what you are, fella," Dunk said as he gripped his cane, "but I didn't survive no Civil War just so's you can come along and tell me what I'm worthy of." He lifted the cane with both hands and brought it crashing down on the alien's head. Fairchild slumped to the floor.

Dunk squinted at the two men. "Angeline there will make sure your letter gets where it's goin'," he said. "But I think you better take that whatsit and git yerself outta here."

They nodded as they grabbed Fairchild and headed for the door. They stopped when two men burst in brandishing pistols.

"You men, come with us. And bring Fairchild."

It took the four of them to haul Fairchild outside and load him into a waiting horse-drawn carriage. Zach was not surprised to find that it was something else entirely once they got inside.

"This time machine is bigger than ours," Zach observed.

"It's not yours," one of the men said. "You stole it."

"Who are you?" Deke asked. "And how'd you find us?"

"I'm Harold." The man shook his head in disbelief. "Do you know how many cousins you have after ten generations? And how many of them are named Harold?" He pulled a yellowed, tattered envelope from his pocket. "This has been in my family for hundreds of years. Angeline Whitman willed it to her youngest."

"But—" Deke started.

"And so on," Harold continued. "It was willed to me by my mother. It just so happens that I'm the head of security for the firm that developed time travel. I guess I'm not the cousin Harold you were hoping for?"

Deke slapped his forehead. "No," he moaned. Of all the rotten luck!

"What's going to happen?" Zach asked.

"There'll be a trial," the man said. "Your friend here for crimes against humanity, and you lot for grand theft."

Deke was incredulous. "But we exposed an alien plot!"

Harold nodded. "That'll be taken under advisement." He faced the console at the front of the machine. "Now, let's get you home."

The hologram sat in the second row of the TTX-1000 Prototype Time Craft and adjusted her shawl. She looked at the door and consulted her internal chronometer. The power supply would last for ten thousand years, but without the tachyon-infused beryllium, all she could do was wait, and hope that they hadn't forgotten her. And so, she waited. And waited.

And waited.

Steve Chappell is the chosen servant of four feline overlords, who tolerate his service in the outskirts of the NJ Pine Barrens. He is currently working as a systems engineer. Besides writing, he enjoys photography and reading.

Sarah's Assistant
Karen Eisenbrey

Sarah Pearson rode up front, the first person Jaden Byrd picked up in the streamlined white FuturePast Associates van. No, she was *Susan* now. Susan Perry, her alias for the next month. They picked up Joe next, then Billy. Though also using an alias, Billy looked familiar. Maybe they had worked together years ago. She had been retired long enough for the old faces to blur. Considering how much she had changed in a few years, it was no wonder he wouldn't look the same.

She was ready for the moment when Byrd touched a button above the radio and the tinted windows darkened, a deeper hum drowning out the quiet electric motor. They parked in front of a downtown apartment tower.

Byrd passed Sarah—no, Susan, she had to remember—a manila envelope. "You'll be staying in apartment 305."

"Easy to remember. Same number as my condo unit."

"The key's in the envelope, along with general instructions and other incidentals. Can you find your way to work from here?"

"Yes, I know the neighborhood. How do I reach you if I have questions?"

"There's a business card in the envelope. Our office is staffed in this time."

She grinned, eager to start her adventure ...ten years in the past. That van didn't just look futuristic. It was a fully functional time machine.

"All right, then. See you in a month!" She stepped from the van and grabbed her bag from the back. She had only an overnight bag for a whole month. Byrd had assured her FuturePast would provide period-appropriate work attire in her size, on loan during her stay. Her bag held only underwear, socks, toiletries, and a few changes of casual clothes for off-hours.

Sarah—Susan—found apartment 305, an efficient studio equipped for her temporary stay with a sofa bed, a comparatively small flat-screen TV, and a clunky e-reader loaded with classic literature and (to her) decade-old bestsellers. Sometime deeper in the past, Joe and Billy were also settling in here with even older tech. The three were roommates who would not meet again until Jaden Byrd returned them to their own time.

She pulled the instructions from the envelope:

REMEMBER: You are here to do a job. Focus your energy and attention on assisting your past self with job tasks.

DO NOT involve yourself in your past personal life.

DO NOT offer stock tips, future predictions, or anachronistic tech to ANYONE.

DO NOT use your future knowledge to benefit yourself (past or future).

DO NOT socialize with anyone you knew in this time or become romantically entangled with ANYONE.

DO enjoy this visit to your past. When not working, you are allowed to leave the apartment, as long as you observe the above restrictions. Transit tickets and a small amount of cash have been provided to facilitate leisure activities. Funds remaining are yours to keep at the end of your contract period.

In case of emergency or questions, please call the office of FP Assoc.

Blah, blah, blah. Don't change anything, don't have any fun. Story of her life.

In this time, the small fridge was stocked with mixed salad greens and assorted nutritious, low-carb toppings, enough for a week's lunches, plus breakfast yogurt and assorted reasonably healthful frozen dinners. Not much variety, but tolerable for a month. These provisions would be replenished at FuturePast's expense each week. She was free to eat in restaurants on occasion, if she wished, as long as she didn't interact too closely with the people of this time and used the vintage cash provided (no chip cards or payment apps back in this day). As promised, the closet held a few pairs of business-casual slacks with a week's worth of coordinating tops. She'd brought her own sensible shoes, the same style she'd worn for fifteen years at least. Comfort over fashion.

Sarah had retired early, mostly for health reasons. Five years later, she had resolved her health issues and then some, almost by accident. Part of the severance package included extended health coverage. She'd been limping around on an excruciatingly sore knee for years. She finally had someone look at it as soon as she had time, while she still had good employer-provided insurance. Knee surgery followed by physical therapy had led to a discovery: She didn't hate exercise; she hated her old gym teacher. Water aerobics, yoga, and strength training followed PT, with Zumba and spin classes for variety. She'd changed her eating habits upon learning her blood sugar was higher than normal. At sixty, she was in the best physical condition of her life and ready for something new. She'd been considering swing dance or a vegetarian cooking class when she received the invitation from FuturePast Associates to participate in their pilot program. "Improving today's bottom line by improving yesterday's."

And so, here she was, back at her old cubicle, being introduced to a woman she remembered well from the mirror.

"Sarah, this is Susan Perry," the woman from HR said. "Susan, Sarah Pearson. You'll be assisting her with her backlog."

"Call me Sue," she improvised as she shook Sarah's hand. *Susan* had never sat right. She could live with Sue.

"I hope you can help with this mess." Sarah gestured at the stacks and boxes of files on and under her desk. "You can use the cubicle next to mine if you can find enough open space. Get settled and then I'll walk you through it."

Sue put her things away in an empty desk drawer. File folders had already begun to encroach on this desk, too. She remembered this time all too well. The real estate market was red hot, but management was reluctant to add staff because things could cool off by the time the new hires were up to speed. They chose to overwork current staff instead. Until Jaden Byrd showed up with his time machine and a proposal: pay a single salary plus increased retirement contribution and have a retiree from the future assist her past self, saving on overtime and employee stress. It was crazy enough to work.

"You don't look old enough to be retired," Sarah said from her cubicle.

"Thanks, I think." Sue rolled her chair over to begin training, or more accurately, reminding. "I'm only sixty, but I took early retirement five years ago, after a merger. The deal they offered was too good to pass up."

"Ooh, I'd like to retire in five years rather than wait ten or more. What made you want to come back?"

"Just keeping my hand in. A change is as good as a break, right? And the extra money doesn't hurt."

Sue tried not to stare at Sarah's long brown hair while they talked. She'd been dyeing it since the first gray hair appeared, as her mother had. It had always been brown, but this color didn't look natural. And the length was habit more than style. When she was young, she'd aspired to be pretty. Pretty girls were tall and slim with long flowing hair. Her body type precluded both *tall* and *slim*, so she'd settled for long hair. It never really flowed, though. It just hung there, limp.

Sue had gotten a short haircut before her knee surgery to simplify things in recovery. It turned out the short, layered bob suited her face. As the brown grew out, she'd discovered a nice streaky, dark/light mix in her natural color, and the cut played up the contrast. She stopped dyeing and never looked back. Now, her hair was almost entirely silver, and still looked better short than long.

She had also forgotten she almost always wore dresses in those days, casual knitwear without a tight waistband. She'd believed she was fat, and the style was supposed to be slimming. *Oh, honey, you have no idea*, Sue reflected. She might have been technically overweight but far from where she'd end up in a few years. Today's dress, though comfortable, announced, "I'm wearing vertical stripes to look slimmer." Sue always wore long pants now to cover the scar on her knee. She hadn't lost all her vanity.

Her job today would be handling incoming phone calls while Sarah concentrated on clearing files. Sue took a few files to work on between calls, making slow progress. In retirement, she had not missed the constant interruptions, the customer in her ear taking priority over the one on paper. Having an assistant would have made a huge difference, and now she *was* that assistant. Weird.

It was so busy, Sarah took her morning break at her desk.

"Kind of defeats the purpose of a break," Sue said.

"I walked across the office to get a muffin, and I'll go to the restroom when I finish my coffee," Sarah replied. "If it gets me off my chair, it counts."

Sue stayed to keep herself company and regretted it when Sarah started to chat. She knew how much effort it took Sarah to make small talk. And how much she longed for connection. She still did, though Sue had made peace with her solitary life. Her real concern was that she wasn't supposed to make friends in the past, especially not with herself. Too much conversation and she might blow her cover. The whole experiment would be over. With a time machine, Byrd could make it never happen.

"So, got kids?" Sarah asked. "Grandkids?"

Sue tried not to cringe as Sarah bit into her huge muffin. All those carbs. "Me? No."

"Me, neither. Single for life. Well, I was married a long time ago, but it was so short, it barely counts."

"I can relate," Sue said. They had been fixed up by college friends and kept seeing each other because it was what people expected. When all their friends were getting married, they did, too, only to conclude after a few months that it was a mistake. They got along okay, though there'd never been much chemistry. They parted on friendly terms but hadn't stayed in touch. It was another life.

Sue went for a walk at lunchtime. She needed to move after a morning at a desk. How had she lived that way? Better late than never to discover the joy of a brisk walk and fresh air. She found a bench and ate her salad outside. When she returned, Sarah was finishing a cheeseburger and fries from the food court downstairs. Sue resisted commenting, though she regretted the unhealthy emotional eating. It helped to know she'd eventually figure it out.

Later in the afternoon, Sarah limped back from the copier and sank into her chair with a barely stifled groan. "This knee ..." she said.

"Mm?" Sue replied. She remembered the knee pain, which had started around this time. She'd never mentioned it to anyone else except to make and cancel doctor appointments. Work had always been too busy to take the time off.

"I made an appointment to have it checked out," Sarah said. "I thought I'd have to cancel again, but maybe I won't, with you here. Think you can cover for me Friday afternoon?"

"Oh, um, sure. I'll take messages if I can't handle it myself."

Sue returned to the apartment after work, equal parts satisfied and unnerved. It felt good to be useful and productive again, but her mere presence was changing Sarah's responses to things. She was talking aloud about things she'd always kept inside. Sue would have to be careful how much she gave away in conversation. She'd known going in she was forbidden from betting on sports or deliberately changing major events. Those were easy to avoid. It was going to be trickier knowing what little things might change what other little things.

Sue's second day on the job presented a new challenge when Sarah commented on the surging real estate market, and not in a job-related way.

"I've always rented, but I want to own a place so I can get a cat," she said. "I may have missed my chance, though, the way prices are going through the roof."

Just wait, Sue thought. "Don't give up your dream. These things never last."

"Yeah, I've seen more than one bubble burst."

Sue knew this bubble would burst hard in less than a year and bring the rest of the economy down with it. She'd somehow survived the ensuing layoffs, and with housing prices crashing, she'd gotten a sweet deal on her one-bedroom condo. She'd delayed getting a cat while she got her own life in order. She couldn't reveal any of that to Sarah. Worse than betting on sports. Jaden Byrd claimed FuturePast would know if she broke the time-travel rules, and she would be retroactively disinvited from the project.

Sue got through the week without breaking the rules and spent the weekend in darkened theaters, watching movies she'd missed on the big screen the first time around. There was something to be said for a vacation in one's own past. When Monday rolled around again, she found she was nearly back in the old routine, minus regular visits to the office candy bowl. She had forgotten how close it was to her desk. She bit her tongue to keep from saying anything when Sarah walked over there for a handful of M&Ms.

Sarah picked up the bowl and disappeared around a bank of filing cabinets. She returned empty-handed, with a relieved smile on her face.

"Out of sight, out of mind," she said. "They can have it in Unit Ten for a while."

Sue raised her eyebrows, unsure what she could even say at this point. This was not the Sarah she'd been. Not until years later, anyway.

"Well, I finally had my doctor's appointment. They say my knee doesn't need surgery yet, but it most likely will someday," Sarah explained. "They gave me a shot to reduce inflammation and a page of strengthening exercises. And suggested it might help if I lost a few pounds. So ..." She nodded toward the relocated candy bowl. "They found out my blood sugar is on the high end of normal. Not quite diabetic, but it won't be long if I don't do something. I have a phone consultation with a dietitian this afternoon." She sighed. "I'll miss my French fries. Maybe I can learn to like salads. I peeked at yours the other day—it didn't look half bad."

"Okay." Sue felt faint. This was familiar, but happening five years early.

"You know what's weird?" Sarah seemed not to notice her assistant was having an episode. "I dreaded the exercises, but I actually enjoyed them. They're hard work, in a good way. And I swear, I'm seeing muscle definition after only three days. Look!" She raised her hem a few inches to show the muscles around her knee.

Sue couldn't recall how her legs had looked back then. There might have been a slight improvement in muscle tone. "Good for you. Congratulations."

"Thanks. I thought I hated exercise; turns out, I only hated my gym teacher! I think I'll sign up for a water aerobics class."

Sue pretended calm until she could get away at lunchtime. She called the FuturePast office in a panic. She was reassured to reach Jaden Byrd himself.

"I'm not doing it on purpose!"

"What are you not doing?" Byrd sounded amused and unruffled.

"Things are changing, but I'm not changing them! Things are happening that didn't happen, or not until much later."

"It's all right. Some minor shifts are inevitable," Byrd explained. "Your mere presence will trigger small alterations. You're not going to be disinvited for that. Keep up the good work."

Minor shifts? Small alterations? Sue had two sets of memories: the ones she considered "real," her dumpy, loner self creaking along on a bad knee; and these new ones, feeling empowered as she took charge of her health at long last. But if she wouldn't be disinvited, what Byrd didn't know wouldn't hurt him.

Sarah came in the next day with short hair—an inch or so longer than Sue's and in a different style, with highlights.

"I'm not getting into a swimming pool with long hair," she explained. "I don't know why I waited—I probably lost at least a pound at the salon!"

"And highlights?" Sue tried to sound noncommittal. Once she'd stopped dyeing her hair, she discovered she had natural highlights, albeit gray ones.

"To make it less obvious when I stop dyeing it," Sarah whispered.

"Really? I didn't know."

Their coworker Will Stephens passed by, whistling. He paused and smiled at Sarah. "New haircut? Nice for summer."

"I thought so. My neck feels cold, though." Sarah laughed and rubbed the back of her neck. "You seem extra happy."

"Laurie's ten years' cancer-free," he replied. "We're going out this weekend to celebrate."

"Wonderful! Give her a hug for me."

As he proceeded to his own cubicle, Sue belatedly recognized him as Billy from the van. She was right, she had worked with him. In this time, he was older than Sarah and younger than Sue, whom he didn't recognize. But Laurie, cancer-free? Sue had gone to her funeral. When was that? A few months from now. What had Billy changed in the past?

"I lost two pounds!" Sarah exclaimed when she arrived on Friday morning.

"Good for you!" Sue knew she might have to lose eighteen more before anyone else could tell. There was already a difference, not in appearance, but in confidence. Sarah carried herself with the pride of accomplishment after only a few rounds of daily exercise and better nutrition. Two pounds was huge, if only as a start.

"They offer all kinds of classes at the community center where I swim," Sarah added. "Swing dancing sounded like such fun; I signed up before I could change my mind. It starts tonight. Who cares if it's mostly women who show up? They're better dancers, anyway."

Sue laughed. She'd taken ballroom in college, and it had been three-quarters women—who were in general, if not better dancers, better leaders than most of the guys. The dance at the end of the term had been disappointing, though. All the guys brought dates and danced only with them, leaving the girls from the class to dance with one another. It was a good thing they'd all learned both to lead and to follow.

In those days (and later), Sue had been attracted exclusively to men who would never notice her. She had lacked the confidence to even consider asking one out. Hence the fix-up with the eventual (failed) husband. She was capable but not talented, a solid B student with little ambition. She majored in English because she enjoyed reading. She didn't want to write or teach or go to law school. In those days, though, a liberal arts degree could get you into a decent entry-level position with room for advancement if you were willing to work and learn on the job. She had found her niche in an office job with regular minor promotions and small raises, ever-increasing challenges, a chance to excel in a small way without having to supervise others or manage anything except her own desk. And she'd enjoyed her coworkers, the closest to a social life she could have expected to get. She had happily retired from that career to take charge of her own health.

Her past was not in her control now. Things were changing. She didn't know anymore what the future held.

Sue was already at her desk when Sarah arrived on Monday morning. She looked different, though she wore her usual style of dress. It was more than the haircut, the muscle definition, or the two pounds. It was more, even, than confidence and pride. She …sparkled.

"Well, you must have had a good weekend."

"I *met* someone." Sarah plopped into her desk chair and spun it around.

"Say more?" Sue kept her voice level so she wouldn't shout. This hadn't happened. There was no *someone*.

"At dance class on Friday. I ended up partnered with Chris several times, and we …clicked. It was so much fun."

Sue breathed a relieved sigh. The swing dance teacher had paired Sarah with a pleasant guy who was a decent dancer and now she had a crush. She tried to picture this Chris: probably mid-fifties, not too tall, still had his own hair but receding, well mannered …

"We talked all through the break," Sarah gushed, "and after class, she asked me out!" A huge smile split her face, wide enough for teenage Sarah to climb out.

Wait. *She?*

"Oh. I didn't realize you were —"

"Bi? I didn't either, but it kind of explains a lot."

Did it? Sue had always enjoyed women's company. She'd figured that was because men didn't notice her. Some of those friendships had been intense, though, and hard to lose.

"And did you go out?" Sue's voice sounded as faint as she felt.

"Chris—Christina—couldn't this past weekend. She had an event. She's a chef. She owned a restaurant, but she sold it and now she teaches vegetarian cooking classes and does catering. This Saturday, we're going to walk around Green Lake, and if it goes well, she wants to cook for me!"

"Wow, that's…that's great. Will you excuse me? I need to—"

Sue waved vaguely toward the restrooms and made as dignified a retreat as she could manage. Conflicting memories threatened to overwhelm any calm she had left. She remembered the fizz of new infatuation, though she hadn't had a real crush since …when? Middle school? Now, she could dimly see a broad face topped with a dollop of short gray hair, smile lines framing bright blue eyes, a dash of freckles across a strong nose. Christina.

This hadn't happened. Nothing close to this had happened. Sarah looked too happy for Sue to spoil it for her.

Christina cooked for her.

By the time Sue's assignment ended, Sarah had lost eight pounds, turned pescatarian, and made plans for a second date with Christina. Sue almost regretted she wouldn't get to hear the rest of the story. But in a way, she would. When she got back to her own time, she'd know how it turned out.

When Jaden Byrd picked her up, Billy was riding up front and Joe was in the back. Silent anticipation filled the van as they returned to their own time, to the evening of the same day they'd left. Anyone who might have missed them would think they'd gone back to work for only one day. Sue—Sarah again, now— hesitated in front of her building.

"Anything wrong?" Byrd asked.

"It'll sound silly, but …I can't remember the number of my unit. Is it 305 or 503?"

"Time travel will do that to you. Minor shifts, remember? You've lived in 503 for the past four years."

"Right, right." She knew from when she toured the place, 503 was much larger than one person would need.

New old memories shoved old old memories into the background. "I bought it with my wife, Christina. She needed enough space for her cat."

Karen Eisenbrey lives in Seattle, WA, where she leads a quiet, orderly life and invents stories to make up for it. Karen writes fantasy and science fiction novels, as well as short fiction and the occasional poem or song if it insists. You can find her at https://kareneisenbreywriter.com/.

Time Changes Everything
Jon McGoran

Strunk7D was a barren, airless rock, but as of the first of the month, it was Dominic's barren, airless rock. Soon it would be neither barren nor airless, although looking down on it—dusty beige, lazily spinning below their low orbit—that was hard to imagine.

"Ace Xenobio Surveyors?" said Tillman, Retroforma Corporation's on-site rep. He was looking at the printed, certified, and embossed affidavit that officially declared Strunk7D lifeless. He said it with distaste—even more than usual. "Never heard of them."

He said it like an accusation.

Dominic sipped his champagne. Retroforma served champagne on the observation deck for the actual process—and they damn well should, considering how much they charged. "Well, you really should try to keep up on that sort of thing, shouldn't you?" he replied, "I mean, isn't that, like, part of your job?"

He threw a wink at Bronson, the humorless toad his mother had insisted on sending along as a business advisor—and almost certainly her spy.

Tillman scowled.

Bronson looked down and shook his head slightly. "Don't aggravate him," he whispered.

Dominic ignored him, as he usually did. The planet had been bought and paid for. Ace was an officially registered surveyor, and the survey affidavit was legally binding. There was no evidence of any of the corners that had been cut. As far as Bronson and Tillman knew, everything was on the up and up.

Technically, Tillman was primarily a salesman, but he had the authority to shut the whole thing down, and he seemed the type who might do it. Still, as busy as Retroforma was these days, there was a lot of money on the table. It would take more than Dominic behaving like a jerk to make them back out.

"Now," Dominic said, putting down his champagne and rubbing his hands together briskly. "Shouldn't we be getting on with it?"

Tillman studied the affidavit in his hands one more time, then studied Dominic with even greater scrutiny. "I'm going to have to make a call," he said. He turned on his heel and strode out of the observation deck.

Dominic felt a surge of anxiety that almost weakened his knees. He put one hand in his pocket and rubbed the fossilized claw that had become his good luck charm. The other hand he braced against the wall as he struggled to maintain the air of unassailable confidence he had been trying hard to exude to everyone involved: Tillman and his colleagues at Retroforma, a dozen different bureaucratic agencies, Bronson, and of course, Mom.

It all came down to what happened next.

Hard to believe it had been less than a year since Mom had given him the last in her long series of lectures regarding Dominic getting his act together, making something of himself, growing up and becoming his own man. He had been on the receiving end of that lecture at least a dozen times before, but he could tell that the tone was different this time. It had a little more *oomph* behind it, a little more conviction. As Mom had approached the lecture's customary conclusion, Dominic had sensed, to his horror, a new twist. And he'd been right.

"I've come to understand that the allowance I've been giving you simply enables your bad behavior," she had said. "It allows you to delay the reckoning that must someday occur, a reckoning that will only grow harder the longer it is put off. That is why I have decided it would be best for everyone, especially for *you*, if, from this moment on, you must rely on yourself to make your way. I'm cutting off your allowance."

Dominic could still remember the bitter taste of his one-word reply. "But…"

"I love you, son," the old lady had said. "But you need to get your shit together."

During the ensuing two-day bender of spite-drinking and debauchery—one last, glorious run-up of Mom's credit account—Dominic had caught a tip, a solid rumor about a new wormhole secretly being planned just outside the Strunk system.

It gave him an idea.

Dominic had returned contritely to his mother to apologize and to ask for one last chance, an audacious one: A planet of his own, that he could terraform. He didn't share the part about his illegal insider knowledge of the impending wormhole and the skyrocketing property values that would result from all that traffic. Instead, he focused on the metaphorical aspects of the proposal, hoping that might appeal to his mother: Taking something useless and transforming it into something of great value.

It took some doing, of course, some convincing, but as dependent as he was on receiving that money, his mother had been almost as dependent on giving it to him. Neither of them had the wherewithal to quit cold turkey.

Still, she didn't simply roll over. The old lady might have even been impressed by the proposal and relieved to appease her youngest son, but it was a big ask. Along the path to "yes," the proposal evolved from a last massive lump of allowance to, "This is your inheritance, so don't expect anything more in the will."

That had given Dominic pause. The old lady was old, and if he forgot about Strunk7D and simply stayed the course until she died, he'd have his inheritance with no strings attached, free to spend it on whatever reckless decadence he wished. Part of him wanted to just hunker down, endure a few years of relative poverty while he prayed for whatever stroke or aneurysm or cancer would make him rich again. But a part of him had become genuinely enthusiastic about owning and running his own planet. More importantly, if he backed out over that, his mother's opinion of him would have been irrevocably downgraded once again. Shockingly, it turned out that still mattered to him, and not just because of the negative impact it could have on the amount she might leave him.

Mom had insisted on sending Bronson along to help him. He was a dreadful sort, humorless and officious, and physically short, bald and ugly, even though he had more than enough money to change all that if he wished. To be fair, he'd been invaluable in navigating the Byzantine bureaucracies involved in the legitimate side of things, but his presence had necessitated an increased level of deviousness regarding the less legitimate aspects of the plan.

Terraforming had always been highly regulated, but once Retroforma introduced their method, the red tape tripled or more. It was completely justified, of course—even Dominic had to acknowledge that—but it was hugely inconvenient. It was also ungodly expensive—though worth every cent.

Conventional terraforming, even the most aggressive program, was *slooow*. You could put thousands or even tens of thousands of terraforming units onto a sterile planet—with each house-sized unit sucking in whatever toxic soup passed for an atmosphere and churning out breathable air and drinkable water—and it would still take decades to create a decent atmosphere and functioning water cycle. Dominic was young, but he wasn't patient. He didn't have that kind of time to wait.

Luckily, Retroforma had figured out a way to accomplish all that virtually instantaneously, using the one technology even more highly regulated than terraforming itself: time travel.

When the chronolator was invented, making time travel possible, criminals, unscrupulous businessmen, religious zealots, and plain old idiots had all rushed to exploit it, going back in time to invest in the right stocks, profit from futuristic technologies, witness—and interfere in—pivotal moments in religion or history, or simply wander around like ignorant tourists. By the time the government could put in place any kind of regulatory framework, such a mess had been made that the final regulations said: time-travel is illegal, under penalty of death.

A bit of an overreaction, maybe, but it took ten years, and countless memory recovery interviews, to identify all the paradoxes that had been created, and decades more to litigate them.

The most famous case involved the Chakrabarti quantum battery, or CQB, which years earlier had revolutionized nanoelectronics. Long an essential mainstay of modern technology, one day, all the CQBs in the world disappeared, vanished from every application, replaced by a slew of bulkier and less efficient substitutes. More unsettling, it wasn't just the physical batteries that disappeared, but also every mention of them, anywhere.

People remembered the CQBs. They knew how they worked, in principle, at least. But they also now remembered an alternate timeline in which the batteries had never been invented. The reality of these dual memories answered many questions about what happens in a time-travel paradox, but it raised many more.

While the world was understandably going nuts trying to figure out what the hell had happened, one smart young reporter went looking for Chakrabarti's heirs, to get their thoughts on the situation. As it turned out, in this new timeline, those people no longer existed. Eventually, it was determined that, in this timeline, Chakrabarti had been killed and his laboratory destroyed before he could announce his discovery or file his patent—or father his children.

Meanwhile, within days of the batteries' disappearance, thousands tried to take advantage of the situation by filing quantum battery patent applications, mostly based on the recollections of engineers intimately familiar with them. But one application was different from the others. It was complete. It was exact. And it hadn't been submitted by a scientist or engineer, but by a venture capitalist named Gordon Rails, who had helped fund development of the chronolator, then apparently used it to go back and kill Chakrabarti.

Rails was arrested but not immediately charged. He hadn't violated the laws against time travel or timeline manipulation, because those laws hadn't been written yet. And he couldn't be charged for murder, because Chakrabarti's murder had taken place before he was born, and while there was no statute of limitations on murder, the body and any possible witnesses or evidence had long since turned to dust.

Law enforcement scratched their heads before figuring out that he had lied on his patent application. He was prosecuted to the fullest, and a deep dive into every aspect of his life turned up enough other misdeeds to keep him in jail for the rest of his life.

A proposal to use the chronolator to undo Rails' paradox was abandoned for fear of other unintended consequences, and that's when time travel was made illegal on Earth and on every other inhabited planet in the Association.

For the next thirty years, apart from a few well-publicized criminal violations, people left time travel alone. But in that time, most of the settled exo-planets had begun to feel population pressures. For years, humanity had been expanding, settling every habitable planet within travelable distance. Humanity needed more habitable planets, and the conventional terraforming projects were taking way too long.

That's when Retroforma unveiled their idea for "Retroforming." They faced universal opposition at first, but as people got used to the idea, they had to concede the logic behind it.

Time travel was illegal on all the *settled* planets, because of the paradoxes that could arise when you interfere with people's backstories. But the time travel laws didn't technically apply to all the *uninhabitable* rocks littering the galaxy. Since those planets were lifeless, there would be no paradoxes to worry about.

The Retroforma technique was brilliant in its simplicity, and surprisingly affordable compared to conventional terraforming. Retroforma could terraform an entire planet, instantaneously, using a single terraforming unit.

"A single unit?!" the critics had said at first. "But that would take a million years!"

They were right, of course, but Retroforma had figured out that a million years was no problem if you used a chronolator to retroactively start the terraforming process a million years earlier. Instead of using thousands of terraforming units, Retroforma used just one, but paired it with a chronolator to send it a million years into the past. You simply had to orbit the barren planet of your choice, drop the paired devices onto its surface, and watch from a safe distance as both devices disappeared into the distant past. After a few moments, *boom*, the planet below was instantly transformed into a lush oasis, courtesy of a million years-worth of retroactive terraforming.

It was too good an idea to be denied — the kind of idea that Dominic wished he'd come up with. Retroforma spent trillions in currency to grease the political wheels, refine the technology, sway public opinion, and keep the company afloat while waiting for Association approval. Three years ago, that approval had been granted, and since then the company had terraformed over thirty planets, making back their investment and much, much more. It was projected that within a few years, Retroforma would be the biggest and most profitable company in existence.

Not everyone was crazy about it—especially not the conventional terraforming companies, who had seen their orders dry up. A lot of them probably wished they could go back in time and have the idea first. But of course, on an inhabited planet, that was illegal.

Tillman returned to the observation deck, pinching the affidavit between his fingers like it was soiled. He brushed past Dominic and pushed a button on the console. "Commence the loading procedure."

Dominic swallowed his sigh of relief. Apparently, Ace Xenobio Surveyors had checked out. He'd been fairly certain they would, but they were such a half-assed operation, there was a substantial chance that they might have incurred some penalty or even lost their charter since the last time Dominic had checked.

It was their half-assedness that had brought them to Dominic's attention. The bio survey was one of the most important—and most expensive—parts of the terraforming permit application. In an excess of caution and to avoid wiping out any indigenous life, a planet had to be bio-surveyed and certified "aseptic," free of life, in order to be approved for retroforming.

Dominic had initially hired the cheapest planetary survey company in the sector, Torvald Planetary, but damned if they hadn't actually found a vein of fossils, roughly six million years old, alongside the banks of an ancient river. Legally, that should have led to an amended application and an extensive level-two survey, which would have been catastrophic. The resulting delays could have prevented the retroforming from being completed before the public announcement of the new wormhole, and the added expense would have exceeded what Mom was willing to cough up. And that would have been far from the end of it. Next would be the cataloging and radiometric dating of every potential fossil discovered. Retroforming would only be allowed to proceed if it could be determined that there were no signs of life from the last two million years. If there were, you had to file for a special exception—more delays and expense—after which you would receive either a denial or a qualified approval, which meant you could only send your retroformer and chronolator back as far as one million years *after* the date of the youngest fossil found.

Dominic shuddered at the thought of spending all that currency and only being able to send the retroformer back 600,000 years or even 400,000 years, ending up with some thin-aired desert planet no one would ever want to visit.

It was the second worst-case scenario.

The worst was that something went wrong with the terraform itself and the company decided—and it was clearly stipulated in the contract that it was *solely* Retroforma Corporation's decision—to undo the terraforming. Undoing involved dropping a second chronolator—this one paired with a powerful explosive instead of a terraformer—and sending it back in time to destroy the previously launched terraformer, preventing/undoing the terraformation.

The contract also stipulated that the customer had to pay for both chronolators, plus the terraformer and the nuke. They would be left with nothing to show for it, other than an ancient scar on a still-uninhabitable planet.

That would not do.

Dominic had doubled Torvald's fee in exchange for a non-disclosure agreement, then shredded the report, buried the fossil site under a rockslide, and hired the second-cheapest survey company, Ace Xenobio, to do another survey.

Mercifully, they were as lax in their work as Torvald should have been.

All that remained of Torvald's discovery was a single fossilized alien claw, which Dominic now carried in his pocket.

The server returned with a tray of champagne. Bronson shook his head, politely declining. God, what a bore.

Tillman, too. He wordlessly took one of the flutes but placed it on a ledge without a sip. Dominic suspected the company reps were required to take a glass, presumably so that the customer wasn't drinking alone. He also got the sense that Tillman's refusal to imbibe was due, at least in part, to his personal disapproval of Dominic. Whatever. Tillman might assume the worst about Dominic, and he might be right, but he couldn't prove any of it.

"Okay," Tillman said reluctantly. "We're about to launch."

Dominic wondered how much of the man's demeanor had to do with their interpersonal dynamic and how much he was just like that. Try as he might, Dominic couldn't picture him smiling or laughing or being pleasant in any way. And the man was in sales, for God's sake. He should at least be able to fake it.

A panel above the observation window came to life, counting down from ten.

Dominic took out his fossil and rubbed it with his thumb.

Tillman glanced over, then did a doubletake, squinting at it. "Interesting piece," he said in that vaguely accusatory tone.

Dominic reminded himself that virtually everything Tillman said was in that tone. "Thank you," he said. "It's one of a kind." Then he aimed a forced smile at Bronson. "When this thing drops, I'm going to want to clink with somebody, so get yourself a goddamned glass."

Bronson jolted into action, scrambling across the room to get a glass of champagne and returning to his spot next to Dominic by the time the countdown reached two.

Then it reached one. Then zero.

The screen said, "LAUNCH SUCCESSFUL" and all three of them leaned forward to get a better angle.

Bronson glanced over nervously, but Dominic wasn't prepared to clink until he saw the damn thing.

Then there it was, drifting into view from the bottom of the window, an egg-shaped capsule studded with thrusters, falling slowly toward Strunk7D. It released a small puff of exhaust and surged forward, picking up speed as it descended toward the planet's surface.

Dominic smiled. It was actually going to happen. Tillman smiled, too, just a bit.

Bronson held up his glass and Dominic clinked it. The capsule shrank and fell, accelerating as the planet's gravity grabbed onto it. The three of them watched until it disappeared into the planet's thin atmosphere.

They watched another few seconds, then Dominic said, "Now what happens?"

Tillman shrugged, still smiling, but didn't look at him, as if doing so would ruin the moment. "Depending on conditions, it should take five or six minutes to reach the surface. The chronolator should activate immediately upon landing. Then we'll see how it turns out."

For several long minutes, they stared without moving, without sipping their champagne or speaking or seemingly even blinking. It almost felt like time itself had stopped for them, and in the back of his mind, Dominic entertained the notion that something had gone wrong with the chronolator, that it somehow *had* frozen them in time. But it hadn't. Everyone was breathing. Bronson shifted his posture. They just had to wait.

Then, in a flash, it happened. The three of them gasped simultaneously. Dominic felt like he had blinked, but he was pretty sure he hadn't. He felt a tingle in his hand, but his attention was fixed on the planet below them, which a moment earlier had been a featureless dusty beige and was now a lush green with a swirling bluish atmosphere.

Even more striking than what they saw, however, was the violently disorienting feeling of an entire unfamiliar lifetime of memories flooding their minds.

Dominic's brain struggled to assimilate it all, to sort it into meaning, to separate out the two lifetimes competing for his identity. And the new memories were winning.

He could feel whoever he had been for his entire life up until that moment fading—all that he had experienced and everything that had been real was becoming less and less vivid, like a dream in the moments after waking.

Tillman staggered. "Oh, fuck," he whispered.

Bronson stepped back, holding his head and retreating from the observation window.

Somehow, despite their precautions, there'd been a paradox.

The newly green Strunk7D took up most of the observation window, but the black space that framed it was suddenly speckled with twice as many points of light as just a moment before. Triple. And they weren't stars, they were spacecraft, some small—satellites and shuttles—but plenty of larger ones, too.

Dominic recognized the shapes of them as his new memories continued to assemble in his brain. He knew exactly what they were. He had known it all his life.

Strunk7D was called Coranis. The spacecraft massed around them were warships. The Coranians were at war. With humanity.

Tillman's hand shot out and flipped open the red abort button and hit the button. A machine-voice announced, "Reversal initiated."

Dominic opened his mouth to protest, to say he wasn't going to pay for that. But then he closed it, realizing that without the reversal, he wouldn't be around to pay for anything.

The reversal capsule drifted into sight below them, following the same trajectory as the retroformer. But one of the closer ships swiveled toward it, glowing pale blue, then royal blue, before a searing cobalt beam erupted from it, slicing through space and vaporizing the capsule.

Tillman began to hyperventilate. Bronson dropped his champagne flute, which smashed on the floor. Bronson himself hit the floor an instant later.

Dominic's head pounded as the two sets of memories jousted in his head, two sets of realities, two lives, conflicting, contradicting, vying for supremacy. But sight of that cobalt light cut through it all, bringing up visceral memories of entire planets incinerated in blue fire, and billions of humans exterminated.

In this new reality, Dominic had lost friends in those attacks. He'd lost his entire family, his fortune. He'd lost everything but his own life. In this reality, he wasn't a spoiled punk rich kid, scamming his way to a fortune of his own; he was an emotionally devastated member of humanity's decimated resistance. And that reversal capsule had been humanity's last hope.

He was no longer there to terraform Strunk7D; he was on a last-ditch suicide mission to retroactively prevent the brutal and malevolent but highly advanced Coranians from having ever existed.

The Coranian armada was massed for a final attack, to track down and snuff out the last elements of their galactic rivals: Earth.

Dominic looked down at his tingling hand and saw that it was empty. The fossil was gone. His luck had run out.

When he looked up, Tillman met his gaze with his eyes narrowed in hatred and disgust—and understanding.

Dominic started to apologize, but what do you say when you've singlehandedly ended your entire species?

Before he had a chance to say anything, their attention was drawn back to the observation window. Half the ships out there had turned in their direction, glowing pale blue, then royal blue, then everything disappeared in a blinding cobalt flash.

Jon McGoran is the author of eleven novels for adults and young adults, including the YA science fiction thrillers *Spliced*, *Splintered*, and *Spiked* and the science thrillers *Drift*, *Deadout*, and *Dust Up*. His latest science fiction thriller, *The Price of Everything*, will be out April 2025 from Solaris Books. He can be found at www.jonmcgoran.com.

We hope you enjoy reading this anthology as much as we enjoyed compiling it.

Our open submission call was so successful that we decided to publish Volume I and Volume II. Volume II will be published two to three months after Volume I. You can find out when it will be published, and also information about other open submission calls, by visiting our website: celestialechopress.com, signing up for our periodic newsletter, and/or joining our Facebook group.

About Celestial Echo Press

A few years ago, Gemini Wordsmiths LLC's partner, Ruth Littner, had a crazy idea to expand into publishing. That crazy idea came to be in June 2019 when we formed Celestial Echo Press. Our first anthology, *The Twofer Compendium*, contains 36 stories based on the theme of twins, penned by 34 international authors. *The Trench Coat Chronicles* was our second anthology. *Ruth and Ann's Guide to Time Travel Volume I* is our third, and we will publish *Volume II* later this year.

We are deep in thought about where we go from here. …

Thanks for joining us in our adventure!

About Gemini Wordsmiths LLC

Gemini Wordsmiths, LLC, a woman-owned editing, copywriting, and proofreading business, was founded in 2011 in Abington, Pennsylvania. As karma would have it, Ruth, Ann, and Gemini Wordsmiths were all born under the astrological sign of Gemini.

Every project is given the same intense review, regardless of whether it is a one-page document or a 100,000-word novel. And instead of getting one editor for their dollars, our clients receive a second set of eyes at the same cost, as both editors review each project separately and then collaboratively. For more information visit geminiwordsmiths.com.

Other publications from Celestial Echo Press

CHASING ASHES

In 1992, shortly before a tragic fire on their college campus, Laura Cunningham saw her best friend, Kate McDonald, for the last time. The fire's 20th anniversary elicits Laura's guilt and ignites her passion to learn what actually happened to Kate. Now a journalist, Laura teams up with her hot detective ex-husband to pursue cold leads in hopes of sparking interest in the decades-old mystery of what happened that day.

DRACULAND

A New York City real estate developer decides to buy Dracula's Castle in Romania and turn it into a theme park. Not her best idea.

TIME BLINKED

Just like Dorothy in the Wizard of Oz, college athlete Bobby spends his days with those he loves and stays close to home. But unlike Dorothy, when Bobby's "tornado" bushwhacks his world, it doesn't move him into a fantastical realm of color and delightful beasts. He is propelled into a complicated past, where his dreams come true through a somewhat mystifying, somewhat terrifying wrinkle.

THE TRENCH COAT CHRONICLES

This murder mystery anthology is dedicated to Sam Spade, Hercule Poirot, and Dick Tracy, as well as to all the writers of hard-boiled detective stories of years past, many of whom formed the basis for the crime mysteries we read today. Enjoy this wide variety of storylines, each of which includes criminals, victims – and trench coats.

THE TWOFER COMPENDIUM

"Twins are said to share special bonds, understand each other's unspoken communication, speak their own languages, even possess powers of ESP. Their double-ness continues to fascinate the rest of us. Adored or abhorred, sheltered or shunned, twins have universally and perpetually aroused attention and curiosity. It was that fascination that inspired this collection of twin-themed stories. In them, you'll find all matter of twins: the good, the bad, the fantastic, the fearsome, the magical, the envious, the secretive, the devious, and more. Being a twin. Fun, right? Think about it. *What could go wrong?*"
--From the Foreword by Merry Jones

All Celestial Echo Press publications are available at Barnes & Noble and other fine bookshops, and online at amazon.com.

THANK YOU TO OUR KICKSTARTER SUPPORTERS!

Alana Byrd *** Amy Hollinger *** Antaeus Balevre

Barbara Kaufman *** Bernadette Dougherty

Cathy Green *** Charles Barouch

Christopher Ryan *** Cindy Snyder

Corey Terhune *** Daniel Ogawa

Danielle Ackley-McPhail *** Debra Webb

Dianna Sinovic *** Ef Deal *** Gary Zenker

George W Young *** Irene Darocha

Isaac Dansicker *** Jeff Apps *** Joan Blumberg

Joanne McLaughlin *** John Breiner *** Joshua Webb

Karen Keeley *** LC Allingham *** Liliyana Greer

Maryanne Chappell *** Michael A. Burstein

Neal Wiser *** Richard Novak *** Shaya Deitsch

Shebat Legion *** Stephen W Chappell

Susanna Reilly *** The Creative Fund by BackerKit

Tony Merlo *** Vince Dowdle *** Vivian Sotomayor